HALT STATIO

HALT STATION INDIA

The Dramatic Tale of the Nation's First Rail Lines

Rajendra B. Aklekar

RUPA

First published by
Rupa Publications India Pvt. Ltd 2014
7/16, Ansari Road, Daryaganj
New Delhi 110002

Sales centres:
Allahabad Bengaluru Chennai
Hyderabad Jaipur Kathmandu
Kolkata Mumbai

ISBN: 978-81-291-3497-4

First impression 2014

10 9 8 7 6 5 4 3 2 1

The moral right of the author has been asserted.

Typeset by SÜRYA, New Delhi

Printed by Parksons Graphics Pvt. Ltd, Mumbai

To the Bombay railways and its creators

CONTENTS

EDITOR'S NOTE

In 1995, Bombay was officially designated as Mumbai, and in 1996, Madras as Chennai. In 1974, Baroda was redesignated as Vadodara, and in 2001, Calcutta as Kolkata. In the course of recent Indian history, several roads, suburbs, stations, townships and districts within the city of Bombay and along the fringes have undergone a change in name—Victoria Terminus is now Chhatrapati Shivaji Terminus, Thana is Thane, and New Bombay is Navi Mumbai. In this book, for these specific places, the older spelling has been retained for consistency.

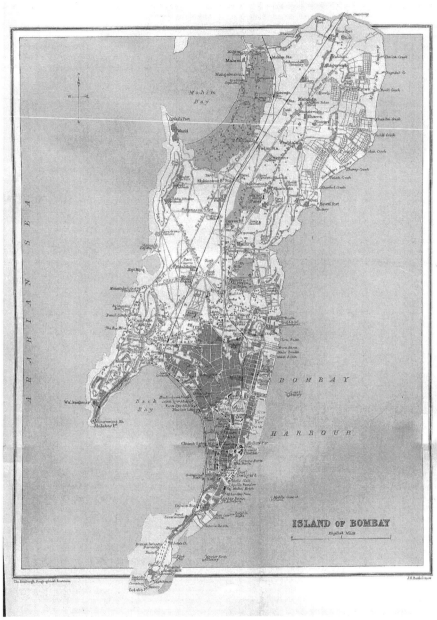

ISLAND OF BOMBAY

The Bombay Presidency, 1909

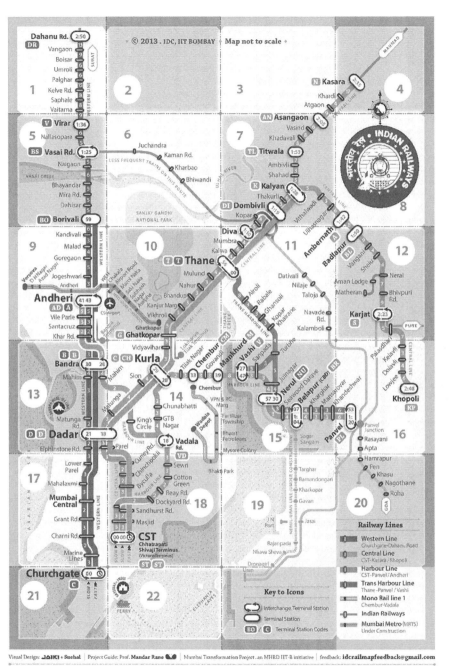

Courtesy: Professor Mandar Rane, Industrial Design Centre, IIT Bombay

Bombay's Railway Map, December 2013

FOREWORD

Sir Mark Tully

On reading Rajendra B. Aklekar's book, packed with fascinating details, I learnt that Bombay, or Mumbai as it is now known, has not just one, but two reasons, to claim to be the birthplace of the Indian railways, and indeed, as the author points out, the birthplace of Asian railways. Not only did the first train in India run from Bombay to Thana in April 1853, but also twenty-nine years earlier the first stationary steam engine operated in Bombay. It was a precursor to the locomotives which would pull the trains that would usher in the age of the railways.

But still, Calcuttans like me would dispute Bombay's claims, or at least cast doubt on them. Having spent the early years of my childhood travelling by the East India Railway, the Bengal Nagpur Railway and the Assam Bengal Railway, I would point out that the first train in India might well have run from Calcutta, if it hadn't been for a careless captain who sank the ship carrying the first carriages for the East Indian Railway, and a careless clerk who dispatched the first locomotive to Australia instead of India.

Rivalries apart, no one can deny that the railways of Bombay and Calcutta made the two greatest cities of British India. The railways were the arteries through which their lifeblood flowed. Rajendra B. Aklekar's meticulous research—and his scholarship which enables him to interpret his findings—throws new light on the way those railways were built—the laying of the lines, why they were laid where they were laid, how the demands on them changed and how they met those demands. We also learn from this book about the people who staffed the railways—including one engine driver renowned for the speed he managed to coax out of his engines, the people who travelled on the trains and the people whose businesses depended on them. These details are not just valuable for railway historians; they provide clues to the past for social, economic and every other sort of historian. Rajendra B. Aklekar provides nuggets that we journalists will be able to use to spice up our writing about the railways.

Bombay was the birthplace of two major railways. One took upon itself from the very start a name which presaged grandeur, the Great Indian Peninsula Railway. The other, in my view, has the most onomatopoeic name of all the Indian railways, The Bombay, Baroda, and Central India Railway. The name always reminds me of the sound of a train passing over an iron bridge, the *bom, bom, ba-bom* sound. The Great Indian Peninsula Railway enhanced its grandeur by building one of the world's great stations, greater in my view than Grand Central in New York—Chhatrapati Shivaji Terminus. Taxi drivers and others in Bombay often still refer to it as VT, the initials of its original title, Victoria Terminus. The Bombay, Baroda, and Central India Railway built two less magnificent termini in the heart of Bombay—Churchgate and Bombay Central—but compensated for that by the Saracenic Gothic extravagance of its headquarters.

Over the last ten years, Rajendra B. Aklekar has walked down the Great Indian Peninsula Railway line from Victoria Terminus to Thana, searching for relics which give clues to the past. During that research, he discovered that the palatial Victoria Terminus stood where gallows once were. During his research on the Bombay, Baroda, and Central India Railway line, he found that in its early days, each train per day took forty-six hours to travel from Bombay's Grant Road Station to Ahmedabad, a distance of 492 kilometres. That makes an average speed of just over ten kilometres per hour.

Rajendra B. Aklekar hasn't just researched the main lines running out of Bombay. He has investigated the branch lines, the industrial lines and the port lines. I particularly like his research on the line to Bombay's Ballard Pier because it conjures up visions of the great days of passenger liners and boat trains—the days before that most faceless and boring form of transport, the aeroplane. I can imagine the Frontier Mail, stuffed with soldiers being transported to the North-West

Frontier, departing from Ballard Pier—and in contrast, the Imperial Mail taking the British 'burra sahibs' from their P&O (British Peninsular & Orient Company) liners to Calcutta. Among the luxuries the passengers enjoyed was a needle bath, two steel pipes punctured with numerous small holes through which jets of water shot—a sort of early Jacuzzi. Mail trains also remind me of the mighty steam engines which pulled them—the steam engine is surely the most human of all the machines mankind has ever invented.

The defunct industrial lines remind me of a sadder story—the story of the railways' retreat in the face of competition from roads. They also tell of the decline of the industries which, along with the railways, made Bombay great. But times change and the railways have to change. Rajendra B. Aklekar shows where they started from and just how much they have transformed.

It's to be hoped that when in fifty years' time another historian walks from Bombay to Thana, he or she will find the tracks still there, and the railways—which are no longer the Great Indian Peninsula Railway and the Bombay, Baroda, and Central India Railway, but the less grandiose and certainly not onomatopoeic Central and Western Railways—still flourishing. If the tracks and the trains are to survive, they will have to change. The transport writer, Christian Wolmar is confident they can survive. In his book, *Blood, Iron, and Gold*, he says:

> Railways may have lost out to the car and the lorry, and in America and other big countries, to the aeroplane, but the fact that they survived and now thrive shows their resilience and flexibility. Trains may be of the past, but they are still the future.[1]

So as we admire and indeed love the trains and tracks of the past, and everything which goes with them, we must make sure that Bombay's railways, and indeed all of India's railways, always look to the future.

---

1. Christian Wolmar, *Blood, Iron, and Gold: How the Railways Transformed the World* (New York: PublicAffairs, 2010), p. 334.

PREFACE

A sun is rising on the darken'd land,
Shaped by civilization's godlike hand,
And thousands soon will gather to behold,
The spectacle of wonders manifold. [...]

Oh, hark its shrill, its thrilling, awing scream;
Oh, see it moves, it glides like some freed stream,
Rising all things with it with ruthless force,
That come upon its unimpeded course.[1]

The railways in India have always evoked nostalgia and romance. Reams of pages have been written about them by authors across the globe. Thousands of researchers have burnt the midnight oil to scour railway records and museums, and publish serious research papers on the rail lines criss-crossing this nation. Fans and enthusiasts have taken journeys and maintained blogs to cover every aspect of the magnificent network. From the fact that on 16 April 1853 the first official passenger train in India (and in Asia) with three engines and fourteen coaches ran the thirty-four-kilometre distance between Bombay (now Mumbai)[2] and Thana (now Thane), to the fact that the railways merged this land of manifold cultures into a national entity—name the subject pertaining to the railways and studies emerge. We know of their contribution to India's freedom struggle, the

---

1. 'The Opening of the Bombay Railway', *Bombay Times*, 18 April 1853.

2. Bombay city was originally an archipelago of seven islands of Bombay, Parel, Mazgaon, Mahim, Colaba, Worli and Old Woman's Island (also known as Little Colaba). The Treaty of Bassein placed the islands in Portuguese possession in 1534. Charles II of England had control of the islands in 1661.

controversies associated with their growth, and the simple pleasures linked to their rhythmic chug-chugging.

'What else is left to say? What's there that's not known?' was the most common question I encountered when I first began work on this manuscript. Lots, was my confident response.

Ten years after I first began the exercise of walking up and down the first of all Indian rail lines—the Great Indian Peninsula Railway (the GIPR, today the Central Railway)—I decided to pause and share my discoveries. I chose to make note of the many marvels I had come across.

Equally, encouraged by the walk along the GIPR line, a similar amble along Bombay's second network—the Bombay, Baroda, and Central India Railway line (the BB&CI, today the Western Railway)—proved to be rewarding. Consequently, there is a chapter devoted to the growth of the Western Railway.

Furthermore, the Harbour Line—originally a chord line between Kurla (then Coorla) and Victoria Terminus (now Mumbai Chhatrapati Shivaji Terminus), and subsequently, spreading to New Bombay (now Navi Mumbai) and beyond—has been recognized as the host to India's first electric train. This has been dealt with in a whole segment, along with the port railway network.

Memories, personal recollections and the stories of those who witnessed the arrival of the first trains lend yet another facet to this book, and conjure clear impressions of the golden days of the past.

~

India's first train ran in 1853. The line was built from Bori Bunder in the southern tip of the vertical island of Bombay—stretching thirty-four kilometres northwards—to the town of Thana. It trundled along the eastern seashore, through open fields, hillocks, swamps and tunnels. It then passed beyond the mainland to Kalyan (then Callian), where it split into two. From here, it ascended the Sahyadri mountain ranges, over 2,000 feet high, and spread out into the subcontinent.

The opening of this network, the GIPR, fascinated the world. Equally, as it was the first ever such line to begin in the East, it not only captivated engineers, but also charmed writers, and sparked off a number of literary works. Jules Verne's *Around the World in Eighty Days* was triggered by the opening of the GIPR; indeed, the protagonist Phileas Fogg found that with the advent of this line, the time taken to circumvent the globe had dramatically reduced—to merely eighty days!

~

The first rail line originally started as an 'experimental' one, used primarily to ferry goods swiftly so that they reached (to and from) the port of Bombay; later, the line was used for strategic military purposes, besides, obviously, for passenger transport.

Around 1853, the East India Company was managing the administration of the Indian empire on behalf of the crown. One of the key items of trade was raw cotton, required for the British textile industry. Cotton grew in the interiors of India. Transporting it from the interiors to the port of Bombay, so it could be conveyed via ship to England, was one of the prime objectives of setting up the rail network. Besides cotton, there were other items too that formed export cargo— hide and leather, oil, spices, salts and fruits, wool, opium, dyes, sugar, precious stones, tea, grains, cashmere shawls, beads, metals—the list is endless. And trade was pursued not just with England, but also with China, parts of Africa, Singapore, France, Mauritius, Java, Ceylon (now Sri Lanka) and North America—all from the port of Bombay.[3] The railways gave a definite fillip to such business dealings.

The introduction of British ideas and technology led to a change in the habits of the local population. From using wheelbarrows for construction, to consenting to English education, the people of India began adapting to new ways of living, albeit with caution. The railways that came in the mid-1850s were a remarkable addition to a long list of British innovations; trains, too, were reluctantly accepted by the resident community. With time, however, trains found overwhelming approval, and their network spread across the length and breadth of the nation like wildfire, with a number of private Indian ventures working on rail lines of diverse gauges.

---

3. *Professional Papers on Indian Engineering*, Volume 3, edited by Major J.G. Medley (India: Thomason College Press, 1866), p.134.

I should make an important point here. While Indians accepted foreign technology with trepidation, awe and surprise, they also, over the centuries, had been building sturdy and magnificent engineering marvels of their own, with rudimentary and traditional methods. Our historical relics stand testimony to this fact.

~

Tracing the original blueprint of the lines is like looking for a hidden treasure; the pleasure is indescribable! However, 150 years later, is it worthwhile looking for relics along India's first railway line, in an attempt to arrive at the network's precise history?

Well, the question isn't easy to answer. The infrastructure for the first railway network—station buildings, structures and the line itself—was built with primitive technology and did not survive for very long. By the late 1860s, less than fifteen years after the first line's construction, many of the original structures had started falling apart and had to be replaced and upgraded. British engineers blamed this setback on insufficient knowledge about Indian building material.[4] This is the first hurdle you face if you attempt recovering the GIPR line's history.

Further, every small and big development, local and global—the 1857 mutiny, the 1861 cotton boom following the American Civil War, the opening of the Suez Canal, the World Wars—had a physical impact on the rail lines in Bombay. Stations were upgraded, rebuilt and expanded as more utilities emerged. The original lines multiplied. About seven decades after the first train run, the railways got electrified, and stations got riddled with steel gantries, masts and a network of power substations. The fact is that railway infrastructure changes in a jiffy. What you see today becomes history tomorrow. The geometries of the lines change, leaving no sign of the past.

Worse, I came to realize that several railway relics and artefacts had vanished—a few had been salvaged by heritage galleries, but many

---

4. Ian J. Kerr, 'The Dark Side of the Force: Mistakes, Mismanagement and Malfeasance in the Early Railways of the British Indian Empire', *Our Indian Railway: Themes in India's Railway History*, edited by Roopa Srinivasan, Manish Tiwari and Sandeep Silas (New Delhi: Foundation Books, 2006), pp. 189-90.

had been doomed to extinction. While the optimist in me is certain
that there are fragments of the past still waiting to be explored and
studied, which I may have missed in this work, I mourn the loss of
parts of our collective history.

What's left, then, of the original lines to document? Faint but firm
footprints, I would say. Few know that that trains on India's oldest
rail line—more popularly known as Bombay's local trains—pass
through forgotten ruins that are centuries old—forts, religious places
and battle grounds. The millions of commuters who use the line every
single day remain oblivious to these vestiges of history.

The fact is that the line still runs along the original blueprint, and
exploring 'ground zero' of the Indian railways leaves you astounded.
Take a studied walk along the country's pioneering line, and you
chance upon remains, scattered like the pieces of a gigantic jigsaw
puzzle. You find bits and pieces of iron and steel, once shipped across
the seven seas. Many old, discarded rails of the early railway lines are
still 'alive' within the station premises, and have been creatively used
to construct fences and pillars. Indeed, *The Locomotive* magazine of the
1920s acknowledges that in the early days of the railways, old rails had
to be used inventively if they were meant to be disposed:

> In the construction of permanent erections in India, it is
> interesting to note the very common use of old rails withdrawn
> from track. The short running 'life' (due to wear) of the first
> iron rails sent out to the G.I.P. Ry. formed an early nucleus of
> the supply of such material in almost unlimited quantity, for, as
> there were no iron works or industries to utilize such, they
> became almost a 'drug in the market' from a sales point of view.
> Station roofs, supporting columns, sheds footbridges, telegraph
> poles and signal posts, all have their fundamental construction
> dependent on old rails, and very often these are so skillfully used
> that it is difficult to recognize the components.[5]

These stone and metallic relics tell you a story—the story of how the
country's first railway line was formed, and how trains edged out

5. *The Locomotive*, 15 December 1926, p. 395.

primitive modes of transport. This is also true of the location of many stations, and their social and historical contexts. Their careful study tells you a fascinating tale of how the railway network grew. Every time you go back to them, something new emerges, to take you back to an era when the railways were a novelty and trains were the future.

Moreover, the lines pass through a city that was once a cluster of seven mosquito-ridden islands with shallow walkways. On following them, you find narratives of love and loss, tragedy and ambition, birth and death. Many of these narratives can be traced to this day through forgotten plaques, bridges running across railway lines, or within station alleyways.

The railways' engineers, who planned and laid down the lines, were in fact *Bombay's* engineers—for, townships grew around these lines and morphed into the booming city of Bombay.

~

Our journey begins from the southern tip of Bombay, from Victoria Terminus or Churchgate. We proceed further north, exploring, documenting and deciphering the relics that lie along the original railway lines. Many of them are significant, many stray and trivial, but they go a long way towards explaining the development of the country's first rail network, its history, the technological trends of the era, and more importantly, the growth of a megapolis. To this end, efforts have been made to explain the design of the GIPR and the BB&CI Railway, or the Central and Western Railways network, and of each station.

The research has been conducted over the course of the various train journeys undertaken along the line with authorized tickets and permits. Much has also been uncovered during walks along the line, which have been conducted with the formal permission of local railway authorities. The relics, found and documented, are the undisputed property of the Indian railways, and I am grateful to the Central and Western Railways for the images and archival material. My research has been limited to identifying and analyzing the remains of the past.

RAJENDRA B. AKLEKAR
Bombay, 2014

THE STORY OF AN EXPERIMENTAL LINE

Camberwell Old Cemetery, London. At this address one can find the grave of James John Berkley. Above it is the statue of a reclining female, and the oval bust of a serious-looking Berkley.

Berkley's grave is no tourist attraction, nor is he known to today's generation. But here lies the man who built India's first railway line and its most difficult sections along the Lonavala-Khandala and Kasara Ghats (Bhor and Thal) in the Sahyadri mountain ranges. From here, the trains fan out across India.

Within the cemetery, there is a monument in Berkley's memory that has been a Grade II building since May 1992. It was erected by Berkley's peers after his death, and a detailed inscription on it reads:

> This monument is erected by the engineers and contractors of the Great Indian Peninsular Railway in token of their admiration of the distinguished professional career of their chief engineer James John Berkley whilst engaged upon the extensive system of railways designed by him in Western India which comprised the Bhore and Thal Ghat inclines up the Syhadree range of mountains and in affectionate remembrance of his high social qualities as well as of the uniform kindness and consideration with which he conducted his official duties.

~

In the last few years of the 1840s, an experimental railway was being planned for India. The construction of the line across an unfamiliar terrain came with an element of risk. Even as things were being finalized in England, on 14 November 1849 the most prominent of English engineers strongly recommended the name of a thirty-year-old fellow engineer, Holloway-born James John Berkley. Given the number of endorsements against his name, Berkley was unhesitatingly appointed as the chief resident engineer of the GIPR in India.

Educated at King's College in London, Berkley had been working closely and had trained with Robert Stephenson—the famous son of the famous father, George Stephenson, who built the world's first public railway with steam locomotives. For the rest of his life, Berkley would enjoy an intimate friendship with Robert Stephenson. Impressed with his skills, Robert Stephenson appointed him as chief resident engineer of the Churnet and Trent Valley Railways.[1] However, Berkley's future lay elsewhere, and in 1849, backed by Robert Stephenson's effusive recommendation and the commendation of several peers, Berkley found himself in India on a mission to build the railways. The Indian assignment was to be his life's foremost achievement.

Berkley arrived in Bombay by ship on 7 February 1850, soon after his appointment. His first view of the city was from Mazgaon, where vessels of the era docked. Bombay of the 1850s was a semi-urban place where the foundations of a modern city were yet to be laid. The docks were alive, trade was active, steam machines and equipment made the occasional appearance, and ships offloaded new tools and machines—creations of the industrial revolution.

In fact, it was a period when India as a whole was in the throes of discovery and change. On the one hand, Alexander Cunningham, with the Archaeological Survey of India, was digging out ruins and decoding the country's glorious history. On the other hand, William Lambton, as superintendent of the Trignometrical Survey of India, was measuring and mapping every inch of this large British colony.

As early as 1823, the Gun Carriage Factory at Colaba—that manufactured cannon balls and wheels—is reported to have had several machines running on steam at a frantic pace. In 1824, a year before the world's first public railway between Stockton and Darlington opened, Bombay saw another large stationary steam engine (a fixed

---

1. *Dictionary of National Biography*, Volume 4, edited by Leslie Stephen (New York: Macmillan & Co, 1885).

steam engine used for pumping or driving mills and factories) for public use, with a cattle-driven Persian wheel pumping out water from wells to tanks.[2] Inaugurated on 17 May 1824, this apparatus was built by Parsi merchant and philanthropist Seth Framji Cowasji Banaji to tide over the water crisis in Bombay.[3] The noble act of charity by Seth Framji was in memory of his second son Eduljee, who had died a month earlier at the age of thirty while returning on foot from Madras (now Chennai). Seth Framji spent more than Rs 30,000 on the device, a princely sum at that time, and maintained it at a monthly cost of Rs 200.[4]

Four years later, in 1828, far away from Bombay, at Calcutta's (now Kolkata) Agro-Horticultural Society's meeting, an Indian blacksmith from Titigur, Goluk Chandra, built and demonstrated (without any Englishman's help) a stationary steam engine and won a prize of Rs 50! Chandra had been closely observing William Carey's steam engine of twelve horsepower that had been bought to run a paper mill—it was the first steam engine to have been imported by India.[5]

---

2. Govind Narayan Madgaonkar, *Mumbaiche Varnan*, edited by Narhar Raghunath Fatak (India: Marathi Granth Sangrahalaya, 1863), p. 61. Translated by the author.

3. Khoshru Navrosji Banaji, *Memoirs of the Late Framji Cowasji Banaji* (Bombay: Bombay Gazette Steam Printing Press, 1892), pp. 28-32.

4. Around 1814, as the local population expanded, the Bombay government decided to develop a new area at Kamathipura to meet an urgent need for habitable space. This area faced an acute shortage of water. Therefore, two large water reservoirs were dug up and connected to the larger water tank that had been built by Seth Cowasjee Patel at Khetwadi in Girgaum, named Cowasjee Patel (CP) tank. But the arrangement of pipes worked only when the CP tank was full, leading to regular crises. It was another Parsi, Seth Framji Cowasji Banaji who saved the day, by sinking three wells and pumping water from these wells to the tanks by a Persian wheel run by bullocks and a steam engine. Centuries later, the areas, now changed beyond recognition, are still called Do Tanki (Two Tanks) and CP Tank. Ref: Kalpana Desai, 'The Role of Parsis in the Urbanisation of Mumbai in the 19th Century', *The Parsis in Western India: 1818 to 1920,* edited by Nawaz Modi (India: Allied Publishers, 1998), p. 156.

5. Ian Jack, *Mofussil Junction: Indian Encounters (1977-2012)* (UK: Penguin, 2013), p. 85.

But with no communication and primitive transportation methods, such local adventures were quickly forgotten. While India may have been at the brink of major discoveries, one must remember that entire generations in the country stayed in one place and followed tradition; the major mode of transport was cattle and water canals. While 'palkhees' or palanquins were used to transport people, animals—which changed as per the region and terrain (elephants, camels and oxen)—and ferried goods.[6] Horses and water ferries were probably the fastest means of communication and passage on land and water respectively. According to Captain Edward Davidson, deputy consulting engineer for railways in 1868 to the government of Bengal:

> From time immemorial, droves of pack bullocks had struggled with the utmost difficulty and delay by two tracks, barely passable even for animals, from Central India to Bombay, carrying sacks of grain and other things in which a small and uncertain trade was maintained between the two districts The track which led towards Agra and Calcutta was known as the Thull Ghat and that towards Poonah and Madras as the Bhore Ghats.[7]

Consequently, prominent railway historian, Ian J. Kerr is known to have said: 'No railroads, no India.'[8] Until the iron horse arrived, India was doomed to be stuck in time.

Fortunately, the idea of steam and communication was fast catching on. Two years before Berkley stepped on to the shores of Bombay, thirty-six-year-old James Andrew Broun-Ramsay, more popularly known as the Earl of Dalhousie or simply Lord Dalhousie, had taken over as India's youngest governor general. Dalhousie had arrived with experience as the vice-president of the board of trade in England

---

6. Romila Thapar, *The Penguin History of Early India: From the Origins to AD 1300* (India: Penguin, 2002).

7. Edward Davidson, *The Railways of India with an Account of Their Rise, Progress and Construction* (London: E. & F.N. Spon, 1868), p. 231.

8. Ian J. Kerr, *Engines of Change: The Railroads that Made India* (USA: Praeger Publishers, 2007).

during an era marked by railway mania. Once he set his foot in this country, he began promoting the railways with renewed vigour, along with the postal system and the electric telegraph—the three engines of social change.

Before the 1840s, it took five to eight months for a letter to travel between Britain and India, and 'the writer could not expect to receive an answer in less than two years'.[9] Even after steamships took over mail services, it took six weeks each way. Within India, mails were just as slow. When the first telegraph lines between Bombay and Calcutta were set up, a letter written by Lord Dalhousie to a friend shows the marked improvement in communication systems:

> The post takes ten days between the two places. Thus in less than one day, the government made communications, which before the telegraph was, would have occupied a whole month— what a political reinforcement is this![10]

The migration of newer technologies from England was slowly set to change the face of India and other English colonies. Lord Dalhousie, who had been working over sixteen hours a day, now pushed for trains, and wrote detailed railway minutes to strategically connect the dots on the empire. This, he believed, would be of military and trade significance. He began by charting out two experimental lines—one from Bombay and the other from Howrah—and sought their construction. The minutes became the blueprint of the Indian railways, a central document in the history of the Indian rail network.

~

Thirty-one-year-old Berkley had arrived in a Bombay where hotels were still a rarity. On getting off the ship at Mazgaon, he was offered accommodation in the vicinity, at the Hope Hall Hotel, a fashionable lodging house of the era that 'had a bathing place attached in every

---

9. Daniel R. Headrick, *The Tentacles of Change: Technology Transfer in the Age of Imperialism* (England: Oxford University Press, 1988), p. 97.

10. *Ibid.*

room and a very desirable accommodation for single gentlemen'. It was owned by T. Blackwell, and Berkley eventually married his daughter, Annie.[11] Opened in 1837, it had 'long maintained its high respectability with aristocratic exclusiveness'. It was a spacious inn, and additionally, had an annex to accommodate families, known as the Hope Hall Family Hotel.[12] In today's Bombay, this lodging house would be located east of Hancock Bridge—at the base—opposite the site where Mazgaon Station once was. However, instead of a respectable hotel, one will find shabby informal settlements. It's hard to imagine the site's glorious past. An ancient bracket of a lamppost, plastered up and painted over by a local corporator, is all that is left as a memory.

Once in Bombay, an enthusiastic Berkley got down to work the very next day with his two assistant engineers, C.B. Kar and R.W. Graham. In a letter written on 8 February 1850, he reported his arrival the previous day and, in subsequent letters, sought permission of the provincial committee to 'engage a draughtsman and four peons'; additionally, he asked for a tradesman who could help him with drawing tables and planning presses. With local merchants and traders pooling in support and with government permissions in hand, the planning, studies and surveys proceeded without too many hurdles. Within eight months of Berkley's arrival, on 31 October 1850, the first sod for India's first railway—the 'bhoomipujan' of the Indian railways—was turned at Sion by John P. Willoughby, chief secretary to the Bombay government.[13]

The minute mathematical details surrounding the railway project are mind-boggling! Describing the first line, Berkley documents:

> The principle works upon the Experimental line are the crossing of the Sion Marsh, which is effected by an embankment; the

---

11. S.N. Sharma, *History of the GIP Railway (1853-1869)*, Part I, Volume I (Bombay: Chief Public Relations Officer, Central Railway, 1990), p. 6.

12. Sir Dinshaw Edulji Wacha, *Shells from Sands of Bombay; Being My Recollections and Reminiscences:1860-1875* (Bombay: The Bombay Chronicle Press, 1920), p. 287.

13. S.N. Sharma, *History of the GIP Railway (1853-1869)*, Part I, Volume I (Bombay: Chief Public Relations Officer, Central Railway, 1990), pp. 5-6.

crossing of the arm of the sea from the island of Salsette[14] to the Concan [now Konkan], comprising two viaducts, the length respectively of 111 yards and 193 yards, in the latter of which there is an opening for navigation of 84 feet, spanned by wrought iron plate girders; beyond this, there are two tunnels of the respective length of 103 yards and 115 yards. The railway is protected by post and rail fences, and prickly pear and cactus hedges. The station buildings are masonry. The permanent way is chiefly laid with transverse wooden sleepers and six miles [approximately ten kilometres] of it with iron pot Greaves' sleepers. The rails, which are of the double T form, weigh 81 lbs per lineal yard as far as Tannah beyond which they weighed only 65 lbs and 68 lbs per yard.[15]

Confronted by the practicalities of India's western terrain, Berkley planned to build a railway of fifty-three kilometres straight from Bori Bunder to Thana and then to Kalyan, at which point the line would divide and veer towards the northeast for forty-two kilometres to Thal Ghat, and southeast for sixty-one kilometres to the foot of Bhor Ghat.

In January 1851, the gauge of the railway was fixed at 5'6". This was Lord Dalhousie's master stroke as he chose a middle-sized gauge for India, between the traditional British 4'8.5", and Brunel's 7'1". The dimensions had an immediate impact on land acquisition deals and related procedures.[16]

With the gauge dimensions in place, in the same year, the contract to build the first thirty-four kilometres from Bombay to Thana was finalized. On the recommendation of Berkley, who trusted English contractors over Indian ones, it was given to Faviell and Fowler, an English construction firm. Work was also let out to contractors George Wythes and William Jackson, along with Parsi contractor Jamsetjee

---

14. Back then, the island of Rewa was situated between the bigger island of Parel-Matoonga (Matunga)-Dharavi in the south and the island of Salsette in the north.

15. *Professional Papers on Indian Engineering*, Volume 3, edited by Major J.G. Medley (India: Thomason College Press, 1866).

16. S.N. Sharma, *History of the GIP Railway (1853-1869)*, Part 1, Volume 1 (Bombay: Chief Public Relations Officer, Central Railway, 1990), p. 8.

Dorabjee Naegamwalla, to build the line from Thana to Kalyan; this involved constructing a large viaduct after Thana and a tunnel in Parsik Hill.

In October 1851—a year after the ground-breaking ceremony and earthwork had been completed—the railway project slowed down due to heavy showers. Shortly thereafter, orders were issued by the court of directors for the construction of a three-kilometre line to the port of Mahim—a hub for goods and passenger traffic.[17] The project began at full pace, even as debates persisted on whether the first thirty-four-kilometre segment from Bori Bunder to Thana should be a single or a double line. Though the contract had originally been inked for a double line, there were second thoughts—after all, the other 'experimental line' at Howrah, along the Indian east coast, was for the most part a single line; some engineers believed that the same pattern ought to be followed in the Bombay Presidency to save money. But the suggestion was overruled by the government of Bombay, in view of contractual and financial complications. Consequently, the Bombay Presidency retained a double line.[18]

~

The story of William Frederick Faviell and Henry Fowler is as interesting as that of India's first line. Faviell was born in Yorkshire in 1822 and educated at a private school at Lincoln. At the early age of seventeen, he assisted his brothers—also railway contractors—with the construction of various lines. He joined his father in 1846 to successfully complete a contract for a line between Harrogate and Ripon on the Leeds-Thirsk Railway, and also helped with an extension of the same line in partnership with his brother-in-law. In 1850, he joined hands with Henry Fowler to bid for India's first railway.[19]

17. *Ibid.*, p. 25.

18. G.S. Khosla, *A History of Indian Railways* (India: A.H. Wheeler & Co, 1988), p. 34.

19. 'Obituary: W.F. Faviell, The Engineer', *British Industrial History*, 18 July 1902, in<http://www.gracesguide.co.uk/The_Engineer_1902/07/18>, accessed on 9 February 2014.

The professional career of Henry Fowler—born near Sheffield in 1821—began at the age of sixteen as a pupil to John Towlerton Leather, who, at that time was the resident engineer of Sheffield Waterworks. Fowler gained experience from the construction of a portion of the North Midland Railway, in the vicinity of Chesterfield. He was offered the position of a permanent resident engineer of the Great Northern Railway Company. But in 1850, he resigned to join hands with Faviell to build Bombay's rail network; he sailed to India on 19 December 1850 with hope in his eyes.[20]

Faviell and Fowler got down to work immediately by employing nearly 10,000 workers from Bombay and the surrounding regions.[21] For the very first time, British rail engineers had to engage with 'native' workers. This led to a giant clash of cultures, with British engineers trying to extract their money's worth, and the workers, in turn, demanding respect for their ways and religious practices.

Ian J. Kerr in *Building the Railways of the Raj* documents how a harried Henry Fowler shot off a letter to his mentor in England on 2 May 1851, stating that he had been trying to get the workers to start work at 6 a.m. instead of the customary 8 a.m., but 'it is a most difficult thing to alter the existing system as almost every custom the natives have is founded on absurd but invincible prejudices—generally of religious character'.[22] Fowler lamented the fact that the workers' groups were divided along caste demarcations, and that they refused to work alongside one another.

The Bombay Quarterly Review of 1855 reported a rare strike by workers at the Coorla (Kurla) Cutting; they demanded a change in work timings so they could have a hot water bath.

> In the month of November soon after the commencement of the Coorla Cutting, a deputation of native workmen waited

20. 'Proceedings of Institution of Civil Engineers, 1855: Obituaries', *British Industrial History*, in <http://www.gracesguide.co.uk/Henry_Fowler_(1821-1854)>, accessed on 9 February 2014.

21. Dr A.K. Arora, *History of Bombay Suburban Railways: 1853-1985* (Bombay: The Indian Railway Electrical Engineers Association, 1985), p. vii.

22. Ian J. Kerr, *Building the Railways of the Raj: 1850-1900* (UK: Oxford University Press, 1995), p. 32.

upon the contractor with a complaint about the hours of working, which were then from 8 am to 6 pm. They solicited their master to allow them to begin their day an hour earlier so that they might leave work before sunset, because at 6 o' clock the water was too cold for them to bathe.[23]

Yet another story states that one day in the 1850s, during the construction of the line, there was a sudden strike by workers due to misperceptions regarding their wages.

One day, the Engineer who was engaged at Sion was surprised to observe all the native labourers from the large cutting in that neighbourhood were walking away as no one had assured them of payment. Only when the engineer guaranteed them the wages, they turned round.[24]

The relationship between local labourers, contractors and British engineers remained strained. Conditions only worsened when the line reached the difficult Bhor Ghat terrain near Khandala in the late 1850s. So tense did the situation become that the British were compelled to enact a full-fledged labour-law in 1860 — the Employers and Workmen (Disputes) Act — which gave magistrates full power to settle wage disputes. Additionally, the law allowed the British to keep a police force on call to handle difficult situations.

About twelve months into his arrival in India, Fowler fell ill; the harsh tropical climate in India did not suit him and he went back to England. Poor Fowler never recovered from his illness and died soon after, on 26 January 1854, at the young age of thirty-two.

By March 1852, Faviell had to proceed single-handedly, totally dependent on the local workforce. A year later, *The Illustrated London News* went on to describe his many trials and tribulations.

The work appears to have been one of great labour and difficulty. In addition to a most trying climate (in which the constitution of Mr Fowler, the partner of Mr Faviell, as well as that of many

---

23. *The Bombay Quarterly Review*, July-October 1855.

24. *Ibid.*

English labourers they took out with them, failed), Mr Faviell found himself, in March, 1852, working single-handed, his partner having gone to England for the benefit of his health. Mr Faviell was then dependent principally on native labour: the men are scarce, and, in the rice-harvest time, always difficult to manage; alteration in the arrangement of the work, or strict orders given by the contractor, often gave offence when the men went away in a body of fifty or a hundred at a time. It was also difficult to get then to earn their small rate of wage. Snakes abounded on the line; the cobra di capello, and a small dark snake were very common among the stones; the former is an object of worship, and both have a deadly bite.[25]

While attending to the project, one of the biggest challenges to confront Faviell and his men was the swamp between the two islands of Parel-Matoonga (Matunga)-Dharavi and Salsette. How were they to fill this up? Fortunately, by this point in time, rail mania had taken over the globe, and railways were being built across multiple countries, on every possible terrain; there were ready solutions.

Robert Stephenson, the GIPR's consulting engineer, replicated the approach used by his father George Stephenson during the construction of the Liverpool-Manchester Railway, the world's first twin-track inter-urban passenger railway that opened on 15 September 1830. Along the Liverpool railway line was a swamp at Chat Moss. On this swamp, George Stephenson constructed a railway line by 'floating' it on a bed of bound plants and branches, topped with tar and covered with rubble.

Work at Salsette began using George Stephenson's model. The Sion Hill—then located on the small island of Rewa between Bombay and Salsette—was acquired for land filling, and Faviell and his team got down to work. The hill, that had ruins of an old fort tower and ramparts, was quarried by Faviell's team, though the central portion of the tower, an important piece of Bombay's history, was kept intact. One must congratulate this careful railway contractor; most others had a reputation for destroying relics of bygone eras. The

---

25. *The Illustrated London News*, 4 June 1853, pp. 436-38.

contractor in charge of the Lahore-Multan line, for instance, unknowingly used bricks from the ancient Harappan city as track ballast. Similarly, Faviell's contemporaries, Wythes and Jackson, in charge of the Thana-Kalyan line, demolished an old seventeenth-century fort on Parsik Hill while boring tunnels. Fortunately, the footprints of time are still visible at Sion. The ruins of the old watchtower can be seen even today, if one looks closely from Sion Station.

At Sion, mattresses were made from mangrove trees and spread across the mud; then soil was placed on top to press the mattresses; another mattress was superimposed, and more soil placed, until a sturdy bed emerged, sufficient for a solid road and tracks. This, and a small stone bridge, made it possible for the railways to enter Salsette. (Sadly, this small bridge at Sion cannot be spotted today.)

As attempts were made to install new technology in a new country, there were problems that required novel solutions. The track of the first section was laid 'true to gauge'—that is, the tracks were precisely 5'6" in width, with no change even at the curves when required. This challenged the contractors and supervisors no end, who could not get the local workers to insert the correct cotters (pins) in the tie-rods. Instead of using thin cotters on the outer side, thick ones would be used, with the result that the rails were drawn in where they should have been spread out! The gauge became tight and vehicles often got derailed. Berkley therefore decided to make suitable allowances in the wheels of the vehicles.[26]

~

Faviell and his team worked at a furious pace, and when the line to Thana was finally ready, everyone was surprised! The cost of constructing the line was 20 per cent less than had been estimated. Moreover, work was done ahead of schedule.[27] By the end of 1852, the line from Thana to Sepoy Lines (near today's Masjid Bunder Station)

---

26. *The Locomotive*, 15 November 1926, p. 366.

27. S.N. Sharma, *History of the GIP Railway (1853-1869)*, Part I, Volume I (Bombay: Chief Public Relations Officer, Central Railway, 1990), p. 25.

was almost ready. In the same year, the GIPR took the first end-to-end trial run of the train.

As for Faviell, he was to later accept the contract to build lines in Bhor Ghat. But he abandoned this project midway, claiming it was unaffordable. Soon after, he went to Ceylon (now Sri Lanka) to successfully build rail lines to cover the 117-kilometre distance between Colombo and Kandy.

What of Berkley? Ill and exhausted from all the hard work in a tropical nation, the country's pioneering railway engineer returned to England in April 1861, and died a year later in August 1862. Back in the 1850s, newspapers had questioned Berkley's skills and the alignment selected by his team. However, upon his demise, directors of the GIPR in Bombay passed a resolution, mentioning him in terms of the highest praise. Today, a small railway colony in his name exists at Byculla along the Central Railway line and his forgotten bust on the walls of Bombay's Victoria Terminus looks over a municipal bus depot.

Dalhousie had died two years earlier in 1860 at the age of forty-nine. The British named a town in today's Himachal Pradesh after him.

What do we know of the original line? We know that the quality of the work was poor. This was inevitable, given the engineers' sketchy understanding of the land they had been allotted and the quality of labour (largely untrained). Besides, this was the first time such work was being attempted in the country. In fact, the Khopoli (then Campolee) line at the foot of the Sahyadri ranges, till as late as 1861, was washed away every year during the monsoons and had to be rebuilt afresh. Today, over 150 later, the stations along the Khopoli line, while primitive, survive; nobody remembers Berkley in this region, but his line offers respite to the villages.

THE GENESIS: A RAILWAY LINE FOR COTTON

A paper presented in October 1847 before the House of Commons discussed trade relations between India and England, focusing specifically on cotton.

Cotton, it said, grew in the interiors of India, in places without transport and communication facilities. Therefore, by the time cotton reached the shores from the country's villages, it was badly damaged, scarred by unpredictable transport and capricious bullock-carts. Worse, during times of drought and famine, bullocks had been unreliable; on such occasions, ships had been kept waiting at the ports for goods that never arrived.

With a rail line, things could change. Cotton, and indeed, every raw material, could get transported with remarkable speed to the seaports. From here, cotton could be sent by ship to the hungry textile mills in Britain.

Back then, cotton, a crucial commodity for the textile industry in the UK, was mainly purchased from America; this had been the case since the 1830s. Though India too used to export cotton, the quantities were miniscule. However, Britain did not want to be dependent exclusively on America for cotton production, and from the 1840s, showed deep interest in cotton cultivation in India.

A promotional pamphlet entitled 'Railways for Bombay', published in Bombay in 1849, decided to address this issue. Four points were raised. First, the Americans were flooding English markets with their cotton. Second, they could do this, and at a low cost, because of their railway infrastructure. Third, the most important reason for the decline of commerce in western India, especially its cotton trade, was problematic internal transport. Fourth, this evil could best and, indeed, *only* be remedied by the construction of railroads in India.

J.A. Turner, president of the Manchester Commercial Association went on to write a letter in 1847 that clearly explained the vision guiding the establishment of the railways.

> I believe that if Indian cotton is sent home clean, there will be an increased demand for it; and that it is very unlikely that the spinners will discontinue using it, even if American cotton recedes from its present value; though of course they would, in such case, only use it as its relative value compared with the American.[28]

---

28. John Chapman, *The Cotton and Commerce of India Considered in Relation to the Interests of Great Britain; With Remarks on Railway Communication in the Bombay Presidency* (London: Strand, 1851), p. 3.

A railway network would also help the British fortify their position in India. It was believed that organizing and dispersing the growing native population and the quick deployment of troops could be best handled by trains. A letter by Thomas Williamson, revenue commissioner of Bombay, to the chairman of the GIPR Company, Lord Wharncliffe, in May 1846, confirms this stance. Williamson said:

> I need not remind your Lordship that Bombay is the great focus of our military strength in Western India. Its admirable harbour, at the most central point on the west coast of the Peninsula, has since the time of our first connection with India, pointed it out as the key of our possessions in this quarter. There are our Dockyards, our Arsenals, our Manufactories of Ordnance and other stores; and it is the only point on the whole coast where troops can, at all times of the year, be embarked and disembarked without difficulty or delay.
>
> In Europe, the importance of a railway as a military work is limited to the speed and comfort with which large bodies of troops may be conveyed to their destination; but in India its value is enhanced by the mode in which it would spare the health and save the lives of European troops.
>
> Should an arrangement at any future time be concluded for the passage of troops through Egypt, the importance of the Great Indian Peninsula Railway would be vastly increased.
>
> The great trunk line, running by the Malseje Ghaut [Malsej Ghat] in the direction of Nagpoor [Nagpur], would be the most direct which could possibly be selected to connect Bombay and Calcutta.[29]

By this time, India was also pursuing the dream of a rail network, with various traders, local groups and administration representatives making feeble attempts at building lines in various provinces.

Technically, a small standard-gauge industrial railway, called the Red Hill Railroad, with rotary steam locomotives, had been started as

---

29. Thomas Williamson, *Two Letters on the Advantages of Railway Communication in Western India, Addressed to The Right Hon. Lord Wharncliffe, Chairman of the Great Indian Peninsula Railway Company* (London: Richard and John E. Taylor, 1846).

far back as 1836 in Madras, ferrying material for road building. Though the network shut down by 1845, it could qualify as the first ever rudimentary railway in India. A study done in 2011 by Simon Darvill, senior member of the Indian Railways Fan Club Association (IRFCA), reveals that the rails in Madras had been manufactured locally at the furnaces of the Porto Novo Steel and Iron Company, which had received an 'order from the Government for six hundred cast iron gun carriages, as well as another for a large quantity of road-rails.'[30]

The Madras Herald of 1838 narrates an amusing account of the locomotive run on the Red Hill Railway—amusing, since while the line was for the conveyance of road-building material, the account seems to be that of a passenger train!

> We had another most gratifying sail on the Red Hill Railway last Monday afternoon. [...] the wind was favourable going and returning. The carriage is a small conveyance fitted up with springs; it is large enough to carry four or five persons, and is furnished with a small lug sail. The wheels are low, and in some places the road has suffered much by the last monsoon, yet in spite of these obstacles, the carriage travelled at least twelve miles [nineteen kilometres] an hour; and when the wind freshened, it was necessary to ease off the sheet to prevent the vehicle going at a greater velocity than would be agreeable, or, in the present state of the rails, safe.[31]

By the early 1840s, rail plans were drawn almost simultaneously in Calcutta and Bombay. The railways had raised interest among local intellectuals and businessmen, so much so that many schemes were in place and many planners and investors were queuing up for the

---

30. *The Asiatic Journal*, Volume 22, January-April 1837, p. 170. Porto Novo was the Portuguese name for the town of Parangipettai in the Cuddalore district of Tamil Nadu and the iron-works company there was one of the first industrial establishments in India, having been founded in 1828.

31. *The Madras Herald*, 16 January 1838. See also Simon Darvill, 'India's First Railways', *IRFCA*, December 2011, in <http://www.irfca.org/docs/history/india-first-railways.html#ftnr1>, accessed on 3 September 2014.

approval of their plans. But the looming question remained: how was one to build a rail network?

~

A formal proposal to build a railway line in India was first floated in 1843. With encouragement from Bombay governor, George Arthur, a civil engineer, Colonel George Thomas Clark, prepared tentative plans for a line on Bombay's island of Salsette, referring to this line as the Bombay Great Eastern Railway.

Clark was an odd combination of an engineer and a doctor. The *Oxford Dictionary of National Biography* refers to him as a surgeon who practised in Bristol. But a few years later, he joined the celebrated engineer, Isambard Kingdom Brunel[32] for the construction of the Great Western and Taff Vale Railway in England.

When Clark came down to India, he was the one who proposed eighty-nine kilometres of rail line from Bombay to the foot of the Western Ghats.[33] Parsi merchant, Seth Framji Cowasji Banaji was a rare, bold entrepreneur who believed in the railways; in 1844, he took up 200 shares of the proposed railway company, worth Rs 1 lakh, and worked with Clark on the plans. In fact, the elaborate designs of a rail line connecting Bombay and the mainland were laid at Seth Framji's estate gardens at Povoy (now Powai) near Bhandup, when Clark visited. In his diary, Clark notes that the estate had trees 'full of fruits of every country', and a bungalow 'for English travellers along the Thana great road'; he further records that the estate was 'exactly half

---

32. Isambard Kingdom Brunel, the iconic British engineer, made his first journey by a steam locomotive in 1831 on the 'shaking' Liverpool-Manchester railway line. He later promised to build a railway line where one could take coffee and write while going noiselessly and smoothly at seventy-two kilometres per hour. Brunel built a line with one of the widest gauges in Britain: 7'.25" inches (2,140 mm). Brunel also went on to build bridges, steamships and dockyards; the first major British railway, the Great Western Railway; and a series of steamships, including the first propeller-driven transatlantic steamship.

33. Ian J. Kerr,'John Chapman and the Promotion of the Great Indian Peninsula Railway: 1842–1850', *Financing the World's Railways in the Nineteenth and Twentieth Centuries,* edited by Ralf Roth and Gunter Dinhobl (Aldershot: Ashgate Publishing, 2008).

way between Bombay and Thana' (and on the island of Salsette). After an enthusiastic Clark chalked out detailed schemes for a line between 'Coorla to Thana', he got down to work.[34]

His plan included ten locomotives for passenger traffic and about 334 horses for goods trains. In his diary, Clark presented the specifics of his proposed line:

* The embankment, four feet in average height, will be sufficient to carry the rails on a level over a considerable portion of the line.
* From the Bombay Terminus to the flats, the line passes over a portion of the island formerly overflowed by the sea.
* From Byculla along the flats to Sion an embankment will be necessary. [...] In the deepest part this would not exceed four or five feet.
* A little beyond Sion some cutting will possibly be necessary, but the distance is very short and the amount unimportant. On approaching Coorla, the land is nearly on the level of the parts of the flats of this island, namely a few feet above high water mark as proved by the tide flowing up to the road side.
* From Coorla to the twentieth milestone, the line runs nearly parallel with the western bank of Tannah river; it has been surveyed by Captain Crawford [...and] he states that along the whole of this line there need not be a rise of [over] ten feet.
* From the twentieth milestone to Tannah, the line passes an extensive tract of rice fields.[35]

A group of local officials, prominent citizens and wealthy Indians took the plan further by instituting a provisional committee in July 1844. After months of private discussion, on 9 November 1844, the project was submitted to the government, with a letter delivered by senior judge Thomas Erskine Perry, Jagannath Sunkersett, Cursetjee

---

34. S.N. Sharma, *History of the GIP Railway (1853-1869)*, Part I, Volume I (Bombay: Chief Public Relations Officer, Central Railway, 1990).
35. *Ibid.*

Jamsetjee Jeejeebhoy, among others.[36] A public meeting was held in the town hall a few months later, on 19 April 1845; a resolution was passed in favour of forming an 'Inland Railway Association'. Colonel Clark's plan was taking flight.[37]

~

Even as the Bombay plan chugged ahead slowly, proposals for an Indian rail line were simultaneously being developed in England. In Britain, another enthusiastic English gentleman, John Chapman— who had originally been manufacturing carriages and precision parts, designing a flying machine, and improving the functionality of horse-drawn cabs[38]—played a key role in getting the railways to India. The story[39] goes that in 1841, when Chapman got in touch with British member of parliament, George Thompson, and learnt about his efforts to 'improve' India, Chapman advised him that better roads and railways were seminal to any development plan. These, he said, would help bring cotton to the coast at a low cost, and would contribute greatly to India's and Britain's progress. In his work, *Cotton and Commerce of India*, Chapman further emphasized the need for railways in light of the difficulties faced by those transporting cotton to Bombay's ports.

> More or less of such disappointment occurred every season, from different and even opposite causes. Rain too early, too scanty, or too plentiful; drought; epidemics amongst cattle; and many other varieties of misfortune, contribute to render the transit [of cotton] uncertain, insufficient and costly.[40]

---

36. See Dr Teresa Albuquerque, *Urbs Prima in Indis: An Epoch in the History of Bombay, 1840-1865* (India: Promila and Company, 1985), p. 4. See also Shaheed Khan, 'The Great Indian Railway Bazaar', *The Hindu: Metro Plus, Bangalore,* 18 April 2002.

37. *The Civil Engineer and Architect's Journal: Scientific and Railway Gazette,* Volume 8, 1845.

38. Ian J. Kerr, 'John Chapman and the Promotion of the Great Indian Peninsula Railway: 1842–1850', *Financing the World's Railways in the Nineteenth and Twentieth Centuries,* edited by Ralf Roth and Gunter Dinhobl (Aldershot: Ashgate Publishing, 2008).

39. *Ibid.*

40. John Chapman, *The Cotton and Commerce of India Considered in Relation to the Interests of Great Britain; With Remarks on Railway Communication in the Bombay Presidency* (London: Strand, 1851).

This was the turning point. The idea of a railway line in India was being championed like never before, and Chapman supported his arguments with detailed research and surveys, highlighting which lines would be profitable and where. A route from Thana to Malshej Ghat was deemed fit by Chapman in his initial survey. In a letter to the directors of the company on 17 July 1844, Chapman said:

> The Malsejee Ghaut, which was carefully surveyed by Lieutenant Stuart, Bombay Engineers, in 1837, seems to possess every requisite by which we can hope such an ascent shall be favoured and to be situated very favorably for both the northern and the southern traffic. Dismissing then, the Thull and the Bhor Ghats for the present, with a hope that increasing traffic will require them also to be fitted up as railroads at no distant period.[41]

After the East India Company officially issued a dispatch in May 1845 indicating they were prepared to receive detailed plans for railways in India, Chapman was on a roll. He formed a group in England, called it the Great Indian Peninsula Railway, and created a provisional committee to turn the GIPR into a joint stock company.

As the 'projector' of the company, Chapman spent three months examining the records of India House and collecting information. Messrs White, Borrett and Company, solicitors of Whitehall Place, helped him organize venture capitalists in London, and on 10 May 1845, the committee held its first meeting. By July the same year, the prospectus was ready, calling for subscriptions from India and Britain. Support for Chapman's project was only growing, with the Liverpool cotton merchants, on the lookout for new sources of cotton, backing him.[42] Consequently, by August 1845, Chapman was off to India to turn his dream into reality.

~

---

41. *Ibid.*

42. G.S. Khosla, *A History of Indian Railways* (India: A.H. Wheeler & Co, 1988), p. 33.

It took Chapman one month and four days to reach Bombay.[43] He came with a letter addressed to the governor of Bombay, seeking local support to make field investigations. First, he got in touch with the committee members of the Bombay Great Eastern Railway and persuaded them to assist him. The London and Bombay committees were merged to form a common commission with a singular aim— laying a railway line in Bombay to run steam trains.[44] John P. Willoughby became its chairman, and Robert Stephenson its consulting engineer. A crack team of three men—the dreamer, John Chapman; the planner, Colonel George Thomas Clark; and the young civil engineer, Henry Conybeare[45]—began to survey and work on the proposed line. The survey sought to study the movement of people in Bombay. To this end, a note was sent to offices and establishments in Bombay.

> It is being desired for the purpose of the railway company to ascertain as nearly as possible, the existing local passenger traffic of Bombay. Send a statement of various individuals employed in your office, with their places of residence and the manners in which they come into the Fort in the morning and return on the termination of their day's work. The list should include all persons who travel in vehicles of all description, and all persons whose pay is above Rs 15 per month, who come and go on foot. In remarks, write if the person keeps a vehicle of his own, or hires one, or hires jointly. If he walks sometimes, mention.[46]

On 1 August 1846, the company formally applied to construct a line at Byculla, to pass through Girgaum, Grant Road, Bellasis Road and Parel, from where a railroad up to Thana was to be opened, with a

43. S.N. Sharma, *History of the GIP Railway (1853-1869)*, Part I, Volume I (Bombay: Chief Public Relations Officer, Central Railway, 1990), p. 2.

44. *Ibid.*, p. 3.

45. Conybeare, later as Bombay's civic engineer, was the one who developed piped water supply systems for the city that still remain in use.

46. Dr A.K. Arora, *History of Bombay Suburban Railways: 1853-1985* (Bombay: The Indian Railway Electrical Engineers Association, 1985).

branch to the port of Mahim.[47] It requested the Bombay government to permit building a terminus on the esplanade opposite Churchgate for the proposed Thana line.[48] But the alignment was soon found to be unfeasible as it passed through congested areas. (The plan would have changed the Bombay we know today, if the arrangement had worked.)

A subsequent simpler alignment was planned from Bori Bunder along the eastern shore to the mainland and Thana. Conybeare submitted a report on 21 June 1849, highlighting the problem of swamps at Sion, and the difficulties in acquiring properties—for, the line at certain stretches here had to pass through dense residential colonies. There were disputes and cases and compensation issues. When Bombay's collector of land revenue, Hugh Poyntz Malet (who later, as district collector of Thana, discovered the hill station of Matheran in 1850) was asked to provide a list of lands to be acquired, with details of their revenue assessment and compensation rates, he too highlighted the land acquisition problem and emphasized the need for special legislation for lands to be acquired from private individuals.

A year later in 1850, the Bombay government's financial department set up a 'railway branch' to centralize land purchases with the railway's superintending engineer. Captain J.H.G. Crawford was required to maintain records of all deals and report the transactions to the government at regular intervals. Those who resisted were ordered to present their case before a jury panel for arbitration. Ultimately, Crawford played a key role in acquiring land for the first railway.[49]

Meanwhile, the bill to incorporate the GIPR Company came up before parliament in England, first in March 1847 when it was withdrawn after opposition from the East India Company over certain clauses, and two years later on 1 August 1849 when it was cleared. With the bill cleared, and the act to incorporate the GIPR Company now in existence, a formal contract was signed on 17 August 1849

---

47. *Ibid.*

48. *Ibid.*

49. Mariam Dossal, *Mumbai: Theatre of Conflict, City of Hope: 1660 to Present Times* (India: Oxford University Press, 2012), p. 117.

between the East India Company and the GIPR Company to lay a thirty-four-kilometre 'experimental line of railway' from Bombay to Thana. The GIPR Company would build and operate its own line with a guaranteed 5 per cent return on the investment of stockholders. The directors of the East India Company advised the government of India to remain economical and not spend money on ornamental structures, as had been 'erroneously done in England.'[50]

Once this act was in place, Berkley was appointed as the chief engineer and sent out to India. The rest, as we now know, is history.

A FIRE CHARIOT ARRIVES

As English contractors Faviell and Fowler struggled to complete the line, a steam locomotive arrived in Bombay in 1852. It was a grand, new attraction for one and all.

However, it was not the first steam locomotive on Indian soil. Kilometres away in North India, at Roorkee, just a little earlier, in December 1851, a six-wheeled giant Thomason had landed. It was a standard-gauge tank engine built by the E.B. Wilson railway foundry in Leeds. It had been brought for the construction of the Solani aqueduct, a part of the River Ganges canal project, which had begun in 1845. According to the Indian Railways Fan Club:

> It did not last very long, and after about nine months, India's first steam locomotive died a spectacular death with a boiler explosion, reportedly to the delight of the construction workers who had viewed it more as a hindrance than a help.[51]

Much before that, in 1836, as we know, the Red Hill Railway line had been running.[52]

---

50. S.N. Sharma, *History of the GIP Railway (1853-1869)*, Part 1, Volume 1 (Bombay: Chief Public Relations Officer, Central Railway, 1990), pp. 5-6.

51. 'IR History: Early Days', *IRFC*, in <http://www.irfca.org/faq/faq-hist.html#first>, accessed on 3 September 2014.

52. Captain J.T. Smith, *Reports, Correspondence and Original Papers on Various Professional Subjects Connected with the Duties of the Corps of Engineers: Madras Presidency*, Volume 1 (Madras: Vepery Mission Press, 1839).

Like the one that had arrived at Roorkee, the giant that reached Bombay was an E.B. Wilson creation, but met the requirements of a 5' 6" gauge line. The locomotive drew crowds by the thousands and was promptly named after the Bombay governor of that time, Lucius Bentinck Cary, the tenth Lord Viscount of Falkland. Though stationary steam machines and steamships had been in regular use, it was the first time that the local populace was seeing a *moving* steam apparatus on rails. 'Lord Falkland'—as the locomotive was named— created a wave of euphoria. Its hissing, puffing, whistling, its smoke and smell provoked awe. Indeed, when 'Lord Falkland' arrived, it had to be pulled down a public road by more than 200 coolies for its first operation. Its sheer size scared many, but fascinated several others.

The engine's shunting operations began near Byculla from a grove that belonged to an Englishman, William Phipps (and others). The grove—that had been used to cultivate toddy trees—also had stone

Courtesy: Central Railway Archives

The Byculla Loco Staff with a Decorated Steam Locomotive

quarries, later used as ballast for the railway line. As quarrying would destroy toddy plantations, it was necessary for the railways to have absolute rights over the land, so as to make radical changes. The GIPR bought it over at a cost of Rs 4,000.[53] The land that now housed the engine began to attract crowds from all parts of town and the site became a virtual fair.[54]

Locals, who had by then seen a working steamship, started calling the rail engine an 'aag-boat', or sometimes a 'fire chariot'. English newspapers of the day had debates over what to call the locomotive in the local language—was it a steamship, a steam chariot, or perhaps, something else?

> By what name is a railway locomotive to be known among the natives? This is not an utterly uninteresting question. They have already commenced to call her 'Ag-boat', which is the name given by them to a steam-vessel; but this is absurd. It is suggested that the proper appellation would be 'Bauf-ka-Rutthee', which means a steam-chariot. Now is the time to settle this important matter. If the term 'Ag-boat' is allowed to prevail at this time, it will infallibly stick.[55]

Meanwhile, the 'fair' at Byculla's grounds to watch the locomotive in action also attracted media attention. The *Bombay Telegraph* dated 17 February 1852 reported:

> The native population appears to evince great interest in the 'Fire Chariot' as they name her, and crowd round to have a look. The weight and massive character of the whole is quite at variance with their notion of speed; and, after observing the slow progress she made when being dragged along the public road by 200 coolies, their incredulous look of astonishment is

---

53. Mariam Dossal, *Mumbai: Theatre of Conflict, City of Hope: 1660 to Present Times* (India: Oxford University Press, 2012), p. 117.

54. *The Locomotive*, 15 June 1926, pp. 182-83.

55. *Allen's Indian Mail, and Register of Intelligence for British and Foreign India, China, and All parts of the East*, Volume 10, January-December 1852, p. 196, quoting *Bombay Telegraph*.

not to be wondered at, when told, that in a few days she will be able to pass the race course swifter than their fleetest Arabs.[56]

~

The first trial run of the locomotive, Lord Falkland, was on 18 February 1852, from Byculla to Parel (where the Bombay governor then stayed). A frenzied crowd ran along with the locomotive and people lined up in every conceivable spot along the route. The railways had arrived in Bombay and had received a jubilant welcome! A news report in the *Bombay Telegraph* documented the trial 'wonder run'.[57]

> Not above a dozen Europeans were present, but thousands and thousands of natives were attracted to the spot, gazed with an expression of wonderment at the smoking, hissing machine as it stood at the entrance of its shed at Byculla and as it moved slowly onwards, this expression changed into one of gratified surprise, as if they had scarcely expected that the huge affair could be got into motion. A loud whistling was heard, a cloud of spray fell like a shower on the crowd, and the engine moved on her way, first at a walking pace, then at a trot and latterly at a speed of about 15 miles [24 kilometres] per hour. It went as far as Parell (a distance of two miles), where she stopped for some time, probably for the Governor, after which she was named, to have an opportunity of looking his namesake and came back as before. A second trip was soon performed with slight stoppages to put it in mechanical order.

On Thursday, 18 November 1852, at noon, at the instance of contractors Faviell, Jackson and Wythes, the directors of the GIPR Company took the first end-to-end trial run of a train, with the giant Lord Falkland at the helm. The journey took forty-five minutes.[58]

---

56. *Ibid.*, p. 165.

57. *Ibid.*, p. 196, quoting *Bombay Telegraph*.

58. Dr A.K. Arora, *History of Bombay Suburban Railways: 1853-1985* (Bombay: The Indian Railway Electrical Engineers Association, 1985), p. vii.

A report in the *Bombay Times* describes the trial run of 1852 with the great Lord Falkland:

> From Bori Bunder, the railway proceeded by a very densely peopled district till, skirting along the shore, it passes the lofty precipice of Nowrojee Hill. [Nowrojee Hill is today's Sandhurst Road Station, West.] After passing under the Mazagon viaduct, opposite the Sudder Adawlut, which was crowded with people, and which commands an excellent view of the line, and also of the engine and its train on both sides, the railway describes a very graceful double cone of large radius, and then crosses the Byculla road near the bishop's house, and passing under the still unfinished viaduct, and across the temporary public road beyond, which not being provided with gates was protected by a strong body of police, it so reached the flats near the race-course. [...] From the curious gravel bank called Phipp's Oart, it stretches along the flats to Sion, over a dead uninteresting level for the space of six miles [approximately ten kilometres] in almost a perfectly straight line. [...] At Sion it passes under the public road and along the base of the hill, on the summit of which is an old Marathi fort and a Portuguese church contiguous. Here it is joined by the branch which goes along to Mahim, at present an unimportant fishing village, but likely to be transformed by the railway into a port of importance. The branch is about ten miles [sixteen kilometres] in length, and has just been completed.

The old Marathi fort described here are the remains of the Rewa Fort watchtower; the church is next to Sion Station. The report goes on to say:

> From this, the line sweeps across Sion marsh, the embanking of which at one time threatened to be very troublesome—the material thrown in sinking amongst the mud, which afterwards rose up, forming a little island on each side along the line. Here, immediately adjoining and nearly parallel to the railway, we have the Sion causeway on one side, and full in view two miles [three kilometres] off the magnificent work of the like kind, constructed by Jamsetjee Jeejeebhoy, first constructed in 1844.

[...] The railway now bends considerably to the right, and passing through a long line of salt pans, it enters Salsette, and encounters the only formidable obstruction on the line; a beautifully wooded ridge traversed by an open cutting about half-a-mile [about a kilometre] in length, and about 120 feet across where it is widest, and about fifty feet in depth. Here the fire-steed stopped, and took a vast quaff from the cellar close by.

This is today's Kurla East, where the badly demolished ridge still stands; the remains are now called the Kasaiwada hillock, and can be spotted from passing trains. *Bombay Times* goes on to marvel at the train's speed and the views it offers:

The nine miles [fourteen kilometres] had been performed in eighteen minutes; the speed at one time being above 50 miles [80 kilometres] an hour, and the average 30 [48 kilometres]. From this, for the next fourteen miles [22.5 kilometres], the line is perfectly level, the rails being laid along the surface of the ground, with merely so much embanking as to save them from the risk of flooding during the rains.

[...] The country for a considerable distance is open on both sides, and the view extremely beautiful. To the left are the low rocky wooded ridges of Salsette—woodlands and richly cultivated fields, hamlets and cottages, filling up the intervening space. On the right, parallel to and close beside the railway for about eight miles [thirteen kilometres], is the salt water creek called the Tanna river, and just beyond are the magnificent ghauts.

Today, on the left of the line, one can still see the wooded ridge at Vikhroli, but festooned with houses and slums. Parts of the hill near Powai are now being quarried to accommodate towering residential apartment blocks. On the right of the line, the Eastern Express Highway has come up, beyond which still stand the salt pans and the creek.

~

The locomotive in action caused a cultural shock, and a number of opinions emerged; gossip flew. To those unacquainted with the industrial developments taking place on the other side of the world, the smoke-belching locomotive, spitting steam and pulling wagons, was a mystery! Some locals believed that an evil force was powering the engine. 'How can this thing move so fast without mediation? There must be something to it, either evil or godly, more likely evil.' Many were confident that the monster would soon spread its malice across society. They called the train the 'lokhandi rakshash' ('the iron demon' in Marathi); no native of a good caste would ever 'defile himself by entering a railway carriage'. [59]

Still others whispered that if the great saints of India had failed to discover such a thing, how could mere mortals presume to be inventors of a running engine? If the creation of a steam-powered locomotive had really been possible, it would have been put to use much earlier. This engine was an ogre!

While there were a handful of enterprising businessmen who knew the importance of railways, there were others who were neither superstitious nor ambitious. For them, Lord Falkland, the steam-run machine pulling a row of wagons, was just a 'bluff', a hoax to cheat poor Indians of their land! Taking this theory to fantastic extremes, some said the wagon was a ploy by the English to collect all of India's money and run away.

As people saw Lord Falkland in action every day, another set of superstitions emerged. The rumour was that one had to bury children and young couples under the rail sleepers to 'power' the rail engine; British sepoys, therefore, were perpetually looking for and catching hold of young couples and children on the streets, who would then be put under the tracks as food for the beast!

There was also the belief that if one travelled by rail, one's lifespan would dramatically decrease. After all, if one reached one's destination so much faster, one was bound to speed up life and age!

There was also a wave of resentment, as old taboos were being eroded. The author, K.R. Vaidyanathan describes the unfavourable response of a 'high-caste Hindu' in 1874, when he learnt that 'the

---

59. Balkrishna Bapu Acharya and Moro Vinayak Shingne, *Mumbaicha Vrutant* (India: Rajya Sahitya Sanskriti Mandal, 1889), pp. 220-21.Translated by the author.

sweepers, the chamars and the like classes of people [were] in the same carriage along with Hindustanis of the higher order.' Equally, upper-class Muslims were uncomfortable sharing seats with the general populace; a 'Muslim paper in Lucknow pressed for the "provision of separate carriages for the respectable classes of the Hindus and Mussalmans on the one hand and the lower classes of the natives on the other."'[60]

Courtesy: Mumbai Port Trust Archives

The 'Fire Chariot'

---

60. K.R. Vaidyanathan, *150 Glorious Years of Indian Railways* (India: English Edition Publishers, 2003).

Fortunately, as the benefits of easy, clean and swift transport became obvious, both rumours and objections vanished. What started as a vehicle to ferry cotton and goods, soon became a passenger service, and an extremely lucrative one. Therefore, it was said:

> The steam engine was overturning prejudices, uprooting habits and changing customs. A man who, before railways existed, on no account would have walked or carried a pound weight, but must have had a palkhee and bearers, now cheerfully marches to the station with a carpet bag; and, strange to say, even unpunctuality and apathy vanish before the warning bell of a station master. Railways, which had gone far in England to annihilate distance, were in India to reduce to a manageable extent the vast distance of the continent; were to strengthen the Government; to bind races together; and by giving an impetus to commerce, to vivify and give such a bias to the character of the peoples of India, as ages had not effected, and ages would not efface.[61]

~

On 16 April 1853, fourteen months after Lord Falkland had been seen trundling from Byculla to Parel, India saw its first commercial passenger train service.

At 3.30 p.m., Lady Falkland, wife of the governor of Bombay, boarded the train, followed by 400 invitees: royalty, 'burra sahibs', rich zamindars and other VIPs. At exactly 3.35 p.m., to thunderous applause and a twenty-one gun salute, the train whistled and rolled out from Bombay's Bori Bunder Station to Thana. This train was hauled by three locomotives—ceremoniously named Sindh, Sultan, and Sahib. (These were three among eight locos that had arrived from the Vulcan Foundry in England, a firm partnered by Robert Stephenson.) It took fifty-seven minutes to complete the thirty-two-kilometre journey, with a halt at Sion to refill the train's water tanks.

Krishnashastri Bhatwadekar, a Marathi scholar, describes the

---

61. Edward Davidson, *The Railways of India with an Account of Their Rise, Progress and Construction* (London: E. & F.N. Spon, 1868), p. 231.

opening day of the 'iron road' of Bombay as a memorable occasion, and says that the atmosphere was one of celebration.

> Exactly at 3:30 pm, the cannons boomed from the Dongri Fort [the new St George's Fort] and the governor's band that was in one of the wagons started playing the national anthem. [...] This was a wonder, and men, women and children from the town had gathered to watch the spectacle from their terrace or roofs. Most of the high places along the way were taken to watch this run. [...] After the engines pulled the garland of wagons till Byculla, and once they crossed the viaducts of Sion and Mahim, there were more crowds.[62]

The billowing smoke of the train drew gasps from bystanders. *The Overland Telegraph and Courier* famously reported that 'the natives salaamed the omnipotence of the steam engine as it passed.'[63] Rail enthusiasts affirm, 'To [the onlookers], this miraculous entity was nothing short of god, as they applied red tilaks on the smoke stacks, left food and money on the footplate, and reverentially placed flowers on the tracks.'[64]

For the British, the arrival of a rail network in India was the ultimate victory. *The Overland Telegraph and Courier* asserted this fact, when it said:

> [The railway is] a triumph, to which, in comparison, all our victories in the East seem tame and commonplace. The opening of the Great Indian Peninsular Railway will be remembered by the natives of India when the battlefields of Plassey, Assaye, Meanee, and Goojerat have become landmarks of history.[65]

---

62. *A Short Account of Railways, Selected from Lardner's Railway Economy*, translated by Krishnashastri Bhatwadekar (Bombay: Ganpat Krishnaji Press, 1854), p. 2.

63. *The Overland Telegraph and Courier*, 16 April 1853.

64. Anurag Mallick and Priya Ganapathy, 'Boribunder to Thana: 1853 Revisited', *Redscarab*, 14 April 2014, in <http://redscarabtravelandmedia.wordpress.com/2013/04/14/boribunder-to-thana-1853-revisited/>, accessed on 2 September 2014.

65. *The Overland Telegraph and Courier*, 16 April 1853.

The *Bombay Times* reiterated this jingoistic stance, when it carried a poem on the opening of the island city's railway line:

Hark, hark, reverberating over land and sea,
The kind of cannon's boom and jubilee,
And lo! Solemnly standing, wroth'd in clouds,
Hissing steam, amidst the breathless clouds,
The sight of wonder, in whose grasp appears,
The flag that's brav'd its foes a thousand years.[66]

~

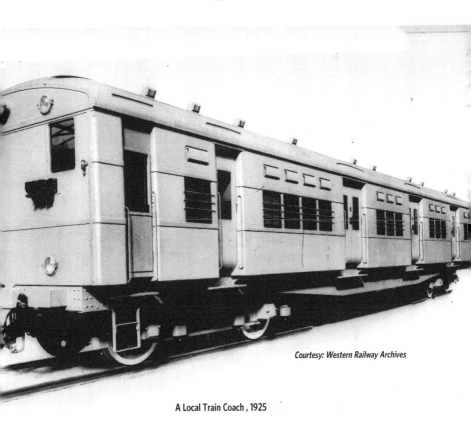

Courtesy: Western Railway Archives

A Local Train Coach , 1925

---

66. 'The Opening of the Bombay Railway', *Bombay Times*, 18 April 1853.

Though images of the early railways, taken with primitive photo technology, do not have colours, the real locomotives and stations of the time were suffused with colour and life. Bombay's earliest locomotives were painted a bright green, with black bands; they were polished, clean and well-maintained. The initials 'GIPR' appeared on the tender panels and driving splashers of many engines in small yellow letters. Several were decorated with brass stars, had polished lamps, and designs scratched on the smoke box.[67] A few decades later, between 1875 and 1889, the locomotives got a coat of lead grey with red lines. This style continued till 1901, when a dark red shade, made of roasted laterite—red-brown coloured earth found freely in India— took over.

How did the first of all carriages in India look? The first carriages were built in England with varnished teak panels (and shipped out when it was time for the first section of the railways to start). These carriages were fairly primitive, with well-built bodies on short wooden underframes, running on four open-spoked wheels.

Class determined everything! The framing of the superstructure was external for third-class carriages, but for the first and second classes, woodsheeting was used outside to grant carriages a smooth finish. The upper classes, of course, had bright-green sunshades. Furthermore, each class was colour coded, in the hope that the 'more ignorant of the native travellers' would be able to make distinctions. Consequently, reports from 1885 reveal that the first-class carriages were white, the second-class was khaki-buff, and the third-class was a dark red-brown. With time, though, the British discovered that these 'native travellers' followed the 'birds of a feather' precept, rather than colour schemes. Therefore, the British abandoned colour codes and adopted uniform colouring for all carriages. The initials of the railway appeared on a small cast-iron plate attached to the sides. With no diagonal brace, the roof used to sway endways and sideways alarmingly.[68]

---

67. *The Locomotive*, 15 June 1926, pp.182-83.

68. *Ibid.*, 15 December 1926, pp. 395-97.

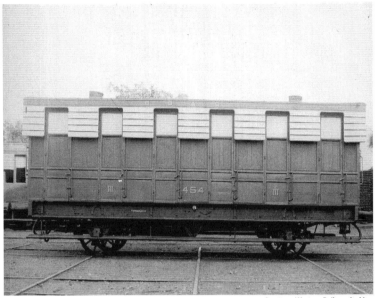

Courtesy: Western Railway Archives

A Third-Class Carriage

THE MATERIALS THAT BUILT THE FIRST LINE

Berkley, in his minutes, documents that the first railway had rails with a 'double T form, weighing 81 lbs per lineal yard as far as Tannah, beyond which they weighed only 65 lbs and 68 lbs per yard.'[69] Many of these double-head rails can still be found today, extensively used as station furniture.

The laying of the tracks was a crucial step in actually building the railway line. To lay a line of a 5'6" gauge, a wooden sleeper, sized 10'x12"x6", was required; this sleeper had to be placed on a bed of stones. A whopping 1,700 sleepers were required for a kilometre-and-a-half-long track. There were debates regarding the kinds of sleepers that could be used to lay the tracks. Would wood or iron sleepers suit Indian conditions? Wood proved to be the most popular

---

69. *Professional Papers on Indian Engineering*, Volume 3, edited by Major J.G. Medley (India: Thomason College Press, 1866).

choice, but sourcing the right kind of wood and guaranteeing its steady supply was always a problem. Inevitably, the right kind of wood would be available only in distant places.

Consequently, a railway engineer was deputed to survey forests, and locate a depot in the vicinity where the wood could be stored. This would be transported by wheeled carriages to the work site with the permission of the local collector. There are reports of wood being imported, but generally, wood was sourced locally. Timber was found to be most suitable for India, especially in the wet, windswept, sun-scorched, vermin-ridden and weed-infested ghats. Occasionally, blackwood, teak or khair were also selected.

The first broad-spectrum forest surveys in India were done in the 1840s, followed by a detailed survey per district. Scottish surgeon and botanist, Alexander Gibson, also the conservator of forests and superintendent of gardens, and William Fenner, the first assistant conservator of forests, were in charge of the forest administration survey of the Bombay Presidency for the years 1856-1860. This included a physical inspection of the Khandala rail line by Gibson. Later, as work proceeded and the trees were felled, the destruction was monitored, even as the revenue earned by the forest department was meticulously registered.

THE CHRISTENING OF THE STATIONS

Most station names along the first section of the railway line referred to ancient villages that had existed at those locations.

Mahikavati's Bakhar by Keshavacharya is a fourteenth-century chronicle of ancestries, events and places in North Aparanta (North Konkan, including the islands of Bombay). It covers historical events in the region across a period of 400 years, from the fourteenth century till the arrival of the Portuguese. The chapters have been written in different time periods and by a range of authors. *Mahikavati's Bakhar*, consequently, helps shed light on the names of the villages. These are the names that entered British revenue surveys; the Britons anglicized them as a matter of convenience, and these became the names of railway stations.

The revenue villages mentioned in *Mahikavati's Bakhar* include

Kuraley, Chembhoor, Nawoor, Bhandoop, Mulunda, Vikharoli, Kanzhurey. These are all stations and suburbs in today's Bombay. The British surveys—the first one was done by Thomas Dickinson in 1812, followed by a survey of Salsette by William Tate in 1827— reinterpreted the names. Kuraley became Coorla (and still later, Kurla; even today, suburban trains carry the initial 'C', despite the station being known as Kurla) and Chembhoor became Chimboor (and still later, Chembur). Many 'newer' stations were subsequently named after British public figures or important places in their home cities—Sandhurst Road, Currey Road, and Cotton Green being some examples.[70]

Incidentally, if you have wondered why some stations have a 'road' or a 'marg' as part of their names, here is the reason. Diseases and epidemics were quite frequent in British India. Many Englishmen who came down to this country succumbed to fever and ailments. To avoid the menace of infection, British engineers made a conscious effort to keep the rail alignment straight and away from cluttered Indian habitations or villages. However, so the rail network could be accessed, a road would often get constructed from the settlements to the stations. The station would carry the name of the village, and the lane leading to it would be acknowledged with that commonplace tag, 'road' or 'marg'.

THE BIRTH OF THE ROUNDEL

The popular blue-and-red roundel—or 'bull's-eye' and 'target' as it is commonly known—is now a part of all station signage in India. It comes with a fascinating story, one that has its origins in London.

A precursor to the roundel was a winged, spoked wheel with a crossbar, originally used by the London General Omnibus Company, the city's principal bus operator between 1855 and 1933.

In 1908, the Underground Electric Railways Company of London, the direct ancestor of today's London Underground, used a version of this wheel for its stations' name boards; it fashioned a bright red

---

70. From the extensive preface by V.K. Rajwade, on Keshavacharya's *Mahikavatichi Bakhar*, originally published in 1924 by Chitrashala Press, Pune.

circle, with a blue bar across. Frank Pick, 'the Lincolnshire solicitor who became London Transport's first chief executive and imposed a passion for excellence in design on every aspect of his work',[71] enlisted the help of calligrapher, Edward Johnston, to chisel such signage. The

The Roundel in India

two replaced the solid red disc with a white circle framed by red; within this were 'plain block letters of Roman proportions in which the main strokes were of equal thickness and there were no end strokes or serifs.'[72] The font—called 'Johnson Sans'—followed a strict palette: white on a dark blue bar. The design became popular across the London Underground, and its centennial year was celebrated in 2008.

Somewhere along the way—the precise date remains unclear—this roundel found its way to Indian rail stations, and remains very much in use.

---

71. 'In Praise of Frank Pick', *The Guardian*, 17 October 2008.

72. 'Frank Pick: Designing Modern Britain', *Design Museum*, in <http://designmuseum.org/design/frank-pick>, accessed on 12 September 2014.

ALL IN FAVOUR !

------ · ------

BRIEF POINTS ON TRAVELLING BY TRAIN

Peace of Mind.—The responsibility for every journey is taken by trained staffs of engine drivers or motormen, signalmen are in charge of the most modern equipment along the linesides, and guards travel with every train.

Regularity of Departures and Arrivals.—A higher standard of punctuality is maintained by railway trains than by any other form of transport.

Private Steel Highways.—Prepared tracks are maintained at high standards of perfection, giving smoother travel than by any other means.

All-Weather Journeys.—Weatherproof trains, controlled heating and sheltered stations enable comfortable travel to be accomplished irrespective of weather conditions.

Freedom of Movement.—Corridor carriages, with toilets, restaurant, buffet and sleeping cars form part of long distance trains.

Meals on the Move.—Table d'hôte or à la carte refreshments may be obtained without loss of travel time.

Time to Think.—Quietude and the opportunity to think, or for conversation—and perhaps romance.

Detached Observation.—A moving panorama to be seen through the carriage windows. Fields, old and new buildings, towns, cities and unusual views.

Adequate Artificial Lighting, enabling reading, writing, needlework, study or relaxation to be enjoyed without strain.

Unconscious Speed.—Many trains now touch 90 miles an hour. It's quicker by rail.

Complete Safety.—Railway trains are the safest form of travel, and railway tracks are the safest and best kept highways in the world.

Courtesy: ISR Magazine: GIP Railway Supplement, Central Railway Archives

An Early Advertisement for the Railways

AFTER THE FIRST RUN: PROTESTS AND UNUSUAL
ANCILLARY INDUSTRIES

The first month of the first-ever railway was a runaway success.
Regular runs of the train had begun from 18 April 1853, and by 30
April 1853, the trains had ferried 21,922 passengers, earning Rs 9,109,
three annas and eight paise! The next month, in May 1853, the figure
rose to Rs 40,071, and by December 1853 to Rs 61,413.[73]

Yet, even as the rail network took root, there was resistance from
an unlikely quarter. Bullock-cart owners took up a fight with the
railways. They were irate, not only because of the dwindling number
of passengers, but also because of falling cargo supply. The railways
were ferrying everyone and everything!

To take control of the situation, bullock-cart owners began
charging a fixed rate from the hinterlands to Bombay; it now made
little economic sense for passenger traffic and cargo to disembark
midway at railway stations. The bullock-cart owners' plan was a
success and proved to be a headache for the railway managers. In
1868, fifteen years after the first run, the agent of the GIPR wrote a
harried letter to the railway board, suggesting that the railways appoint
a person to solicit traffic.

> We are, I regret to say, threatened with a severe competition on
> the part of the Bullock Cart drivers from cotton markets in the
> south eastern district. The whole of the cotton markets on the
> south eastern district are situated at a distance varying from 20
> to 120 miles [193 kilometres] from our station and the bullock
> men have combined to charge the same rate to our stations as to
> Panwell (the latter place is situated at the foot of the ghats on
> the Bombay river) from whence the cotton is conveyed by boat
> to Bombay. The saving by boat to Panwell is some forty pc as
> compared by rail. I had this week been to the south eastern for
> the purpose of seeing what can be done to retain traffic by the
> rail. I shall, I find, have to establish carting agencies same as on
> the Up district as well as appoint a person specially to solicit
> traffic and report as to what is being done at the various markets.[74]

---

73. *Ibid.*, pp. 1-3.

74. S.N. Sharma, *History of the GIP Railway (1853-1869)*, Part I, Volume I (Bombay:
Chief Public Relations Officer, Central Railway, 1990), p. 89.

The agent did execute the plan for a while. Eventually, the bullock-cart owners' protests died a natural death, just like the strange rumours that had spread when the railways had arrived.

~

The arrival of the rail network gave rise to a host of local publications describing what a train was and how it worked—a sort of dummy's guide to the railways! These guides, in a range of languages, are a joy to read.

The Marathi scholar, Krishnashastri Bhatwadekar translated a few chapters of a book by Dionysius Lardner[75] into Marathi to help introduce the concept of railways to the local population. The translated version[76] is probably the earliest available local literature, with the oldest possible photographs, on India's first rail line. With no local vocabulary for railways, rail wagons and engines, the concept of a train was explained through the use of a rather simple set of words: a machine ('yantra') pulling a garland of wagons ('gadyanchai haar'). To clarify these rather strange ideas, there were sketches of the earliest railway stations and locomotives. Compare these with the original builder's drawings of the Vulcan Factory locomotives, and the images match perfectly!

Bhatwadekar's book tells us that while the first train had single-journey tickets, season tickets were introduced in 1854. The book also documents twenty-four local laws for travel framed by the GIPR administration on 11 March 1853. 'Regulations for the GIPR Railway of Bombay Region' reveals that India's earliest trains had a separate compartment for the women—not unlike today. The GIPR urged male commuters to stay away from this compartment; disobedience would provoke a fine of Rs 20. Additionally, the rules specified that it was compulsory to buy a 'chitti' (a ticket) before boarding the 'women's room' on any part of the 'iron road' in Bombay.

---

75. Dionysius Lardner, *Railway Economy: A Treatise on the New Art of Transport* (London: Taylor, Walton and Maberly, 1850).

76. *A Short Account of Railways, Selected from Lardner's Railway Economy*, translated by Krishnashastri Bhatwadekar (Bombay: Ganpat Krishnaji Press, 1854), pp. 56-62.

G. I. P. Railway Supplement.

Baloo the Careless
or SAFETY FIRST

RUTHLESS RHYMES FOR RAILWAY FOLK.

By W. B. B.

Drawings by K. W. M.

Baloo thought it would be fun
To play with " hammers S. B. one "
   Later on they found him dead,
   Laid out by the hammer head.

N. B.—" S. B." is short for " Sledge, Blacksmith."
     not for " Silly Baloo."

Moral: Watch the wedge
        Don't play with tools.

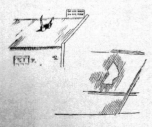

Through the roof of asbestos
Baloo took a nasty toss
   A new " Big Six " came from the store
   But Baloo had a broken jaw.

8

Courtesy: W.H. Burford, ISR Magazine: GIP Railway Supplement, Central Railway Archives

A Dummy's Guide to Trains Released by the GIPR in the early 1900s

According to the third law in the charter of regulations, the fine for most offences, including ticketless travel or lighting tobacco in the train, was Rs 20. While grazing cattle in the railway's premises invited a fine of only Rs 10, not locking the doors of level-crossings once they were used, or the removal of boards and lights, and the destruction of railway property, invited a fine of a whopping Rs 50! If railway property suffered severe losses, the person responsible would be sent 'sumudra paar'—banished from his land for life.

WHAT HAPPENED TO THE FIRST LOCOS?

The first shunting locomotive, Lord Falkland, that had created a ripple in Bombay, continued in service on the regular line. After a number of years, it was sold to the neighbouring BB&CI Railway, and converted into a tank locomotive.

The regular locomotives, built at the Vulcan Foundry, come with interesting specifications. A neatly handwritten table of the dispatch data of the Vulcan Foundry reveals a constellation of numbers: the rotation numbers of the locos were from 324 to 331, the working numbers were 680 to 687, and they had a water capacity of 800 gallons. These were the first of the 2,750 locomotives supplied to India between 1852 and 1952. The locos came in windjammers and landed at Bori Bunder. They were probably sent in a knocked down condition and assembled in Bombay.

The first locos remained in service for quite some time and the last one was seen 100 years after it was first put to use; it was commemorated for the centennial year of the Indian railways.

A detailed history of the first nine locos shows where they went and for what—numbers 1, 2 and 8 were sold to the BB&CI Railway and converted into tank engines, while numbers 3, 4, 6 and 9 were used as stationary engines for workshops. Of these, number 3 was serving the Parel loco shops in 1916 rather well, driving a rolling mill! Number 5 worked as a stationary engine till 1906, driving the saw mill at the railway depot of the West of India Portuguese Railway,[77] while number 7 was sold to Ebrahim Dadur—where this one eventually went remains a mystery.

---

77. *The Locomotive*, 15 June 1926, pp. 182-83.

THE DISSOLUTION OF OLD LAWS

The British government scrapped reams of colonial legislation relating to the construction and maintenance of India's vast railway network, as late as October 2012. The Indian High Commission and the railways' board were consulted as part of the repeal process. In the list of thirty-eight obsolete rail laws was the founding law of the Indian railways, the Great Indian Peninsula Railway Company Act, 1849. Some of the other scrapped acts included the Bombay Baroda and Central India Railway Act, 1942; the Assam Railways and Trading Company's Act, 1897; the Oude Railway Act, 1858; the Scinde Railway Act, 1857; the Great Southern of India Railway Act, 1858; and the Calcutta and South-eastern Railway Act, 1857. With this round of spring-cleaning, an era had officially ended.

A HOME FOR THE GIPR

With the advent of the era of the railways in India, the GIPR decided to establish itself in Bombay. However, for the first few years, it did not have a permanent office address and kept moving locations.

When the construction of the line had begun, the chief engineer's office had been situated opposite the town hall; subsequently he had been transferred to Mount Castle in Victoria Road, Mazgaon.

Around 1863, the GIPR offices were shifted to a lane off Grant Road. But even this was short-lived, and three years later, they were moved to Byculla Villa. During this period the agent's and accountant's offices were housed in the bungalow of one of the native directors of the GIPR, Jagannath Sunkersett, opposite the synagogue at Byculla. 'Those were the days when the railways did not have enough space for themselves, and we opened up our residential bungalow for the railway company to run their ticket booking office,' says Surendra Sunkersett, the fourth descendent.[78]

In 1869, the chief engineer's office was moved to a building on Churchgate Street, known as the old BB&CI Railway office, while the agent's and accountant's offices were accommodated for a short time in the Temple Bar Hotel, in today's Kala Ghoda. In 1870, all

---

78. A conversation with Surendra Sunkersett in 2013.

three offices were removed to Messrs Remington & Co's building at Elphinstone Circle, opposite the town hall.

As for the traffic offices, they had been located in the old station building at Bori Bunder from the outset; the headquarters of the locomotive department was at Byculla (and eventually moved to Parel in June 1882).

It was only after the construction of Victoria Terminus in 1882, thirty years after the first train run, that all the GIPR offices were streamlined. By 1886, all the offices, except those of the locomotive department, were transferred to the splendid Victoria Terminus building.[79]

Ten years later, in 1896, the BB&CI Railway established Colaba as its terminus in Bombay. With that, the GIPR and the BB&CI Railway became the framework of a city that was to be the financial capital of India. In the words of Britain's leading transport commentator, Christian Wolmar:

> The railways have played a more important role in the history of India than in any other nation. And unlike many countries where their role has been diminished, the railways are still at the heart of Indian life. Other large nations such as Brazil either never managed to build an extensive network or, like China, only realized their advantage recently. While the railways did play a key role in the economic development of the United States of America, nowadays they are reduced principally to carrying freight. For India, the railways have been a constant in their history since the first line was opened. [...] And it all started with a little line from Bombay to Thana.[80]

It is this little line that we plan to explore, in an attempt to recreate the past.

---

79. S.M. Edwardes, *The Gazetteer of Bombay City and Island*, Volume I (India: Cosmo Publications, 2002), p. 346.

80. Inputs from Christian Wolmar, author of *Blood, Iron, and Gold: How the Railways Transformed the World* (New York: PublicAffairs, 2010), in response to a draft copy of this book.

WALKING DOWN THE FIRST
RAILWAY LINE

The first train in Asia (and in India) ran between Bombay and Thana on 16 April 1853, at 3.35 p.m. Today timetabled as T-81, the train still runs, more on less at the same time,[1] keeping alive the memory and legacy of the day when the railways first arrived in India.

Of course, there have been changes. The GIPR has become the Central Railway and steam locos now run on electric power. But the train still trails the original blueprint—back then, a forlorn route through woods and swamps; today, a track through dense urban landscapes and stations teeming with unmanageable crowds.

The first train run had been a celebration—not just for India, but for this part of the world. In Bombay of the 1850s, then semi-rural, enclosed by a fort's ramparts, railways had been a novelty; the first train run had received a military salute. Today, over 150 years later, as T-81 trundles along, there are no grand welcoming gestures. Yet, the unspoken, incontestable fact is that trains are the city's lifeline.

It is this lifeline that we trace.

VICTORIA TERMINUS: THE BEGINNING

26 November 2008, 9.30 p.m. Terrorists Mohammed Kasab and Ismail Khan entered Bombay's Victoria Terminus, and sprayed bullets and threw grenades across the concourse; they killed fifty-eight people and injured 104 others.[2] Even as the attack was captured

---

1. The 3.23 p.m. Thane-81 Down, or simply T-81 in railway parlance, completes a thirty-four-kilometre journey, passing nineteen stations on the way.

2. See 'We Have Got Justice: 26/11 Victim's Wife', *Sahara Samay*, 21 November 2012, in <http://www.saharasamay.com/regional-news/others-news/676518074/we-have-got-justice-26-11-victim-s-wife.html>, accessed on 4 September 2014.

by close-circuit television cameras, there was panic as the security personnel at the station were unprepared for this catastrophe. While Khan was subsequently shot dead, Kasab, captured alive, faced the gallows four years later.[3]

The incident has a strange historical link. For the spot where Kasab and Khan were standing at Victoria Terminus, was once a public gallows where criminals were executed. In a bizarre twist, this was exactly the fate the terrorists would meet.

Two hundred years ago—where the UNESCO-listed Victoria Terminus today stands—murderers 'were subjected to the raillery of the populace and had to submit to being pelted with rotten eggs, old shoes, mud and brickbats'[4] before being hanged. Victoria Terminus was a site of gore and bloodletting, with a tank tellingly called 'Phansi Talao'. Nineteenth-century writer, Govind Narayan Madgaokar has documented Phansi Talao quite vividly.

> The site where criminals were punished was chosen because it was just outside the Bazaar Gate where people were always milling around. Since ancient times, the practice was to condemn criminals in public; such punishment, it was believed, created terror and deterred others from committing heinous acts. It wasn't uncommon for the criminal to be pelted with eggshells. While some were put in a cage and paraded, others were tied to a pole and flogged. Sometimes criminals would be half-shaven, smeared with vermillion, garlanded with onions and paraded on donkeys, with children following them with loud music. Near the pond was the spot where murderers were hanged, and next to that was a wooden contraption that threw cow dung on criminals. In the vicinity, there was a cage that rotated; it would keep spinning till the delinquent inside would fall unconscious.

---

3. Kaustubh Kulkarni and Naeem Abbas, 'Mumbai Attacker Ajmal Kasab Executed Secretly, Sparks Celebrations', *Reuters*, 21 November 2012, <http://in.reuters.com/article/2012/11/21/india-kasab-death-execution-idINDEE8AK01N20121121>, accessed on 3 September 2014.

4. S.M. Edwardes, *The Gazetteer of Bombay City and Island*, Volume 3 (India: Cosmo Publications, 2002), p. 382.

As we can see, there were four to five devices to punish offenders. But recently, the government has banned the machines and shifted the gallows to Dongri behind the old jail.[5]

It was in May 1876—just before the construction of Victoria Terminus began—that the public works department forwarded a letter from the consulting engineer for railways, requesting sanction for the removal of Phansi Talao.[6] The remains of the old Portuguese-era public gallows were soon replaced by the magnificent terminus we see today.

A construction map in 'GIPR contract number one' of 'Bombay station' by the acting chief engineer shows that Phansi Talao was located near the European Hospital and a new proposed road.[7] In other words, it lay next to today's platform eighteen and the public toilet. This is precisely where the 26/11 terrorists first came and loaded their weapons.

Courtesy: Central Railway Archives

F.W. Stevens' Impression of Victoria Terminus

5. Govind Narayan Madgaonkar, *Mumbaiche Varnan*, edited by Narhar Raghunath Fatak (India: Marathi Granth Sangrahalaya, 1863), p. 85. Translated by the author.

6. Rahul Mehrotra and Sharada Dwivedi, *A City Icon: Victoria Terminus, 1887 (Now Chhatrapati Shivaji Terminus Mumbai, 1996)* (India: Eminence Designs, 2006), pp. 63-73.

7. *Ibid.*, pp. 74-75.

The destruction caused by the terrorist attack has now been repaired; the bullet marks on the walls of the station were patched up in 2010. But memories—those of the distant and the more recent past—live on. Today, a granite tablet stands in the station complex with the names of the passengers, staff and policemen who died in the terror attack.

~

Victoria Terminus has been synonymous with the Indian railways for more than a century. It is believed to be one of the most photographed buildings in the world, and UNESCO has described it an 'outstanding example of late-nineteenth-century railway architecture in the British Commonwealth, characterized by Victorian Gothic Revival and traditional Indian features.'[8] Today it is the administrative headquarters of the Central Railway, and is listed as house number 125 in an oval-shaped small metal strip on Dr D.N. Road in Bombay.[9]

In January 1882, nearly three decades after the first train run, the old, ramshackle, wooden structure of Bori Bunder—ground zero of Asia's first railway, the GIPR—was pulled down. This was replaced by a new station, the Bombay Passenger Station. By then, the mega edifice of Victoria Terminus, as we see it today, was in the process of being built.

The construction of the terminus had been facing several hiccups due to land reclamation issues; about eighty acres had to be reclaimed from the harbour. The sea had to be pushed back and the roads had to be aligned. In 1861, the Bombay government signed an agreement with the Elphinstone Land and Press Company to reclaim two-thirds of Mody Bay. Work began in earnest in 1878, and in ten years, in May 1888, the majestic building that we see today was ready at a mammoth cost of Rs 16,35,562.

---

8. 'Chhatrapati Shivaji Terminus', *World Heritage List: UNESCO*, in <http://whc.unesco.org/en/list/945>, accessed on 9 April 2014.

9. D.N. Road has been named after Dadabhai Naoroji, referred to as the 'grand old man of India'. He was one of the co-founders of the Indian National Congress.

It was an exceptional building, the likes of which the denizens of Bombay had never seen. It had a sloping foundation that formed a shape, akin to a web, around the base. With this railway terminus—more majestic than the stations in England—the supremacy of the Indian railways was firmly established. In author Christopher W. London's words, the railways in 'India back then were a symbols of engineering prowess' and 'Victoria Terminus continues to vividly recall the railways' historic dominance over Bombay's fortunes'.[10]

Not surprisingly, the station was named after a reigning queen. In 1887, to commemorate the golden jubilee of Queen Victoria's ascension to the throne, the terminus was bequeathed the name of the English empress. The queen's 9'6" statue, in state robes, holding a sceptre with a globe, was placed in a canopied niche in the central façade just below the clock. Today, we can no longer find this statue; where it has gone remains a mystery.

~

As one enters the premises of Victoria Terminus from the main gates and walks past the lush, elegant gardens—which, till a few years ago, stationed an Orenstein and Koppel steam tank locomotive from the narrow-gauge Matheran Light Railway—the carvings and busts across the two wings and the imposing dome of the main building become larger than life. Around the portico—once lined with horse-driven cabs, and now displaying the official Ambassador cars of Indian babus—one can listen to and feel the wind blowing freely in the corridors, thanks to the strategic positioning of the building by its visionary architect. Indeed, even the platform sheds, though relatively small, had been (and still are) ventilated such that smoke and steam could rise and escape.

The stately building of Victoria Terminus welcomes you with two stone sculptures of a lion and a tiger at the main entrance. The lion and the tiger, representing England and India respectively, have been crouching here for more than a century, watching the changing landscape of the megacity—the shift from horse-driven carriages to

10. Christopher W. London, *Bombay Gothic* (India: India Book House, 2002), pp. 79-89.

trams to the cars of the twenty-first century. The sculptures are the work of British sculptor Thomas Earp who, along with his partner Edwin Hobbs Senior, made them under their company's name, Messrs Earp, Son & Hobbs, and shipped them to Bombay for the railway station. Today, though ageing and ridden with cracks, the statues of the animals still look charming. The lion recently got a 'jaw job' after its real one cracked open and fell off. Sadly, the makeover can easily be spotted, as the new material used is no match to the original Bath stone.

The lion was not the only sculpture to undergo cosmetic surgery. In Victoria Terminus, we also find a towering fourteen-foot-high statue, depicting Progress, atop the dome (again sculpted by Thomas Earp). The Lady of Progress wears a floral crown with a star, holds a torch pointing skyward in her right hand, and a spoked wheel in her left. She, too, got a clean-up recently!

Victoria Terminus also has an association with the novelist, Rudyard Kipling's father, John Lockwood Kipling. John Kipling (an artist) and his students from Jamshedjee Jeejeebhoy (J.J.) School of Arts were responsible for the Indian decorative elements in the building—the peacocks and tigers, tropical plants and reptiles. Interestingly, John Kipling also designed the friezes in Crawford Market (today's Mahatma Jyotiba Phule Mandai), with scenes of Indian rural life.

Today, when you observe the façade of Victoria Terminus, you spot multiple carvings—eleven portraits of the 'big men' of that era; the sixteen communities of Bombay with their distinct head gears; various logos; and the monogram of the GIPR, carved in stone. Besides the two Indian founding directors of the railways—Jagannath Sunkersett and Cursetjee Jamsetjee Jeejeebhoy—the portraits along the front portico include Lord Dalhousie (the governor general who created the first rail line's blueprint); the Earl of Dufferin (who was the viceroy and governor general of India between 1884 and 1888); Bombay governors, Henry Bartle Frere, Donald Mackay (Lord Reay), Mountstuart Elphinstone and John Elphinstone; and the GIPR officials, Colonel James Holland (chairman of the board of directors) and Thomas Watt (managing director). Many forget to make note of the portrait of the railway's chief engineer, the pioneering James John

Berkley, towards the southern side of the building (once known as Bazaar Gate, and open day and night).

On entering the station, a bell in a polished teakwood case welcomes you with bold letters: 'Great Indian Peninsula Railway (GIPR)'. Inside the hall, at the base of a cantilevered staircase, is a stone-framed plaque, with a list of those who fashioned this architectural wonder—the chief engineers, F.W. Stevens ('who supervised the work during its erection') and Wilson Bell; Colonel James Holland and Thomas Watt; and the agent of the company, George A. Barnett.

An Antique Fire Bell in a Teakwood Case at Victoria Terminus

The building's architect, Frederick William Stevens, paid meticulous attention to detail, and designed not only this Gothic building, but even the accessories that went in it. A set of pencil drawings by Stevens, in the possession of the Central Railway archives, show floor plans, corridors and even furniture!

Courtesy: Central Railway Archives

F.W. Stevens' Pencil Drawings of Victoria Terminus

Stevens had arrived in India in 1867, and had been working on proposals for several large building projects in Bombay with the Rampart Removal Committee. (Bombay's governor, Henry Bartle Frere, had issued orders to pull down the ramparts of the old Fort George to allow the city to grow.) The design of the station was to become Stevens' most significant architectural work. The railways were meant to symbolize the power and achievement of the British regime, and the extraordinary station design reflected this. Indeed, a watercolour impression of the station by Swedish illustrator Axel Herman Haig, became hugely popular for its romantic representation of the building's domes, turrets and cupolas, the huge water fountain, and the people of leisure who frequented it; it sold copies worldwide.

While Stevens supervised the project, officials from the public works department—assistant engineer, Raosaheb Sitaram Khanderao Vaidya and supervisor, M. Mahaderao Janardan—did the ground work.

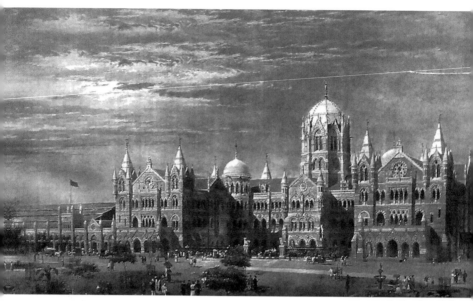

Axel Herman Haig's Watercolour Impression of Victoria Terminus

Let's go back to our tour of the terminus. Walk across, and you'll see that the building had been made with the best of construction material from across the world. The floors within a few offices and chambers display richly patterned Minton encaustic tiles—a common feature in most nineteenth-century iconic public buildings and churches, not only in England but across the world, including in the United States Capitol. While initially a defining feature of Victoria Terminus, many of these tiles have now been removed, replaced by sparking granite or covered with red carpets. Besides, there are rare, circular wooden staircases along four corners (which the railways are now reviving), and solid wooden wall cupboards in the second floor where records are meticulously preserved.

The terminus holds a number of interesting highlights—such as a basement treasury room that is connected with a pulley lift, a narrow tunnel of stone stairs that leads to the dome and a clock room. Incredibly, much of this is still in use, and exploring them is an experience in itself. The basement treasury room is heavily protected with armed guards, who, at any given hour, linger at the entrance. The treasury room was once used to store strongboxes and important documents of the railways. Today, black steel trunks lie there, filled with cash collected from ticket booking counters of various stations. The cash boxes—that are so heavy that it takes over ten people to carry each one—have been manufactured by Thomas Milner, one of the leading suppliers of fire-resistant safes in the nineteenth century.

To get to the room, one has to pass through a small underground tunnel, comprising twenty-three spiral stone steps, to enter a set of heavy iron doors that can only be accessed by a pair of keys—a 'male' and a 'female' key set in a copper ring. The keyhole on these doors is designed such that one cannot easily locate it. The strong room has a small pulley-driven lift that can carry treasury boxes to the basement. The lift, powered electrically since 1967, too has a set of keys for its operation. The guarded basement is surprisingly well-ventilated, with iron windows towards the top (in other words, at foot-level on the ground floor).

From the ground floor, on climbing up the cantilevered staircase built into the walls (that winds inside the two-storey building), one gets close to the dome. The dome has a circular balcony around it, and is supported by walls and sixteen windows that still have the few original stained-glass paintings of Stevens' times. In some of these paintings, one can see a collage of marching elephants, a steam train and locomotives, meticulous floral designs, and the GIPR's logo and monograms.

The large clock that Stevens placed in the centre of the building's façade, with a dial that is a ginormous 10'6" in diameter, is another gem. Along its iron base are the words 'Lund & Blockley, Watch & Clock Manufacturers, Pall Mall, London & Bombay'. The clock is still operated by pulleys and weights. The dial, too, holds a complex system of pulleys and wheels, which in turn make the clock tick. However, some things have changed with time. The gas lamps that were once behind the timepiece have now made way for tube-lights. The clock's original glass front has been replaced by thirty-six pieces of acrylic, like an assembled jigsaw puzzle, to make a dial.

Stained-Glass Floral Paintings at Victoria Terminus

As the huge circular doors behind the dial are opened, light invades the dark room and there is a cool breeze. From here, through the clock, one gets a rare view of Bombay—the once vast maidan and the esplanade, the busy traffic junction and the municipal corporation headquarters building, another one of Stevens' creations. This clock is Bombay's Big Ben.

The clock still needs to be wound every five days with keys that are as huge as the human hand. When the clock is wound, it sends the 175-kilo weights up to a height of fifteen to twenty feet. They make a descent downwards, very slowly, as the clock ticks. B.K. Jadhav, the clock-keeper for over three decades, walks up every day to the terrace (that is accessed by a spiral iron staircase) and then trudges to the barricaded roof of the building, and thence, to the clock room.

The clock room is above the second-floor conference hall of the 'big boss' of the Central Railway, the general manager. It is dark and huge, has a wood-and-stone roof, and still retains what one imagines to be the original ambience of Victoria Terminus. A few broken stained-glass paintings, that once adorned the roof, lie in one corner. Jadhav accesses the huge dial of the clock by standing on a small wooden platform specially raised for it, led by a tiny staircase. He tells stories, several of them. He speaks of how, a few decades ago, the weights had crashed into the conference hall's toilet; the toilet had got entirely damaged, as had the weights. Poor Jadhav had to go hunting for spare weights, and finally found his treasure in the Fort area, with the keepers of the Rajabai Clock Tower of Bombay University.

Jadhav says there are about twenty original 'John Walker, London' clocks, with suspended pendulums, all in proper working condition, in Bombay. They date as far back as 1857, and are in the officials' chambers in Victoria Terminus. There are also several antique wall clocks and a few rare, custom-made ones in various offices inside, with the letters 'GIPR' spread across the dials.

~

Today's clamour at Victoria Terminus is at odds with what the place once was. Back in the 1850s, there was only the nineteen-acre site of the first station of Bori Bunder—named after the locality's 'bor' trees and shoreline.[11] This station was composed of multiple wooden structures (the remains of which can be found north of Victoria Terminus), and overlooked a quiet harbour that was in use primarily for the docking of 'duty-free' goods. In the evenings, when mild westerly winds blew, one could smell the salt and the sea while standing at the jetty. One could also spot adjoining islands—far away, but close enough to discern.

---

11. Samuel T. Sheppard, *Bombay: Place Names and Street Names: Excursion Into the Byways of the History of Bombay City* (Bombay: The Times Press, 1917), p. 38. The book states that Parsi scholar, R.P. Karkaria had written that Bori, or more commonly Bora or Borah, is the name of a well-known Mohammedan sect in Gujarat, whose followers are to be found in large numbers in Bombay. But what particular connection they have with 'bunder' cannot be ascertained. For this reason, the dominant assumption is that the name is derived from the 'bor' tree, possibly once found at the original site of the 'bunder'.

Today, the winds still blow, but one can smell dead fish, and the air is thick with smoke and pollutants. The small islands have survived, but can barely be distinguished. There are endless rows of honking motor vehicles and the multiple arms of steel gantries, loading and unloading cargo from ships behind the tall walls of the Port Trust and the docks. These block any view one could have of the sea.

Near today's mail-express train station of Victoria Terminus, there used to be the old Fort George, its ramparts surrounding the entire English township. In all its life, the fort probably saw fewer people than Victoria Terminus witnesses in a single day. The fortification had three gates on land—Apollo Gate (named after the Apollo pier, the present Gateway of India), Church Gate (to pay tribute to the neighbouring St Thomas Cathedral), and Bazaar Gate (in recognition of the native markets or bazaars in the vicinity, and close to today's General Post Office or GPO). Bori Bunder Station was closest to Bazaar Gate. (While the gate is no more, the market lanes can still be found inside the narrow Bohra Bazaar; houses and alleys here are ancient.)

Late in the 1860s, as the fort's ramparts were brought down ditches filled up and land reclaimed for a newer Bombay, Bori Bunder Station was moved southwards on reclaimed land, almost at the doorstep of Bazaar Gate. What survives of the once-majestic Fort George—artillery had boomed from here to flag off the first train—is now referred to as the office of the government's archaeology department office.

We also see traces of the fort in St George's Hospital which 'partitions' what was once Fort George. Back in the day, St George's Hospital had been known as the European General Hospital, for the use of poor Europeans in the city, sailors, railway officials and their families; this fell into disrepair. The government, therefore, resolved to erect a new European hospital at the cost of Rs 5,69,667 on the ruins of Fort George. Lord Reay, while laying its foundation stone in February 1889, gave the hospital its present name.[12] Since it had been

---

12. S.M. Edwardes, *The Rise of Bombay: A Retrospect* (Bombay: The Times of India Press, 1902).

upgraded and enlarged with stones of the demolished fort, bits and bobs of it can still be found here, such as sloping walls and gun slits, once key to the fort's defence. Sadly, these historic vestiges face a busy road and share a wall with a public urinal. The busy road—earlier named Frere Road, after Bombay's then governor Henry Bartle Frere, who, as we know, pulled down that old fort and its ramparts to open up the city—is today called P. D'Mello Road, after the powerful Port Trust trade unionist, the late Placid D'Mello.

Now, what do we know of Fort George's history? We know that when the East India Company was spreading its tentacles across Bombay, it decided to blow up an old and ruined fortification on a hillock at Dongri in 1768. An account of the demolition of the old fort says that the flattening, that had begun on 23 October 1768, equalled 'about 2,05,000 solid feet.'[13] A year later, on 1 January 1770, the principal engineer, Colonel Keating, laid the foundation stone of a new Dongri Fort, and by order of Bombay's then governor, Thomas Hodges, patriotically named it Fort George, in honour of His Majesty George III.[14]

The fortifying chain of Martello towers that came around Fort George was quite wide, covering the entire area of what we call 'Fort' to this day. Fort George displayed the standard design of 'defensive forts' across the British Empire during the nineteenth century; its fortifications stood about forty feet high with thick walls. The walls protected English occupants from sea and land attack, with six guarded gates, and moats with drawbridges.

Several of these fortifications had basement cells, tunnels and narrow passages, which continue to get discovered under various public buildings. A tunnel with pillars and doors was found beneath a garden manhole cover in the GPO in early 2011. Another such discovery was made at St George's Hospital—tunnels were found going in three different directions, one towards Apollo Gate, a second towards the Blue Gate (near the GPO), and the third towards Church

---

13. J.M. Campbell, *Materials towards a Statistical Account of the Town and Island of Bombay*, Volume 2 (Bombay: Government Central Press, 1893), pp. 377-80.

14. *Ibid.*

Gate. Yet another tunnel is said to have been found in the early
twentieth century in Victoria Terminus, suggesting a network of
basement passages where once the old fort, its ramparts and towers
stood. But where these tunnels lead and where they eventually open
up still remain mysteries. Though, strictly speaking, the underground
networks did not serve as dungeons, most agree that they acted as
escape routes. Some even hypothesize that they were chambers of
punishment.

> The eastern ramparts had on the basement cellars on its northern
> side which were, it is said, used at one time to incarcerate
> criminals. The cellars were really of a most barbarous character
> and suited only to the civilization of the tenth and twelfth
> centuries. They were veritable black holes, with no light save
> that emitted from holes at the top of the ramparts covered with
> large inverted funnels. The only windows at intervals were fixed
> on the roadside. They were fit for the barbarities of a Spanish
> Inquisition but utterly unfit for the civilization of the British of
> the early part.[15]

Fort George in Bombay was strengthened to deal with a series of
potential, and actual, invasions—by the French led by Napoleon, the
Portuguese, the Dutch and Siddi Yakut Khan of Janjira (the African
general who blew up the fort at Mazgaon). Everyone was keen to
capture strategically positioned Bombay. Around this exciting and
historically rich neighbourhood stands today's Victoria Terminus.

~

If a visitor from the 1850s, from the original Bori Bunder, were to
visit, he would not recognize today's Victoria Terminus at all. These
days, the public entrance to Victoria Terminus is through a maze of
wood-framed metal detectors. The main station hall is crowded,
cacophonic and teeming with people. There are blinking red digital
train indicators, scrolling television screens and trains coming and

---

15. Sir Dinshaw Edulji Wacha, *Shells from Sands of Bombay; Being My Recollections and
Reminiscences:1860-1875* (Bombay: The Bombay Chronicle Press, 1920), p. 63.

going every other minute. The terminus witnesses nearly 1,000 train trips and millions of commuters every single day. There are eighteen platforms that buzz with activity—seven for suburban trains that keep Bombay ticking, and the rest to ferry trains that reach every nook and corner of the subcontinent. The suburban complex's seven platforms were remodelled in December 1991 to hold a 'double discharge' facility—in other words, platforms were built on either side of each train entering the station.

When Victoria Terminus had been built, the station's main façade had been approximately 330 feet in height, and train sheds and platform bays had extended 1,200 feet from the main block. Passengers going out of Bombay would use the west opening, and those coming to the city would use the eastern side. Steam trains would neatly line up for commuters.

Today, the suburban concourse of Victoria Terminus sees a steady stream of electric multiple unit (EMU) trains throughout the day. Electric trains were first introduced in Bombay at 'ground zero', at Victoria Terminus, in 1925; train coaches were imported, designed akin to those running in England. Today, ninety years on, the trains here are an advanced version of the old design of 1925.

The electric railway is now switching to an alternating current (AC) model in phases, thus rendering the old, pioneering direct current (DC) controlled EMU trains useless. Today, the fleet is a mix of old dust-brown and pale-yellow DC trains, DC-AC hybrid trains, and the new-age violet-and-white Siemens trains introduced in 2007. Besides, a newer fleet (by Integral Coach Factory or ICF) powered by Bombardier has started arriving.

The old DC trains were manufactured by ICF at Madras and Jessop at Calcutta. While there are still several ICF trains to be found, some receiving upgrades, the ones by Jessop, with symmetrical seats, rectangular windows, leg room and gorgeously proportionate furniture, are fast dwindling. The Jessop models are fit to be called the 'art deco' trains of Bombay. They will serve my generation possibly, but it's unlikely they will survive long beyond.

~

Bombay's 'Art Deco' Trains

The station's interiors, too, have changed since Stevens' era, to adapt to the growing numbers of commuters, their requirements and rapidly advancing technology. The layout of the original platforms, that once served steam trains, has morphed beyond recognition. In 1929, a mail or express station came up. This added three more platforms to the terminus and segregated suburban and outstation train traffic.

Moreover, in the original plans, the ground floor had wide, open corridors and a lot of free area. Today, there is a café where Stevens had recommended 'open space'. The station manager's cabin and the motorman's lobby were once first- and second-class waiting rooms. The chamber where the railway heritage gallery stands (next to the cash office) had formerly been given out to the post office. While the cash office still stands, the post office was later moved to the more spacious GPO building next to Victoria Terminus.

The network of footbridges connecting the platforms, too, has witnessed a makeover. Until recently, at one end of platform seven, there was an old stone wall—the base of a long footbridge that, until 1929, used to span thirteen tracks; this relic of the old station's design has been destroyed to make way for a new bridge that is to span all the platforms and connect suburban and express stations.

A striking nineteenth-century feature that has probably been permanently lost is Stevens' garden kitchen. The original plans of the ground-floor building had a small kitchen laid out in the garden behind the main structure. Today, the garden is all gone, replaced by a scrap depot and multiple offices; the 'kitchen building' with a chimney functions as the railway staff canteen.

Perhaps one of the most prominent modern changes has been the revision of the station's name from Victoria Terminus to Chhatrapati Shivaji Terminus. This was done in 1995, by the Congress' Suresh Kalmadi. While Queen Victoria did not find time from her three royal residences of Windsor Castle, Balmoral and Osborne House to visit the Bombay terminus, traces of her name still linger here in forgotten plaques and fading name boards.

The Remains of the Day

As the new millennium dawned, there was good news for Victoria Terminus: UNESCO listed it as a world heritage site in 2004. And with that came elaborate conservation guidelines and monitoring rules. A heritage gallery was planned and ugly additions and alterations to the building were brought down. There are new strategies to decongest and restore this architectural wonder to its original form.

There are several vintage items within the busy Victoria Terminus—from old wrought iron railings on platform one, to inscriptions on the station's pitched roof reading 'Frodingham Iron and Steel Company Ltd, England'—an iron-works firm established in 1864. The offices in Victoria Terminus, including the chamber of the general manager, still have Stevens' original furniture; these include decorative tables, arched chairs, desks and cupboards with carved letters spelling 'GIPR' (now being restored).

As one walks about the corridors, one can find red fire buckets and equipment provided by Merryweather & Sons. This reputed firm, first set up in 1692, was known to be the fire engineer to the queen herself. Obviously, Victoria Terminus had to enlist this elite firm's services. '12 small fire pumps have been installed on the roof of the building,' notes the railway agent's half-yearly report ending December 1888.[16] Merryweather's red plaques and buckets can still be found on the ground and first floors and towards the rear of Victoria Terminus.

In 2007, while efforts were being made to conserve the roof, a few tiles got dumped in the scrap depot. A close look revealed that they carried the inscription, 'Basel Mission, Mangalore'. This was a rich find, as Basel Mission tiles are of historical value, and the tile-making factory, set up in 1860, was the first of its kind to emerge in Mangalore. When the railway authorities were alerted, the tiles were promptly rescued; now, they sit proudly in Victoria Terminus' prestigious heritage gallery.

A piece of history has been saved for eternity.

MASJID BUNDER STATION: NEW JETTIES, EXALTED CANNONS

As one moves out of Victoria Terminus, one passes a vast electric-mast-riddled railway yard to the east, and old and new houses, warehouses, markets and offices to the west. Along the way, one is assailed by the stench of dead fish and a salt-filled whiff of sea breeze from the market storehouse. A few relics of the original gantries— towering and massive, once supporting the overhead wires across all eight lines, thus eliminating the need for individual masts—still dot the route. But they are now in disuse, many having been dismantled.

The electric yard is one of the last-remaining yards of the Indian railways operated by the direct current (DC) power mode. A little further on, as trains negotiate a curve to pass signal posts S-54 and S-48 (the former site of the old Bori Bunder Station), and pass the

16. S.N. Sharma, *History of the GIP Railway (1853-1869)*, Part I, Volume I (Bombay: Chief Public Relations Officer, Central Railway, 1990), p. 205.

0/0 kilometre markers under 'Carnac Bridge,' they reach Masjid Bunder Station, about 1.22 kilometres away.

~

Before we explore the station, let's consider the historic bridge. Carnac Bridge, opened in 1868, is a solid sixty-foot-wide structure that passes over the lines; it had been constructed by Laxman Harishchandra Ajinkya. It lies between Victoria Terminus and Masjid Bunder Station, and connects P. D'Mello Road to Carnac Bunder.

Walk across the bridge, and you'll see engravings along all four corners. While three corners have the name of the bridge in three languages (English, Hindi and Gujarati), the fourth side carries the symbol of an anchor and announces the date of the bridge's opening.

An Engraving on Carnac Bridge

Today, if you venture towards the centre of the bridge, you can feel the sea's breeze. But the salt and cool air is mixed with fumes. Worse, with the railway tracks below being raised every year to keep away monsoon flooding, the bridge hangs much too low.

The east-west Carnac Road was once the border between old British Bombay and the crowded native township. Today, it mostly ferries cargo trucks to and from the docks, and is lined with shops and buildings. The road itself has been renamed after freedom fighter Bal Gangadhar Tilak; after all, it was along this road, in the Sardar Griha Lodge, that Tilak had spent his last days. The road is also famous for housing the iconic Crawford Market, completed in 1869.

Let's pause at Carnac Bunder now, a jetty associated with 'Bhau' to this day. Laxman Harishchandra Ajinkya, or Bhau as he was popularly known, was born in 1789 in Uran. He had family estates at Naigaum and Parel, and held land rights in Andheri and Malad. A bright student, Bhau found employment with ease as the chief clerk (a high position for a 'native' in those days) at the Gun Carriage Factory at Colaba. His memoir recalls how during visits to Uran, he'd hear of the difficulties faced by the inhabitants of Konkan once they arrived in Bombay; there were no landing facilities. Indeed, right until 1835, Bombay did not have a regular wharf for goods and passengers.

The accounts of these displaced individuals touched Bhau deeply. In 1832-33, the government started leasing out land by the Bombay sea to individuals to build wet docks and basins. Bhau's biographer notes that Bhau, already stirred by the narratives of those landing, grabbed the opportunity and applied to the collector of Bombay, W.C. Bruce, on 17 December 1836. He sought permission to reclaim an area extending from Chinch Bunder to Masjid Bunder in the north, from Masjid Bunder to the meat market (presently in Crawford Market) in the south, and from Dongri Cooly Street (now P. D'Mello Road) in the west to the extensive waterfront in the east! In 1837, the government granted permission to reclaim the entire area, raise the level of Masjid Bunder, and build basins and roads.

Remember, this was the late 1830s, and the railways were yet to arrive and divide the seafront. Bhau proposed to complete all the construction at his own expense. Collector Bruce informed the governor of Bombay, Robert Grant, that the improvements suggested by Bhau were commendable and would serve public interest. His work would not only enlarge and beautify the town, but also put an end to the menace of smuggling. (Building a pier would de-clutter thickly bunched tenements and organize landing facilities; this would curb the rampant smuggling of opium in that area.)

By 1839, work from Chinch Bunder to Masjid Bunder was complete. By 1841, Bhau had constructed Bombay's first wet dock, so commuters could land to safety, and incoming ships could load and berth. The native passengers from Konkan found their fears dissipating with this new, hugely popular landing place. They fondly called the area Bhaucha Dhakka, or Bhau's wharf, a name that remains popular.

In response to the Bombay government's generous commendation of his work, Bhau proposed the name of incoming governor, James Rivett Carnac, for the land reclaimed between Masjid Bunder and the meat market. Ever since, this area has been known as Carnac Bunder. Further, Bhau named another jetty he had built after the Earl of Clare—Clare Bunder. Bhau died in 1858, with Clare and Carnac Bunders in his possession.

With the arrival of the railways, the Bombay seafront was bound to change. Bhaucha Dhakka originally had been at the base of Carnac Bridge. With the subsequent reclamations of the Elphinstone Land and Press Company in 1862 and the formation of the Port Trust a decade later in 1873, a number of wharves and landing places along the eastern shore got realigned.[17] Bhau's wharf, or rather the landing place for passengers, was moved further north to Mazgaon.[18]

~

An 1863 Bombay map indicates that Carnac Road was probably a rail crossing; the area west of the line has been identified as Mandvi and to the east is Kasaiwada.

---

17. *The Port of Bombay: A Brief History* (India: Mumbai Port Trust, 1973), pp. 26-27.

18. Pratap Velkar, *Pathare Prabhuncha Itihas* (Pune: Shrividya Publications, 1997).

The English town ended at Fort George. The areas that represent Masjid Bunder Station (and the next stop, Sandhurst Road Station) had been a part of the lively old native townships of Mandvi, Pydhonie, Umerkhadi and Dongri, with Mazgaon—a hub of the Portuguese— at the northern end. Each of the names of the native townships carry immense significance. While Mandvi traditionally means a custom house, Pydhonie signifies a foot-wash (one could rinse one's tired feet in the ocean's shallow waters). While Umerkhadi is derived from 'umbhar-khadi', meaning a creek spilling over with fig trees, Dongri comes from the Marathi word for a hilly tract, 'dongar', probably in reference to Nawrojee Hill.[19]

Much before the railways had been conceived, Mandvi had been home to the barracks of the native infantry lines, a military outpost of Fort George. Today, in one of its narrow alleys, we find a cannon, buried muzzle down.

Speak to locals and they go down memory lane, to an era much before the infantry lines—when Mandvi was in fact a fishing hamlet (a koliwada) and an island. Back then, the sea had been much closer, and local legend goes that the cannon buried muzzle down had been used by fishermen to tie small boats. This cannon had been a 'saviour', protecting the fishermen's most prized possession from cruel winds and blustery waves. Today, this 'saviour' has been deified and is worshipped as the community's original guardian.[20]

The koliwada survived the onslaught of technology and remained when the rail lines were laid. It was, however, removed in the late 1890s after the bubonic plague epidemic hit the city and the Bombay Improvement Trust decided to build buildings here, many of which stand to this day. Descendents of the old koli families still reside in these buildings that display the letters 'BIT'.

---

19. Samuel T. Sheppard, *Bombay: Place Names and Street Names: Excursion Into the By-ways of the History of Bombay City* (Bombay: The Times Press, 1917), pp. 60, 141.

20. Sadanand Khopkar, *Mumbaicha Mumbaikar* (India: Simant Prakashan, 2011), p. 12. Translated by the author. A few more cannons lying nearby have gone missing.

A Sacred Cannon Near Masjid Bunder Station

~

The train now moves into Masjid Bunder Station. Over a century old and with two island platforms, Masjid Bunder Station has weathered many changes since it was first built in 1877.

Masjid Bunder was named after an old jetty which was near a mosque. The Saat-Taad Mosque, located next to the station, is hidden today within a maze of warehouses and wholesale dealer outlets. Its name, when translated, means seven palm trees, and suggests the presence of toddy palms in the area.[21] (This is further confirmed

---

21. S.M. Edwardes, *The Gazetteer of Bombay City and Island*, Volume 1 (India: Cosmo Publications, 2002).

when we study the streets in the vicinity. Bhandari Street and Bhandari Bridge both foreground the presence at one time of the Bhandari community, the toddy tappers, among the original inhabitants of the city.)

Another set of records, however, suggests that Masjid Bunder Station probably got its name from the 200-year-old Gate of Mercy Synagogue, also called Juni Masjid, one of Bombay's oldest synagogues. It had been built by Samaji Hasaji Divekar (also known as Samuel Ezekiel), a Bene Israeli who along with his brother, Issac, served in the British East Indian Army as an officer. The story[22] goes that during the Anglo-Mysore Wars, both Samuel and Issac were captured by Tipu Sultan. When asked what caste they belonged to, the brothers mentioned they were Bene Israelis. Having never heard of the community, Tipu Sultan was about to condemn Samuel and Issac to death, when his wife intervened, and mentioned that she had come across the 'caste name' in the Koran. Tipu Sultan, a devout Muslim, spared the duo, and later exchanged them for a prisoner with the British. The two brothers returned to the British enclave of Bombay and built a synagogue in thanksgiving. It was originally located near the esplanade and later rebuilt and moved to its present location at Mandvi in 1860, more than a decade before a station came up there.

~

Over time, much has changed in Masjid Bunder Station. For instance, the old sixty-foot-wide Masjid Road Overbridge was demolished and upgraded to a bigger and wider concrete structure in 2009. The demolished bridge had an iron-and-stone structure similar to Carnac Bridge, and even bore comparable inscriptions—the name of the bridge across three corners and an anchor and the opening date on the fourth side. When the bridge was demolished part by part, the huge rectangular stone blocks that had these inscriptions were salvaged by engineers (at my behest), and shifted by truck to the heritage

---

22. Israel Goldstein, *My World as a Jew: The Memoirs of Israel Goldstein* (USA: Associated University Presses, 1984).

gallery of Victoria Terminus.[23]

The process of demolishing Masjid Road Overbridge was completed without halting train operations below, and in just a week. This is incredible, if you consider the fact that the overbridge was more than a century old—not easy to pull down! The general manager and other top railway officials, including those from the neighbouring Western Railway, supervised the operations; they camped on the roof of the new elevated booking office to monitor the proceedings.

The entire project was a part of a Rs 90 crore mission—the Masjid Bunder Remodelling Plan. As a part of this, a seventh line had to be squeezed in and Masjid Bunder's platforms had to be extended to accommodate twelve-car trains. It's important to remember that while twelve-car electric trains had been introduced along the Central Railway network two decades prior, there had been a practice of halting each train twice at Masjid Bunder Station on account of the overbridge. With the demolition of the old bridge, space was created for extending the platforms, for squeezing in a seventh line (that would be put in use for shunting trains from Victoria Terminus to the yard at Wadi Bunder) and for building a brand new road bridge, wider and higher than the original one.

The Masjid Road Overbridge, while no more, has an important place in Bombay's history. *The Bombay Gazetteer* of 1909 documents the overbridge as being the focal point of the plague epidemic. It says that bridge had been flanked by a row of lofty houses, and in one of them the first genuine case of the bubonic plague had been recorded in 1896. This was the epidemic that changed the face of Bombay, and led to the opening up of suburbs to decongest the city. Dr Acacio Gabriel Viegas, a medical practitioner and later, the president of Bombay Municipal Corporation, was the first to detect the epidemic and

---

23. Another relic shifted to this gallery was a beautiful cast-iron lamppost with floral designs, with the inscription 'Turner & Allen, London, 1867'. This firm, then located along the Upper Thames Street in London, had been contracted by the government to provide ornamental lamps across the city of Bombay. Sepia-toned adverts in old issues of *TheBombay Builder* state that the firm specialized in lamps, railings and gates, and offered new sets of designs and patterns on a regular basis.

initiate measures to fight it. Today, he stands in one corner of the
Framjee Cawasjee Hall, overlooking a busy traffic junction.

The Remains of the Day

Before we approach Masjid Bunder Station, we spot a number of
small streets named after cities in Gujarat—Ahmedabad Street, Baroda
Street—as merchants engaged in trade used to come here. Opposite
the station is Sugar Lane, and the area is a wholesale business district,
popularly called Lokhand or Loha Bazaar (iron market). Here, the
remains of GIPR sidings[24] can still be seen; a few old shops along the
street seem to recognize their existence, with signboards announcing
'Carnac Bunder Siding Road'.

Both platforms at Masjid Bunder Station hold the traditional
motto of the GIPR, 'arte non ense' (by art, not by sword), complete
with flags, a crown and an elephant. In the late 1870s, when F.W.
Stevens first stamped the company's insignia on not just the façade of
Victoria Terminus but also its furniture, the trend was replicated
with amazing swiftness at many of the smaller and bigger stations
along the line. Masjid Bunder Station today is a living example of this.
On both the existing platforms of this station, we find not one but
thirteen such monograms, each with detailed ornamental work. Stand
at the southern end of any of the two island platforms and look
upwards to view the arched iron brackets that support the pitched
roof; here too, we see those decoratively carved letters, 'GIPR', ever
so slightly hidden under thick layers of paint. Some of the old and
original water outlet pipes too have 'GIPR' inscribed on them.

SANDHURST ROAD STATION:
EXPLORING YESTERDAY'S MAZGAON

As the train leaves Masjid Bunder Station, one can now see a row of
solid rocks by the rail line. Perched on these are a few ancient buildings.

---

24. A siding, in rail terminology, is a low-speed track that may connect to the
main line or to other sidings. Sidings often have relatively lighter rails, meant for
low speed or minimal traffic, and few, if any, signals.

This is the southern tip of the old Dongri Hill that once had a fort on it, which was demolished for a new one (Fort George, as we know). Later, the hill was bought by a Parsi merchant, Nowrojee Maneckji Seth, and came to be known as Nowrojee Hill.

The line also runs parallel, for a short distance, to a small two-lane pathway, Kuwarshi Raishi Marg. This road was once an old rail link—the Masjid Rail Siding—and a 1914 map shows that the siding merged with the main GIPR line near Elphinstone Road Bridge.[25] In the mid-twentieth century, the siding seems to have been abandoned; a road was built over it, and few traces of the rail line remained. But if you take a walk along Kuwarshi Raishi Marg, its curves and bends still remind you of a formidable rail siding; not surprisingly, the local populace refers to the 'marg' as the Masjid Siding Road. Smaller lanes, such as Kurla Street and Thana Street—named after the stations along the old GIPR line—run parallel to it.

Eventually, you pass the Elphinstone Road Bridge, named after Mountstuart Elphinstone, and built in 1868. Indeed, work on the Carnac, Masjid Road and Elphinstone Road Bridges had begun simultaneously in 1867-68 at the joint expense of the GIPR and the Bombay municipality. With the new millennium, the original Elphinstone Bridge was also demolished and replaced with a bigger and wider concrete structure, as a part of the Masjid Bunder Remodelling Project. The small inscription it once carried (the date of its creation, 1868)[26] has been lost forever. Today all we have of the past are the remains of the ancient stone walls, and one of the oldest electric masts along the Main Line[27]—with an oval seal and the number '32'.

~

25. *The Port of Bombay: A Brief History, 1873-1973* (India: Bombay Port Trust, 1973), pp. 35-36.

26. S.M. Edwardes,*The Gazetteer of Bombay City and Island*, Volume I (India: Cosmo Publications, 2002), p. 508.

27. The Central Railway network consists of the Main (Central) Line and the Harbour Line.

Just after the Elphinstone Bridge, the rail line bifurcates. Two lines rise to reach the Harbour Line, and the rest take a turn to run at a lower level. This rail alignment was formed in 1920s when the harbour branch—which at that point existed only between Kurla and Reay Road—was extended from Reay Road all the way to Victoria Terminus. The lines at the lower level move through a network of steel gantries to reach Sandhurst Road Station.

Today's Sandhurst Road Station was originally Mazgaon Station. *The Bombay Gazetteer* of 1909 lists it as the second of the important nine stations within city limits (that is, till Sion), the first being Victoria Terminus on the GIPR line.[28] Named after one of the seven original islands of Bombay, the original Mazgaon Station catered to a teeming mixed population—locals on the one hand, and old Portuguese and British suburb-dwellers on the other. It was located a bit to the north of today's Sandhurst Road Station, at the base of Hancock Bridge.[29] It was opposite this station, in a 'fashionable' hotel, that the GIPR's first ever engineer, James John Berkley arrived to plan and build the first of all Indian railways.

Today, a visit to the site of the old Mazgaon Station, at the base of Hancock Bridge, offers a few hidden gems. Under the debris and muck, there is the fine stone edge of the Mazgaon station platform. Above it, on the retaining wall, are the remains of glorious arches.

~

The 1896 bubonic plague epidemic, the alterations in rail alignment in the 1920s after the introduction of the Harbour Line to Victoria Terminus, and rapid electrification, all led to the relocation of the old Mazgaon Station.

The new station (built in the place of the old one) was shifted a bit south from its original position. It was two-tiered—India's first such railway construction—to match the alignment of the newly planned

---

28. S.M. Edwardes, *The Gazetteer of Bombay City and Island*, Volume I (India: Cosmo Publications, 2002), p. 348.

29. Pauline Rohatgi, *Bombay to Mumbai: Changing Perspectives* (Bombay: Marg Publications, 2007), sheet number 4.

Harbour Line. It was renamed after the then Bombay governor, William Mansfield, more popularly known as Lord Sandhurst, who took up the city's 'improvement' with a vengeance.

Today's lower-level Sandhurst Road Station is a hub of activity. Passenger coaches come and go from the sprawling railway yard at Wadi Bunder, while people rush across the platform. The upper-level station passes through Wadi Bunder's yard. This yard stands on reclaimed land. While local Marathi writer, Govind Narayan Madgaonkar remembers it in the 1950s as 'a wood quarry, full of mud and silt',[30] much has changed since.

The entry and exit to the station is through a row of buildings, locally called the Chinchbunder Chawls or the Bombay Improvement Trust Chawls; indeed, the building blocks used to bear the inscription 'Improvement Trust Chawls, 1916', till the words were plastered over.

The Remains of the Day

The single island platform at the lower level of Sandhurst Road Station has Stevens' ornamental iron brackets with the GIPR monogram, an old pitched roof akin to the one at Masjid Bunder Station, and old iron pipes to drain out water from the roof, again with 'GIPR' etched in. Relics of the first electrification stand scattered along the line—for instance, one can spot an old electric mast along the main GIPR line, close to platform one, with an oval seal, the number '44', and GIPR in a tiny font. One cannot overemphasize the significance of masts of this kind—they're what we have as reminders of India's first electric railway.

Beyond, deep inside Umerkhadi, hidden behind tall walls, stands the Dongri (Juvenile) Remand Home, an ancient jail that remains unchanged and is probably the 'oldest surviving example of British architecture'[31]. It was here that the gaol at the ancient Phansi Talao had been moved in the early nineteenth century.

---

30. Govind Narayan Madgaonkar, *Mumbaiche Varnan*, edited by Narhar Raghunath Fatak (India: Marathi Granth Sangrahalaya, 1863). Translated by the author.

31. Gillian Tindall, *City of Gold: The Biography of Bombay* (India: Penguin Books, 1992), p. 123.

BYCULLA STATION: OF MRS NESBIT AND LADY FALKLAND

Just as the train leaves Sandhurst Road for the next station, Byculla, it passes under the Hancock Road Overbridge. This bridge, and the one just after—Ollivant Bridge—were once the main links to the colourful Portuguese and English suburb of Mazgaon.

Hancock Bridge, completed in 1879 during the tenure of Colonel H.F. Hancock, who was the president of the municipal corporation between 1877 and 1878,[32] used to lead to the Mazgaon Tram Terminus (today referred to as the Maharana Pratap Chowk or simply, Mazgaon Circle); it had double tram lines on it. The bridge was rebuilt in 1923, and all that remains here of the old tram terminus is a water trough that was once used to quench the thirst of horses, exhausted after pulling tram wagons in the pre-electrification era.

~

At this point, it is important to pause and consider the immensity of these engineering attempts. In Bombay of the 1850s, the facilities for manufacturing iron and steel for lines and bridges were rudimentary at best. Of course, there was the Gun Carriage Factory at Colaba that manufactured cannon balls and cannon wheels; but the requirements of the railways were different and there were few iron foundries in India to meet these specific demands.

England, on the other hand, had advanced processes, including the mass production of cheap steel, a technique developed by Henry Bessemer in 1855; consequently, most of the iron came to be shipped from England. This included not just rails, girders, turntables, locomotives and stationary machinery for wagons, but also assembled structures for bridges, booking offices and station building frames. In the first few years of the construction of the railways, between 1850 and 1853, the GIPR imported about 18,568 tonnes of iron from England. By 1858, the railway web had expanded, and more than 600 ships were being dispatched every year from England with about 5,00,000 tonnes of iron for various lines across the subcontinent.

---

32. The designation of the 'president' of the municipal corporation was changed to that of the 'mayor' from November 1931.

The movement of these ships, however, was regulated by trade. After all, vessels had to return with cargo. This limited the speed with which they could ferry goods to and fro. Moreover, once all the heavy material landed at the Bombay port, it had to be transported with great efficiency to the site of construction, often in the interiors, as the line was growing rapidly.[33] This was quite a challenge. Therefore, the GIPR set up its own small foundries and built its first locomotive workshop in 1854 at Byculla. But sustained supply of finished iron remained a problem.

Finally, in 1858, an Englishman named Noble Carr Richardson started a small foundry called Byculla Iron Works in the compound of his bungalow. It was the right business venture at the right time. Given the great demand for iron, the foundry flourished. Richardson's small foundry, started with the support of his two sons, grew into the massive Richardson & Company by the 1870s. A decade later, it absorbed the business of Nicol & Company of Parel Road. John Cruddas, the manager of Nicol & Company, became a partner, and thus, the firm got a new name—Richardson & Cruddas. With India's Independence, the British partners sold the firm to an Indian, but in the late 1950s, the firm ran into financial difficulties.[34] It was taken over by the government in 1972 and became Richardson & Cruddas (1972) Ltd. While the firm's fortunes are connected with the city's rail network in public imagination, the railways are no longer in the firm's client list.

Today, Richardson's company is a huge barricaded site, located close to the old Mazgaon Station. Until recently, it had a rail siding entering its premises. The siding was removed in 2001, in an attempt to grant trains momentum by dismantling an old rail crossover. In April 2014, the iconic firm's warehouse threw open its doors to host a rock concert that attracted thousands of fans. It's unlikely anyone was aware of the site's history.

~

---

33. Juland Danvers, 'Report to the Secretary of State For India in Council on Railways in India to the End of the Year', 1859.

34. Haridas Mundhra, the Indian entrepreneur the company was sold to, found himself embroiled in one of the first scams in free India.

We move to the next overpass, Ollivant Bridge, which was named after Edward Charles Kayll Ollivant, the municipal commissioner of Bombay between 1881-1890, who drafted and implemented the Bombay Municipal Act of 1888 that is still observed in the city. A stone-carved plaque on the bridge, painted bright yellow, announces the little facts surrounding its creation—that it was erected in 1887; that its construction cost Rs 2,15,000; and that it was built by the GIPR at the cost of the municipality.[35]

Ollivant Bridge has an abandoned one-storey GIPR stone signal cabin near its base. Such signal boxes are, in the words of a famous British rail historian, Paul Atterbury, an 'endangered species' now.[36] The boxes—that exercised control over the movement of trains by way of railway signals and block systems—first emerged in the 1860s and 1870s. The first signals used by the GIPR were of the old-fashioned heavy semaphore type, usually with a blade on each side of the post, operated by hand levers at the base. The blades were painted red with a white spot, in keeping with the Midland Railway Company's signals in England.[37]

~

Ollivant Bridge is synonymous with the historic Nesbit Lane. This lane has been a part of the earliest railway blueprints. Around 1843, when the railroad plans were in their infancy and on the drawing table, Nesbit Lane found an honourable mention. When the GIPR's planning engineer, George T. Clark, charted out the route of the first ever railroad, he wrote: 'The line crosses Mazgaon Road near the entrance to the police office, Nesbit Lane near Mrs Nesbit's chapel and Parel road near the three miles [five kilometres] stone [...]'[38] Mrs Nesbit's road and chapel were to stay linked to the railway lines for generations.

35. *Maharashtra State Gazetteers*, 1987, p. 59.

36. Paul Atterbury, *Tickets Please: A Nostalgic Journey through Railway Station Life* (UK: Newton Abbot, 2006).

37. *The Locomotive*, 15 December 1926, pp. 395-97.

38. *The Civil Engineer and Architect's Journal, Scientific and Railway Gazette*, Volume 8 (London: R. Groomsbridge & Sons, 1845).

But who was Mrs Nesbit? An Armenian Catholic expatriate and 'the wife of Commodore Nesbit, the harbour master of Bombay under the East India Company',[39] Rose Nesbit lived nearly 250 years ago. She built a chapel on her property in 1787 that was transferred to the Roman Catholic Church upon her death in 1819. The chapel is today St Anne's Church. Rose Nesbit, who died on 29 October 1819, remains buried under the chapel she loved, and an old tablet in St Anne's Church still carries her name.

Though Nesbit Lane has been renamed after a prominent post-Independence civic corporator, Balwant Singh Dhody, it is still popular in local memory as the road of Mrs Nesbit.

~

Ahead on the line, we find small yard cabins of the GIPR. We also come across railway quarters, legendarily called Berkley Place, after the line's first engineer. A handsome bungalow once stood as his residence; this was pulled down in the early twentieth century to erect multi-storeyed apartment blocks for railway officials. Walk around these blocks, and you'll stumble upon faint remains of the old world. Chipped octagonal stone blocks, probably remnants of an old wall or Berkley's house, lie scattered along the footpath, too heavy to be moved away or bothered with.

The rail lines, before zooming into Byculla Station, pass under the Y-shaped Byculla Bridge, which came up in 1885. The overpass is about sixty feet wide and once had a double tram line on it. At the base of this bridge is located another landmark that is now a part of railway history: the Byculla Mankeshwar Temple.

To acquaint ourselves with this temple, we must first go through the records of Lady Amelia Fitzclarence Falkland, more popularly known as Lady Falkland, the wife of Bombay governor, Lucius Bentinck Cary (or simply, Lord Falkland), after whom India's first locomotive was named.

Lady Falkland's name is important for Bombay's historians. After

---

39. Govind Narayan Madgaonkar, *Mumbaiche Varnan*, edited by Narhar Raghunath Fatak (India: Marathi Granth Sangrahalaya, 1863). Translated by the author.

all, her diaries extensively document the city's affairs in the 1850s, including the railway run. While witnessing India's first trial train journey, she found a Hindu ascetic looking at the train with awe, as though it were an avatar of Lord Krishna.

> Here and there a religious mendicant standing with his eyes wide open, staring at the puffing, blowing engine, thinking it might be another avatar of Crishna! A bullock gharee creeping on at about two miles [three kilometres] an hour [...and] a bridal-party on foot, the bride walking behind the bridegroom, the progress of the procession being momentarily arrested by the novelty of the sight. The scene was altogether curious, and very interesting.[...] As we rushed along, on our return to Parell, on the occasion of the excursion, of which I have spoken, the palms appeared more majestic than usual, and to look down upon us with contempt and disgust, while the monster of an engine sent forth an unearthly, protracted yell, as it tore over the flats of Bombay where, after sunset, the jackals.
>
> [...] The station from whence we started on a kind of experimental trip, is at Byculla, about three miles [five kilometres] from the fort of Bombay. A very handsome new temple had been commenced even before the railroad was contemplated, actually contiguous to the station (Byculla) and was on the verge of completion when the latter was opened. A railway station, and a Hindu temple in juxtaposition—the work of the rulers and the ruled. Could one possibly imagine buildings more opposite in their purposes, or more indicative of the character of the races? The last triumphs of science side by side with the superstitions of thousands of years ago.[40]

The 'Hindu temple' Lady Falkland (a tad patronizingly) refers to is the Byculla Mankeshwar shrine. The original Byculla Station used to be opposite this. Seth Karamshi Ranmal, a Gujarati merchant, had started building the temple in 1839. However, he died before he could complete it, and his son, Seth Hansraj, took over, after whom the

---

40. Amelia Fitzclarence Falkland, *Chow-Chow: Being Selections from a Journal Kept in India, Egypt, and Syria* (London: Hurst and Blackett, 1857), pp. 46-50.

temple lane has been named.[41] Some temple land, it is said, was given for the building of the rail line. Visit the temple premises today, and you will find a lot of old stone blocks and an ancient covered well.

It was much later that the old Byculla Station was shifted and replaced with a larger building. The shift, however, did harm the railway's earnings, as passengers took time to adjust to the new location. As for the site of Lady Falkland's Byculla Station, it has been lost forever.

~

As the rail line approaches Byculla Station, a small, old bridge over the line acts as another reminder of the past. The bridge, named 'Chamar Lane Footbridge' in railway records, merits close inspection. This, in turn, reveals that the bridge had been raised in height much after its original construction, probably to accommodate electric trains after 1925. A faint inscription on one of the pillars reads 'Dorman Long, England'—three words that link a dull local structure with an international, iconic bridge engineer, the creator of the famous Tyne Bridge in England and the Sydney Harbour Bridge in Australia.

Dorman, Long & Co, originally based in Middleborough, had been founded by Arthur Dorman and Albert de Lande Long in 1875. It became one of the key suppliers of iron and steel to Bombay's rail lines. Today, the company's inscriptions are to be found not only at Byculla, but also at a number of local stations further ahead. (Interestingly, life has come a full circle as the firm's steel-making business is now owned by one of India's key industrial families, the Tatas.)

~

There are famous photographs and sketches one can trace, of well-dressed Englishmen waiting to enter a train compartment; the station in these prints is inevitably Byculla—a pointer to the site's popularity.

---

41. Dr Bhalchandra P. Aklekar, *Mumbaitil Puratan Shiv Mandire* (India: Raj-Pradnya Prakashan, 1996). Translated by the author.

Courtesy: Central Railway Archives

Englishmen at the 'Fashionable' Byculla Station

During the earliest runs of the railways, 'upper-class' passengers boarded from Byculla Station, next to the Mankeshwar Temple.

Byculla is derived from 'bhayakhala', referring to the golden shower tree. Alternatively, the name could signify 'low ground', since locally, 'bhaya' means ground and 'khala' is low. Yet another interpretation is that 'khala' means a threshing ground—perhaps surrounded by golden shower trees.[42]

No matter its etymology, the trendy suburb of Byculla held within it all the favourite pastimes of the British, including a horse-racing course, the Bombay Turf Club, that was once just next to Byculla Station. Around 1864, the race course was to move to a new venue. Fourteen years later in 1878, it finally moved to marshy land donated by the industrialist, Cusrow N. Wadia. It was abandoned for a while since it was difficult to access, and the open drain nearby produced a

---

42. Samuel T. Sheppard, *The Byculla Club (1833-1916): A History* (Bombay: Bennett, Coleman and Co Ltd, 1916).

foul odour. But five years later, in 1883, it was shifted permanently to Mahalaxmi, where it stands today under the name, 'Royal Western India Turf Club Limited'.

Today's Byculla Station, a listed heritage structure with the city's municipal corporation, is vast, with four platforms, an arched decorative roof and a large 'circulating' area. Planned in the 1880s, the design for the 'big station' was revised by the London board in 1885 to cut costs, and a final sanction was given two years later. By this time, the magnificent Victoria Terminus was operational. The work for Byculla was commissioned to the Parsi contractor, Berjoorjee Rustomjee Mistri, who had by then successfully completed the platforms, sheds and upper floors of the new Victoria Terminus.[43]

To facilitate the construction of the new Byculla Station, the pipelines of Vihar (piped water had arrived in the city around 1854) had to be diverted. By June 1891, the station building, platforms, sheds, footbridge, horse-carriage parking areas and staff quarters were ready. The new station was opened to the public in July the same year.

~

Observe the new station's exterior along platform one, and there is a huge arched porch with large iron pillars. This probably was for horse carriages. Today, the wide porch at Byculla is used by taxis to drop and pick up passengers.

There's a story regarding this wide porch that goes back to an era before the 1880s, much before the emergence of the station premises we see today. Back then, Bori Bunder was small and Byculla, as we know, was the more popular station for the English and the upper-classes. Though well-liked, the original Byculla Station was small and had narrow entrances. Now, the surgeon of the GIPR Company, Dr W.C. Eccles, usually used to travel in a brougham—a four-wheeled, horse-drawn carriage. In 1867, during an official visit, one of the shafts of Dr Eccles' carriage broke as it was passing through the narrow gateway of Byculla Station. He presumed that since the accident

---

43. Rahul Mehrotra and Sharada Dwivedi, *A City Icon: Victoria Terminus, 1887 (Now Chhatrapati Shivaji Terminus Mumbai, 1996)* (India: Eminence Designs, 2006), p. 153.

had occurred while he was on duty, he was entitled to get it repaired free of cost.

What followed was detailed correspondence, with claims and counterclaims. Dr Eccles wrote a letter to the agent of the GIPR on 6 March 1867, stating that he was entitled to get his brougham repaired free of cost. But the agent's secretary wrote back promptly saying that such expenses could not be sanctioned.[44] Dr Eccles was far from pleased.

One must ask: Was it Dr Eccles' letter in railway records that prompted the GIPR administration to consider wider entrances at stations? Was that why the new Byculla Station, built fifteen years later, came with a wide porch? One cannot tell for certain, but what we do know is that the new station was ready to welcome broughams by July 1891, and its porch remains wide to this day.

The Ornamental Booking Office at Byculla Station

---

44. S.N. Sharma, *History of the GIP Railway (1853-1869)*, Part 1, Volume 1(Bombay: Chief Public Relations Officer, Central Railway, 1990), p. 96.

The Remains of the Day

The majesty of the past can still be experienced at the station today. Look around—a huge pitched steel roof across platforms one, two and three is supported by fourteen decorative pillars, just like the ones at Victoria Terminus. In the west, there is a huge one-storey stone building with twenty-six arched doorways. While today, many of these have made way for exit and entry points, a few original wooden doors with floral designs still survive, and bear a marked resemblance to the patterns at Victoria Terminus. There's much else of historical value—from wrought iron floral design brackets to hold name plates, to the iron booking office with ornamentally carved iron logos of the GIPR, to decorative wrought iron fences next to the counters. This station houses an old and abandoned stone platform, a forgotten siding and old stone buildings.

Platform number four, outside the roof that encloses the main station, has its own novelties. Here, one can spot old iron pillars, an iron bell holder and hook, and faint inscriptions that read 'Glengarnock Steel'—thus linking this station to an industrial hamlet in Scotland. Glengarnock Iron and Steel lords over a number of suburban stations in Bombay even today.

~

As the lines emerge out of Byculla Station, they pass through the shadow of a towering railway hospital. However, few know that this hospital used to house one of Bombay's premier educational institutions, the Elphinstone School and College.

The structure was built in the 1870s for students by the Parsi philanthropist, Cawasjee Jehangir Readymoney. Indeed, a half-buried cornerstone by the building acknowledges his 'liberality'. This magnificent building later also functioned as VJTI till 1923—after all, by 1888, Elphinstone College had shifted to its present premises at Kala Ghoda.

The birth of VJTI comes with an interesting story. The golden jubilee of Queen Victoria's ascension to the throne, celebrated in Bombay in 1887, was a big event at that time. To commemorate it, there were various official efforts—among them, the Bombay

Municipal Corporation hoped to promote the skills of native artisans and build a new cadre of local technical personnel; the aim was to limit dependence on foreign staff. Money had been collected, but finding land to build an institute proved to be a problem.

This was when the prominent Parsi industrialist, Dinshaw Maneckji Petit presented a solution. After Elphinstone College moved out, Petit donated its former premises, worth a huge sum of money, to the proposed technical institute. To mark the queen's jubilee, it was named Victoria Jubilee Technical Institute in 1888. Today, it is called Veermata Jijabai Technical Institute (retaining its original acronym). The garden and zoo opposite it, once called Victoria Gardens, have seen a similar change in name. In 1923, soon after the First World War, VJTI shifted to Matunga, after the government offered free land there in exchange for its Byculla premises.

Today, the former building of Elphinstone College and VJTI is a 366-bed hospital for employees of the Central Railway and is called Dr Babasaheb Ambedkar Memorial Railway Hospital. Patients, visitors and doctors here are too busy to appreciate the history or the vitality of this building. Indeed, many have forgotten that the structure was named after the architect of the Indian Constitution, because it was here, in this majestic building, that Dr Ambedkar completed his ninth grade and matriculation, between 1905 and 1907. He was the first untouchable to accomplish this.[45]

Daily commuters, too, may forget to notice the amazing architecture of this hospital with overhanging balconies. The stone masonry itself is commendable; the thickness of stone is approximately 1.2 metres. And then there are the towers. The entrance tower is approximately thirty metres high, and is the tallest part of the structure, with Gothic arches, a pitched roof and windows. Expectedly, the railway hospital inspires awe in historians.

~

45. Prakash Vishwasrao, *Dr Babasaheb Ambedkar* (India: Lokvangmaya Griha, Planning Commission of India & Department of Cultural Affairs, Government of Maharashtra, 2007), p. 79.

Past the railway hospital, the line passes beneath another nineteenth-century marvel, an S-bridge. When Seth Teju Kaya, a registered railway contractor, was given the task of building a railroad overpass to connect Victoria Gardens and Jacob Circle Road, he sensed that the mission would be challenging. His visit to the site confirmed his suspicions.

Steep gradients would be required to rise over the rail lines. However, if the bridge became steep, it would cease being useful. After all, how would bullock-carts and horse buggies, the common modes of road transport then, negotiate such a climb? Seth Teju Kaya spent hours at the site trying to arrive at a solution. At his wit's end, he returned to his office and began aligning matchboxes, in a bid to arrive at a workable design. Even as he distractedly moved the boxes, an answer seemed to emerge before his eyes—an S-shaped bridge!

An S-bridge has a reverse curve, shaped roughly like a shallow 'S'. Originally found in the early nineteenth century in America—often to navigate twisting streams and uneven banks—the technology of curves eventually came to be used in the Indian ghats. The peculiar sharp bends at either end of the bridge were viewed as engineering novelties; equally, the gentle gradient help bullocks and horses climb easily.

A stone inscription on the bridge today announces: 'GIPR Gardens Bridge, 1913, Contractors Teju Kaya And Company'. The company still survives in Matunga, and the present-generation owners are proud of their legacy. 'It's one its kind. Our great-grandfather, Seth Teju Kaya took up the challenge when no other engineer in the city was willing. The bridge had to be built in a creative manner and not like conventional overpasses,' says Kantilal Teju Kaya, the present partner.[46] When the railways made an effort recently to flatten and upgrade the bridge for power conversion, there were consolidated steps taken to stop the demolition. The bridge—Seth Teju Kaya's bequest—will now stay.

~

---

46. Based on a conversation with Kantilal Teju Kaya in 2013.

Further on, the lines pass the site that was once the original locomotive workshop of the GIPR. The first workshop was spread across eighteen acres of land, with steam sheds, erecting and fitting shops, metal foundries, sawmills, carriage-repairing quarters and wagon-building sheds, warehouses, timber preservation cabins, offices and dwelling spaces.[47] However, as traffic increased, an open area was selected near Parel in the 1870s for a larger locomotive workshop.

Until recently, the original locomotive workshop at Byculla survived as a spacious, if abandoned, rail yard. Children growing up in the vicinity remember referring to the abandoned Byculla yard area as 'chakri', probably because of the old locomotive turntable that once stood here. Today, that turntable has been replaced by a power substation. The yard itself has been taken over by swank apartment blocks for officials of the Mumbai (Bombay) Railway Vikas Corporation, the city's railway think tank.

CHINCHPOKLI STATION: THE EMERGENCY ZONE

We now inch towards the small single platform of Chinchpokli Station. Just before it appears, trains pass a century-old Jewish cemetery, built by the Jewish philanthropist and trader, David Sassoon, in memory of his son who passed away in Shanghai in 1868. Peek out of slowing trains, and you will spot ageing sarcophagi.

Chinchpokli, if translated from Marathi, literally signifies the hollow in the tamarind.[48] Referred to variously as Chintzpoogly, Chintapooglee or Chinchpugli by English writers and even in numerous official records, the place probably got this name because of the lush green tamarind trees all around. With the old fort gone, and with the suburbs of Dadar-Matunga yet to open up, this area, close to the elite Mazgaon, was one of the growing suburbs of Bombay.

---

47. *Minutes of the Proceedings of the Institution of Civil Engineers*, Volume 19, edited by James Forrest (London: The Institution, 1864).

48. The tamarind tree was brought by the Arabs to India from Africa, and the word 'tamar' is derived from Arabic. 'Tamar Hindi' or 'tamar-ind' signifies 'the date of Hindoostan'. See K.C. Sahni, *The Book of Indian Trees* (New Delhi: Oxford University Press, 1998), p. 230.

Located barely six kilometres from Fort, it came with sprawling bungalows and gardens.

Nineteenth-century English writer, Emma Roberts was a resident of Chinchpokli. She arrived in Bombay in 1839 and lived at Government House in Parel as a guest of Bombay's then governor, James Carnac. She died a year later. While in India, she would spend hours soaking in the rich landscape of Chintapooglee Hill.[49] From here, she could spot a cluster of palm trees along Mahim.

Today, if Emma Roberts were to return, she would fail to identify her beloved neighbourhood. For, modern-day Chinchpokli holds tall residential towers and ritzy malls; the mills barely exist.

~

A few trains began to halt at Chinchpokli around 1877, but it was only about twenty years later, between 1892 and 1894, that sanction was given to open a permanent halt station here.

Chinchpokli Station assumed prominence during the 1896 bubonic plague that killed scores of people—for, it became an important medical transit place. The government's quarantine plan for the GIPR included posting 'barrier inspection staff' at border stations like Kalyan and Thana. All suspicious plague cases were sent at once to a temporary hospital—essentially, fitted up rail carriages in a goods shed—from where the actual cases were sent by trains to Chinchpokli Station. Here, ambulances were kept ready to take the patients to the nearby City Fever Hospital (today's Kasturba Hospital), opened in 1892.[50] An ambulance coolie was constantly on duty at Chinchpokli Station, who, on receiving a telegraphic message from the station master there, provided the necessary ambulances. All compartments in which plague patients were sent were labelled 'to be disinfected'.[51]

---

49. Emma Roberts, *The Notes of an Overland Journey through France and Egypt to Bombay* (London: W.M.H. Allen, 1841), pp. 216, 314.

50. *Maharashtra State Gazetteer: Greater Bombay District*, Volume 3 (India: Gazetteers Department, Government of Maharashtra, 1986), p. 194.

51. Sir James MacNabb Campbell, *Report of the Bombay Plague Committee, Appointed by Government Resolution No 1204/720P on the Plague in Bombay for the Period Extending from the 1st July 1897 to the 30th April 1898* (Bombay: Times of India Steam Press, 1898), p. 36.

The Remains of the Day

Chinchpokli Station is tiny, with a single platform. But there is still much to be recovered. Though the platform has been extended to accommodate twelve-car trains, the original small station can be easily distinguished by its old pitched roof and spiked wooden sunshades. There are also twelve original pillars here, one of which carries the faded inscription, 'Dorman Long, England', that celebrated English firm.

Other remains of the day include an old booking office up the ramp (once used to transport patients and horses) and a road bridge with inscriptions, now hidden under multiple posters that offer to teach fluent English or promise a sure cure for all illnesses. The engraved inscriptions, if salvaged, state: 'GIPR, Arthur Road Bridge, 1911, Contractor: Haji Habib Haji Gunny'. The Arthur Road mentioned here—named after Bombay governor, George Arthur—is the old road that connects Parel Road to Bellasis Bridge.

An ancient milestone still stands tall outside the railway station. It announces: 'IV miles from St Thomas'. These basalt milestones, about sixteen in all, were originally three to four feet tall and placed to mark the distance in miles from St Thomas Church (today's St Thomas Cathedral at Fort), then the city centre. The one at Chinchpokli had been under threat during the construction of the city's monorail, but was saved and barricaded after locals highlighted its historical importance.

CURREY ROAD STATION: CHINCHPOKLI'S TWIN

It's not long before the train chugs into Currey Road Station. With Dorman, Long & Co pillars, it is a splitting image of Chinchpokli Station in layout and design.

Currey Road Station has been named after Charles Currey, born in 1833, originally working with Britain's Great Northern Railway. Currey was brought to Bombay as the agent of the rival BB&CI Railway between 1865 and 1875.[52]

---

52. Samuel T. Sheppard, *Bombay, Place Names and Street Names: Excursion into the Byways of the History of Bombay City* (Bombay: The Times Press, 1917), p. 56.

At first, Currey Road Station existed primarily for loading and unloading race horses. But between 1890 and 1895 a permanent halt station was in place for passengers too.[53] Shortly thereafter, in 1908, *The Bombay Gazetteer* mentions that the station was partially burnt and damaged during riots by mill-hands after the arrest of Bal Gangadhar Tilak for sedition by the British. It's important to remember that Chinchpokli, Currey Road and Parel have historically been the hub of old textile mills and the mill-worker colonies of Bombay. By 1920, Currey Road had recovered and had the distinction (along with Dadar Station) of being one of the first spaces to get colour-light signalling.

The Remains of the Day

Currey Road Station today holds twelve pillars, one with a faint inscription of the English firm, 'Dorman Long, England'; spiked wooden frames; and a road bridge. The bridge had been built by that tireless and innovative railway contractor, Seth Teju Kaya.

PAREL STATION: AN ERSTWHILE SEAT OF POWER

Past Currey Road, the lines run past a row of low houses and the building of the old GIPR stores yard—one of the earlier buildings of the old era with a roof of Manglorean tiles and wooden brackets.

The old GIPR stores yard—that is today a scrap depot—is in fact a treasure house of relics from India's oldest rail line. In 2012, officials from Matunga's workshop discovered and rescued a number of these vestiges of history and put them up on display at a temporary heritage gallery set up at the site. Among the retrieved items were Manglorean tiles from around 1878. How have we arrived at this date? Through the inscription on the tiles, reading, 'Alvares & Co, Mangalore'. We will never know what purpose these tiles served or which building they adorned. What we do know is that Mangalore has been home to the tile industry since the mid-nineteenth century, and that Simon

---

53. Dr A.K. Arora, *History of Bombay Suburban Railways: 1853-1985* (Bombay: The Indian Railway Electrical Engineers Association, 1985), p. 10.

Alvares of Bombay purchased a tile-manufacturing firm in 1878. He worked hard to establish it so it could cater to the growing demand for upscale tiles in Bombay, Jaffna, Colombo and even the east coast of Africa.[54] While Basel Mission Company, whose tiles have been found at Victoria Terminus, is known as the oldest tile-making firm, Alvares & Co belonged to an era when the railways were growing.

Other antiques from here, that have been placed at the Matunga railway workshop heritage gallery, include a 1930 vintage Morris fire engine, a 1948 Indian railway standard bogie and a narrow-gauge bogie designed by British rail engineer, Everard Richard Calthrop.[55]

~

Parel has an important place in Bombay's history—for, it had been the seat of power between 1770 and 1880, after Bombay governor, William Hornby shifted his official residence here. The once-wooded suburb is now a jumble of concrete and tall glass towers. The mills have been pulled down and the trees have all but disappeared. However, the governor's mansion remains to this day.

The site of the governor's mansion, known as Government House, had formerly held a Jesuit seminary; this was when the Portuguese had been occupying the seven islands of Bombay. When Bombay was given to the British as a part of the dowry of Catherine of Braganza, the Parel seminary was converted into an enchanting villa. Admirably suited to the climate in India, it had verandahs running around all the rooms. A civil servant of the East India Company, John Henry Grose, who began his journey across the East Indies in 1750, documents the Parel mansion vividly.

At Parel, the Governor has a very agreeable country-house. This house was originally a Romish chapel belonging to the

54. Arnold Wright, *Southern India: Its History, People, Commerce, and Industrial Resources* (India: Asian Educational Services, 1914), p. 511.

55. Everard Richard Calthrop promoted narrow-gauge lines and old hand-signalling lamps used on non-electrified rail lines.

Jesuits[56] [...] It is now [...] converted into a pleasant mansion-house, and what with the additional buildings and improvements of the gardens, affords a spacious and commodious habitation. There is an avenue to it of a hedge and trees near a mile long, and though near the sea side, is sheltered from the air of it by a hill between. Here the Governor may spend most part of the heats, the air being cooler and fresher than in town; and nothing is wanting that may make a country retirement agreeable.[57]

The hill mentioned by Grose still stands to this day, dotted with shanties and residential colonies. Called Golandji Hill, the battered knoll is no longer majestic. The city municipal corporation warns residents every year about possible landslides during the monsoons as the hill continues to get eroded.

A traveller, Carsten Neibuhr had suggested the villa at Parel be called 'sans pareil' (the peerless) since nothing could compare with it in all of India.[58] Records show that the house had been a centre of gaiety, with balls held regularly. Around 1803, James Mackintosh, then the recorder of Bombay, wrote:

We live about five miles [eight kilometres] of excellent road over a flat from our capital. We inhabit by the Governor's kindness his official country house, a noble building with some magnificent apartments and with two delightful rooms for my library, in which I am now, writing, overlooking a large garden of fine parkish ground. [...] In 1804 the Governor [Jonathan

---

56. Government House had been built at the site of the old temple of Parli Vaijnath, which gave the adjoining village the name 'Parel'. On this site, the Jesuits built a monastery and chapel sometime between 1596 and 1693. It was known as the Romish Chapel of Jesuits. See *Maharashtra Raj Bhavan*, in <https://rajbhavan.maharashtra.gov.in/history/history_sans.htm>,accessed on 9 February 2014.

57. John Henry Grose, *A Voyage to the East Indies: Containing Authentic Accounts of the Mogul Government in General, the Viceroyalties of the Decan and Bengal, with Their Several Subordinate Dependances, with General Reflections on the Trade of India*, Volume I (London: S. Hooper, 1772).

58. *The History of Raj Bhavan, Mumbai*, in <http://103.23.150.141/history/history_sans.htm>, accessed on 7 September 2014.

Duncan] gave a grand ball at Parel, when that sheet of water, to
which succeeding generations of wearied dancers have repaired
to recruit the exhausted energies, became a fairy scene of
gorgeous fireworks, which blazed away far into the night and
early morning over the faces of fair women and brave men.[59]

The gardens around Government House were once the best in the
city, and in fact a model for other power centres in the Indian empire.
There's a rather lovely story regarding the Parel gardens, and how
they came to be replicated at the governor general's house at
Barrackpore near Calcutta.

Around 1856, a year before the Indian mutiny, India's new governor
general, Lord Charles Canning, moved to Calcutta with his wife Lady
Charlotte Canning. The couple had sailed from England a year earlier
in December 1855, and had a brief stay at Government House at
Parel, before moving eastward. Lady Charlotte had been an
accomplished botanist and an artist in her own right; she had been
lady-in-waiting to Queen Victoria and used to send regular updates
to her with illustrations from India.

To the royal children she sent a steady stream of natural history
specimens, while the Queen enamored of India and Indians
(but too fearful of snakes and insects to travel hither), pressed
Lady Charlotte for details of life around her.[60]

The Parel gardens had been a part of the residence of the then
governor of the Bombay Presidency, Lord Elphinstone. These gardens
had charmed Lady Charlotte when she had first set foot in India. She
had delighted in the beauty of all the tropical vegetation. Seated by
her window at Parel, Lady Charlotte would write to Queen Victoria.
In one of her letters to the queen, Lady Charlotte said she could look
out on:

---

59. *Maharashtra State Gazetteers, Greater Bombay District*, in <https://
cultural.maharashtra.gov.in/english/gazetteer/greater_bombay/places.html>,
accessed on 4 September 2014.

60. Eugenia W. Herbert, *Flora's Empire: British Gardens in India* (India: Penguin
Books, 2013), pp. 89-90.

groves and groves of cocoa and palm overtopping round headed trees, then burnt-up ground, mango trees in flower exactly like Spanish chestnuts, tamarinds, peepal trees, higher good deal than the rest with trembling leaves, very green and pinkish stems, a teak tree with a lot of berries.[61]

Some months later, when Lady Charlotte had settled in her home in Calcutta, she attempted making the garden at Barrackpore a mirror image of the one she had witnessed in Parel. Today, at Government House we still see much of the flora mentioned by Lady Charlotte.[62]

Parel remained an important government seat till the mid-1880s, when Bombay governor, Richard Temple shifted his residence to Malabar Point, since Parel, in his opinion, was out of the way. James Fergusson, who followed Richard Temple, occupied Government House in Parel in November 1880. He was the last governor to live there.[63] By the end of his term, Government House had been judged as an unhealthy place. A former Bombay governor, Robert Grant, recorded that every gardener and servant on the premises was 'laid up with fever',[64] and later, in 1883, the wife of James Fergusson, died of cholera in the Parel house. Further, a slum had been developing around the mansion. A transfer to a new locale was deemed best.

The rocky headland of Point Malabar (today's Malabar Hill) with a 'varied and extensive view' was identified as a possible site for a new house. It offered a glimpse of the sea, was sufficiently isolated and came with the amenities the British desired.[65] In 1885, after the governor vacated his Parel premises, his former residence came to be used as the House of Recorders of the Bombay Presidency. In 1895, King Edward VII visited India as Prince of Wales, and stayed there for a week.

---

61. *Ibid.*

62. *Ibid.*

63. Fergusson College in Pune is named in James Fergusson's honour.

64. Manoj Nair, 'Malabar Hill: How a Jungle Turned into a Posh Address', *DNA*, 26 July 2011.

65. *Ibid.*

During the bubonic plague epidemic, Government House stood forlorn in its garden. In 1898, however, it was converted into a plague research laboratory and handed over to Dr Waldemar Mordecai Haffkine, a Ukrainian bacteriologist and a student of Louis Pasteur. The mansion was then referred to as the 'Plague Research Laboratory', with Dr Haffkine as its director-in-chief. So radical were the changes to the building in the early part of the twentieth century that the editor of *The Times of India*, Samuel Sheppard said:

> Government House at Parel had become so severely scientific
> that the ghosts of Duncan and Mountstuart Elphinstone cannot
> walk there without tripping over bottled bacilli or vaccines.[66]

Haffkine is remembered today for having developed vaccines against cholera and the plague. He is also remembered for his long and fruitful association with India. To begin with, Haffkine had worked in Calcutta. But in 1895, he returned to England after a bout of malaria. His stay in England was to be short-lived. The Bombay government invited Haffkine to fight the plague in India, and Haffkine, unable to refuse the offer, reached Bombay's shores on 7 October 1896. Initially, the research laboratory was at J.J. Hospital. By 1898, Haffkine shifted to the governors' former residence, which became a permanent laboratory; in 1906, it was formally named 'Bombay Bacteriology Lab'. Much later, in 1925, the institute was renamed Haffkine Institute, to honour the great scientist.[67] Haffkine wrote back a note of gratitude, saying that he had spent his best years in Bombay.

~

Let's return to the main railway network. Before trains reach Parel Station, yet another overbridge—Carroll Bridge—passes over the line. Around 1905, when the GIPR approached the Bombay municipality to get a bridge built here and close the level-crossing

---

66. Samuel T. Sheppard, *The Byculla Club (1833-1916): A History* (Bombay: Bennett, Coleman and Co Ltd, 1916), p. 164.

67. *The Haffkine Institute*, in <http://www.haffkineinstitute.org/history.htm>, accessed on 20 May 2012.

gate, the civic body refused to bear the cost. The neighbouring BB&CI Railway too refused to get involved. The GIPR then went ahead and constructed the entire bridge at its own cost. Today, one can still see detailed stone engravings along the corners of this bridge and oval metal plaques on iron girders announcing: 'GIPR, Parel Bridge, 1913, Contractor Bomanji Rustomji'. The small metal seals on the girders state: 'P&W MacLellan Limited, Clutha Works, Glasgow', a common enough engineering name on several GIPR creations.

The bridge goes by multiple names. While the engravings refer to it as 'Parel Bridge', the average citizen identifies it as Elphinstone Bridge, since Elphinstone Road Station is right below. As for railway documents, they call it Carroll Bridge, after one of the locomotive superintendents with the old BB&CI Railway, E.B. Carroll.[68] Carroll not only designed train coaches but also played a seminal role in the development of lighting in train carriages.

There were plans to demolish the bridge and rebuild a more contemporary overpass, one that could accommodate the conversion of the alternating current power model. But the project never took off. This was partially because the railways worked out an internal solution to the problem. Equally, local residents at Elphinstone opposed the flattening of the bridge, afraid that their buildings would also get demolished in the process.

~

Further on, trains trundle past Parel's railway workshop on one side and a scrap yard on the other. Eventually, they halt at Parel Station. Here, one gets a clear view of the former BB&CI Railway, today's Western Railway, that runs parallel. There's also a siding, skirting along an old water tank, to enter Parel's locomotive workshop, built between 1877 and 1879 on about forty-three acres of land,[69] when the original workshops at Byculla were found to be cramped. The Parel

---

68. Samuel T. Sheppard, *Bombay: Place Names and Street Names: Excursion Into the Byways of the History of Bombay City* (Bombay: The Times Press, 1917), p. 42.

69. S.N. Sharma, *History of the GIP Railway (1853-1869)*, Part I, Volume I (Bombay: Chief Public Relations Officer, Central Railway, 1990), p. 335.

workshop's history is chequered; there was a point when it manufactured grenades and explosive shells. During the First World War, railway workshops came under immense pressure, and the one at Parel ended up developing ammunition, high explosive shells, Mills grenades and even armoured cars for the army depot.[70] At some point, the Parel workshop was meant to attend to the overhauling of GIPR's steam locos; it was here that one of the nine original locomotives sent by the Vulcan Foundry got destroyed. Today, it has spread its wings to manufacture diesel locomotives for the Indian railways.

The Parel-Dadar yard, that we can spot from Parel Station, has historically been one of the main interchange points between the GIPR and the BB&CI Railway. In fact, it is still used for the exchange of trains and locomotives across today's Central and Western Railways. More than a century ago, on 1 January 1885, the GIPR and the BB&CI Railway signed the very first agreement that would allow for the interchange of coaches and goods stock. Each line acquired power to utilize the tracks of the other via Dadar—therefore, BB&CI Railway could send its goods trains directly to Carnac Bunder, and the GIPR obtained similar privileges and could use Colaba Station. Further, it was mutually agreed that, at a future date, if public interest so demanded, a local passenger train service would be established between Bandra on the BB&CI Railway line and Victoria Terminus on the GIPR line, via Dadar.[71]

Today, in the yard, we find vestiges of the first year of electrification, forgotten sidings and signal cabins. A few signals here still have the inscription, 'MV-GRS Ltd'. MV-GRS signifies one of the biggest industrial mergers of a British and an American company during the mid-1920s. The legendary Metropolitan-Vickers Railway Company, UK, and the General Railway Signal Company of Rochester, New York, formed a joint company in 1926 to sell electric railway equipment in Britain and its dominions. Coincidentally, around the

---

70. *Evening News*, 3 July 1982.

71. S.M. Edwardes, *The Gazetteer of Bombay City and Island*, Volume 1 (India: Cosmo Publications, 2002), p. 345.

same time, the GIPR's Main Line was electrified; MV-GRS sprang into action. The signalling apparatus was designed and developed by the American company; it was then made in Britain.[72] That we can still find remainders of this iconic industrial merger is extraordinary.

~

Parel Station was originally built around 1877. Ten years later, plans for a new, updated station were sent to London in December 1888; subsequently, the station was upgraded in the early 1890s.

Today, Parel Station is congested, teeming with people. With the old mills gone, and sky-reaching offices coming up, the rush and push of commuters and office-goers has grown exponentially. Added to this is the emergence of multiple prestigious hospitals and medical centres—the King Edward Memorial Hospital, G.S. Medical College, the Wadia Maternity Hospital, the Wadia Children's Hospital, the Tata Memorial Hospital (the largest cancer hospital in Asia), the Institute for Research in Reproduction, and, of course, the Haffkine Institute. For good reason, patients from all over India find their way to the station at Parel. Given the high footfall, a project was proposed in 2012 to convert this station into a terminus for suburban trains. The hope is that this will also decongest the next station, Dadar.

The Remains of the Day

You are more than justified if you ask: what 'design perspective' governs this drab-looking station? Well, there's a lot, if you study the space through the lens of a nineteenth-century architect. There's a footbridge with beautiful ornamental floral designs; there are balustrades; there are wooden engravings of the railway company and platforms with inscriptions.

Let's start with the footbridge in the south. It was originally low—with just twenty-four steps. It was also short, only connecting the platforms to the road to the east. Today, it has grown in height—a few

---

72. John Dummelow, *Metropolitan-Vickers Electrical Co Ltd: 1899-1949* (UK: Metropolitan-Vickers Electrical Co Ltd, 1949), p. 84.

additional steps were added, post-electrification, in 1925. It has also been extended, so it acts as a link to Elphinstone Road Station. The pillars have ornamental iron work, and at the base of each of staircase there are large, five-foot-high iron balustrades—all antique.

Look around, and you will spot pitched roofs. Some are higher than the rest, some are cantilevered, some shallow. One of them is set against an old iron pillar with the inscription, 'Glengarnock Steel', linking it to the now-defunct Scotland-based firm.

More than 100 years later, the GIPR's 'design and layout' of the station remains functional, despite the fact that the number of commuters has sharply risen.

DADAR STATION: THE CONNECTOR

Dadar has historically been a connector. When Bombay was just a constellation of islands, a small pathway, almost like a staircase or a ladder—built by silting up the creek waters—connected the islands of Naigaum and Mahim. In the local tongue, 'Dadar' actually means a step, a staircase or a connector. Today, the legacy continues, with Dadar acting as a key junction, a connector of the city's two main rail lines—the Central and the Western Railways. It is a point facilitating the interchange of passengers and traffic.

For the local resident, Dadar carries one of two names—Dadar TT for the east, and Dadar BB for the west. What do these acronyms signify? While TT refers to the old tram terminus that was once located at Khodadad Circle in the east, BB refers to the old BB&CI Railway (now Western Railway) that lies to the west of the station. The BB&CI Railway has ceased to exist by its name; the tram terminus too vanished after trams were discontinued. But the abbreviations have lived in public imagination.

The GIPR's Dadar Station came up sometime in 1856, three years after the line was first built. As mentioned earlier, it has the distinction, along with Currey Road, of being one of the first stations to get colour-light signalling in 1920.

The Remains of the Day

On exploring the platforms at Dadar, you will chance upon ageing balustrades, an old stone signal box with decorative quoins, wrought iron arches for a GIPR brass bell and a GIPR wall clock in the station master's office. While there are no major celebrated relics at this station, the intricate web of sturdy pedestrian bridges here, lost in the crowds and chaos, do have a significant (albeit fading) history.

If we begin our walk from the southern end of the station, the first to pass over the lines is the municipal public bridge, linked to an elevated booking office. One of the beams around the old booking office holds the inscriptions of the popular British engineering firm, Appleby-Frodingham Steel Company. The elevated booking office, in turn, is linked to an iron railway bridge—probably the oldest remaining relic at the Central Railway's Dadar Station, and built around 1942. It is a work of art, with wrought iron railings, wooden sidebars, three ramps and decorative balustrades. The bridge was once longer. But it was subsequently cut, so it would merge with the elevated booking office; indeed, a few old pillars of the demolished bridge can still be spotted beyond platform one.

Moving further, there are three more bridges spanning the station, the widest being a recent construction (1998) at twelve metres. One of the bridges built in 1950 holds the inscription, 'Lanarkshire Steel, Scotland', a company that started in 1897, and got nationalized in 1951 under the Iron and Steel Act, to become part of the Iron and Steel Corporation of Great Britain. Eighty-three-year-old Hammy Jardine, one of the surviving former employees of Lanarkshire Steel Company, recollects, 'Our brand used to be in raised letters; we'd cut the letters into the last pair of rolls, thus leaving the imprint. We had two girder shops, and processed orders for not just governments but private customers too, to keep both shops fully employed. Sometimes, we would get a direct order from a company in India, or a subcontractor from Britain to manufacture railway material.'[73]

There is a small bridge (now partially demolished) towards the middle of Dadar Station, that has faint inscriptions announcing 'Tata

---

73. Personal correspondence.

Steel'. Tata Steel has been one of the major indigenous contractors supplying material for railway infrastructure since the beginning of the twentieth century. The completely Indian-owned Tata Iron and Steel Company Limited (TISCO), the brainchild of Jamshetji Tata, was established by his son, Dorabji Tata in 1907. When British supplies of iron and steel stopped in 1915, the Tatas filled in the gap, and thereafter became a major supplier of steel rails, chairs and fishplates to the railroads. By 1928-1929, railroad requirements for these and many other iron and steel products were met from within India, and by 1939, the Tatas operated the largest steel plant in the British Empire.[74]

With the crowds only increasing exponentially, the railways have now planned for more bridges with escalators for mass transit. Already we see the wheels of change turning; the old footbridge that linked the station to Tulsi Pipe Road was demolished in the early 1990s to build a flyover that runs parallel to the station.

MATUNGA STATION: WHERE THE ELEPHANTS MARCHED

As slow trains leave Dadar Station, they pass the popular Tilak Bridge that came up in the mid-1920s to replace a busy level-crossing. Its girth is vast, connecting Dadar East on the GIPR side and Dadar West on the BB&CI Railway side. Look closely, and you will see that Tilak Bridge is teeming with inscriptions. On the sturdy pillars, we find mention of Lanarkshire Steel; on the solid girders we find inscriptions of Mossend Steel. And then, there is the rare inscription of Alcock Ashdown Limited. Originally a British-owned company, Alcock Ashdown went into liquidation and was taken over by the government of India in 1975 and then by the government of Gujarat in 1994. It is now a shipyard fully owned by the Gujarat government. When in Bombay, Alcok Ashdown was located around Mazgaon and was also one of the key contenders for the laying of pipes for the Upper Vaitarna water supply project of the 1950s.

~

74. Ian J. Kerr, *Engines of Change: The Railroads that Made India* (USA: Praeger Publishers, 2007), p. 121.

In the 1820s, Reginald Heber, the newly appointed bishop of Calcutta, started travelling across India. It all began with a boat trip to the upper waters of the Ganges. He then proceeded overland to the foothills of the Himalayas, and reached the farthest northerly point at Almora. He then turned south to Delhi, crossed Rajputana and reached Bombay, where he spent four months. His wife Amelia joined him in Bombay from Calcutta. In her memoir, Amelia recalls starting an expedition at Matoonga (now Matunga). Based on her descriptions, the area held one of Bombay's vast green spaces; it was also an artillery cantonment and an exercising ground in the centre of the island. Apart from this, it had little to offer of interest.[75]

Since Amelia's excursion with Reginald Herbert, much has changed. The author, Samuel T. Sheppard says that among other things, Matoonga, Matunga, or Matangasthan would mean the place of elephants. He adds: 'It is the merest conjecture that Bhimdeo, or Bimb Raja, may have stationed his elephants in this locality while he was ruler of Mahim.'[76] While in the eighteenth century, all of Matunga was devoted to rice cultivation and salt pans, at the end of the nineteenth century, Lord Sandhurst's Bombay Improvement Trust changed Matunga's destiny and made it a leading locale of the new century. The Bombay Improvement Trust, seeking land to decongest the old Fort township after the plague epidemic, zeroed in on large tracts of the Dadar-Wadala-Sewri and Matunga-Sion 'flats' (empty land) in 1889-90 and devised a 'planned township' along the stretch with public housing.

Matunga Station came up around the same period, in 1906. It is a simple station with two island platforms, an old station office and two footbridges. It is flanked by a railway repair yard to the east (now making way for a power substation) and the Matunga carriage and wagon workshop to the west (where the Tatas originally wanted to build a flour mill). Let's study the history of this space.

---

75. Amelia Shipley Heber, *Memoir of Reginald Heber* (Boston: John P. Jewett and Company, 1856).

76. Samuel T. Sheppard, *Bombay, Place Names and Street Names: Excursion into the Byways of the History of Bombay City* (Bombay: The Times Press, 1917), p. 99.

Owing to a burst of activity and the sudden rapid development of the Indian railways during the viceroyalty of Lord Curzon, the directors of the GIPR in 1904 decided to form a separate carriage and wagon department to look after the upkeep of wagons. They identified land near Matunga to build fine new workshops.[77] However, there was a problem. The Bombay Improvement Trust had already made a survey and had plans for public housing in that precise area; adding to the confusion, the Tatas were keen to build a flour mill on the plot.[78] This was much to the chagrin of the Bombay Improvement Trust that believed that the presence of any industry in the vicinity would affect a planned residential neighbourhood and the city's expansion. The Bombay Improvement Trust went on to oppose the GIPR's plan to build a workshop and appealed to the Bombay government. Ultimately the trust's sound and fury led to nothing—the area between the two rail networks was omitted from the housing plans and the GIPR was given first preference to build the carriage and wagon workshop there in 1904.

Today, within the spacious workshop on the land that was once reserved for public housing, there are criss-crossing rail tracks and brightly painted rail wagons ready for dispatch and public use. The workshop has old plaques dating back to 1909 on its tall steel pillars, similar to those found along the Parel Bridge, acknowledging P&W MacLellan Limited, Glasgow. In one corner of the workshop lies a small heritage gallery that possibly retains some of the oldest relics of the Indian railways.

Now, a century later, as the train pulls out of Matunga Station, one can see a row of small two-storey buildings; the only evidence of the Bombay Improvement Trust's involvement with this area are two small engravings reading 'BIT'. Many of these BIT dwellings are in the process of being pulled down to be rebuilt as high-rises.

---

77. *The Locomotive*, 15 May 1926, p. 144.

78. Nikhil Rao, *House, but No Garden: Apartment Living in Bombay, 1898-1984* (USA: University of Minnesota Press, 2013), p. 49.

The Remains of the Day

The old booking office in Matunga Station is untouched and has survived the onslaught of commuters and construction. Its original wooden brackets, the GIPR logos and the pitched roof are, quite incredibly, still in place. Also in place are the thirteen pairs of pillars on each of the two island platforms, with faint 'Dorman Long, England' inscriptions.

SION STATION: THE PLACE OF BIRTH

The train trundles forward towards Sion. The popular Sion Hospital that lies in the vicinity was originally a military infirmary. During the last phase of the Second World War, in 1944-1945, the Indian military needed a base hospital, and they established one with 1,500 beds on a vast piece of land belonging to the Bombay Municipality that had fortunately already been earmarked as a sick bay. The hospital consisted of forty-four barrack-like structures connected to each other by roofed passages.

As the war ended, the need for a base military hospital in Bombay was rendered redundant and the site remained idle till it was handed back to the municipality in October 1946 for Rs 2,00,000. The municipality then established a 300-bed infirmary, and named it the Municipal General Hospital, Sion. It was intended to be an annexure to the existing King Edward Memorial (KEM) Hospital and was meant for chronic, long-stay patients of KEM's orthopedic department. From May 1948, however, Sion Hospital came to be recognized as an independent establishment. Two years later, in 1950, the Bombay Municipal Corporation passed a resolution to rename Sion Hospital; it is now Lokmanya Tilak Municipal General Hospital, Sion.[79] Opposite this hospital, in one of the lanes behind the main road, stands a milestone, probably the last one before 'Salsette' begins.

~

---

79. S.V. Joglekar and D.D. Vora, *Sion Hospital: A Historical Sketch, Inception to 1947 to Beginning of Sion Medical College in 1964*, in <http://www.indianjmedsci.org/text.asp?1999/53/2/53/12196>, accessed on 20 January 2012.

Sion or Shiv is a Portuguese corruption of the word 'simva' or 'sima', which means 'boundary'. Sion is still the island city's border, the start of the suburbs in municipal records.

Well before the railways arrived, the only connections between Bombay and Salsette were two causeways—Mahim Causeway, which came up about a decade before the rail lines, and Sion Causeway that emerged in the early part of the nineteenth century. Both causeways were survey points for assessing how the first railway would fare. After all, John Chapman, the promoter of the GIPR, had stationed men at each of the causeways to gauge the amount of the traffic that passed both ways, and thus decide if setting up the railways would be profitable.

Today, Sion Causeway, formerly Duncan Causeway, runs parallel to the railway lines in the east. Work on the causeway began in 1798 and was completed in 1805 during the administration of Jonathan Duncan. In 1825, nearly thirty years before the first train run, Lady West, the wife of Edward West, chief justice of the king's court in Bombay, who used the causeway to travel with Bishop Heber and his family, described it in her memoir[80] as 'a very narrow road, two miles [three kilometres] long, which joins the island of Salsette to Bombay'.

Records state it cost a whopping Rs 50,374 to build the causeway. The writer, Govind Madgaonkar, who documented Bombay in 1863, however, begged to differ, and said that the cost was Rs 50,575—Rs 200 more than what was recorded! He went on to say that the cost was recovered quite easily by charging a tariff to those using the causeway—bullock-carts were charged half an anna, horse riders paid four annas, one-horse carriages had to cough up half a rupee, and two-horse carriages had to pay as much as one rupee. The government consequently earned between Rs 10,000 and Rs 20,000 per year.[81] It

80. F. Dawtrey Drewitt, *Bombay In the Days of George IV: Memoirs of Sir Edward West, Chief Justice of the King's Court during Its Conflict with the East India Company with Hitherto Unpublished Documents* (London: Longmans, Green, and Co., 1907), p. 178.

81. Govind Narayan Madgaonkar, *Mumbaiche Varnan*, edited by Narhar Raghunath Fatak (India: Marathi Granth Sangrahalaya, 1863), p. 85. Translated by the author.

was in 1831 that the government realized that the cost of constructing the causeway had been recovered; tax collection was thus suspended on orders of a generous English official. Interestingly, this becomes one of the oldest case studies of tolls levied by the government on the city's roads.

Along the causeway, at the border between today's Kurla and Sion, there was once a check post, with large gates that were shut at 8 p.m. at cannon fire, and opened at dawn after another round of cannon blasts. A small temple and a pond, located at the edge of the bridge, still exist.[82]

The Duncan Causeway is today named after senior bureaucrat, N.S. Mankikar, though the civic pumping station here retains Duncan's name.

~

Sion is the beginning. It's where the railways were born. It was here that the first sod-turning ceremony had taken place on 31 October 1850. It was also here that the chief secretary to the Bombay government, John P. Willoughby had allowed work to begin on the first rail line. Willoughby left Bombay in May 1851, a proud man for initiating this ceremonial beginning. He was confident that the railways in India would bring good tidings,[83] and was assured that their construction was progressing well. He is not remembered today, but his letter on the rail line he inaugurated is worth a mention.

> I am happy to be able to state to board that when I left Bombay on the 3rd May last satisfactory progress had already made in its [the railway's] construction and that as you doubtless have been informed it has since withstood without any serious injury one of heaviest monsoons perhaps ever remembered. I cannot therefore foresee any circumstance to impede its early completion.[84]

---

82. *Ibid.*, p. 69.

83. *The Railway Record Mining Register and Joint Stock Companies Reporter*, Volume 8, Number 41 (London: Railway Record Office, 1851), p. 719.

84. Archives of the GIPR.

Though trains did halt at Sion when the railways first ran in 1853, it seems there was no permanent station here. But as trains became popular and the crowds swelled, it became imperative to have a station. With this end in mind, in 1872, 107 local inhabitants of Sion and its surrounding villages sent a 'humble petition' to the GIPR, pointing out that there was no station between Kurla and Dadar.

> Your petitioners at present experience great difficulty in consequence of the Coorla [Kurla] and Dadar stations being far off stationed. In fact, your petitioners have to travel a distance equal to an hour's walk morning and evening to and from the stations and in reality they get much fatigued after their laborious work in the town, and much more felt during the monsoons, and to alleviate these difficulties your petitioners pray for a station between these two stations and which they consider should be styled 'Sion Station'.
>
> Your petitioners humbly beg to venture and to consider a poor suggestion and hope you will not deem it irrelevant. That if a common shed be erected at a trifling cost and allowing the train, that runs daily, to stop there for a couple minutes, your petitioners feel confident, and there is no doubt you will observe, that it will cover the outlay by the daily revenue of the passengers travelling by the train in a short time, and will also enable the Company to have a permanent shed erected. In this suggestion you will not only relieve your petitioners from the difficulties they experience but it will be a manifest gain to the company, and in conferring the boon solicited for, your petitioners shall in duty bound ever pay.

Fifty such petitions were signed in English, four in Urdu, and fifty-three in Hindi, Marathi and other scripts. Of the fifty who signed in English, twelve were non-Christians. On receiving such an appeal, a rough marketing survey was undertaken, which revealed that a good number of inhabitants, who were almost all fishermen, attended the Bombay market at the other end of the city daily. They generally went by the Baroda train. If the GIPR were to open a small station at Sion, some of these passengers would opt for the GIPR network; equally, the 1,500 inhabitants in Dharavi, the 1,000 in Sion and the population of 500 at Matunga would choose trains more frequently as the preferred mode of transport. A monthly average revenue of about Rs 600 could be expected! After some time, therefore, sanction was given for officially stopping passenger trains at the proposed site which was to be called 'Sion Station'.[85]

~

Sion used to be located on the island of Rewa. Rewa had an old fort (that was referred as an outpost), a watchtower and a Portuguese church, which can still be spotted in different forms.

When the East India Company began strengthening all of Bombay's fortifications, it also focussed on the structures in Sion. Two hundred years later, in the 1850s, as Bombay was being refashioned for the railway line, parts of the by-then ruined watchtower were nearly demolished along with a once-extensive hill. Today, about 350 years later, if we stop at Sion's platform three, we see the crumbing remains of the watchtower, flanked by tall concrete buildings.

Folklore has it that once upon a time, there was a witch in this watchtower who could read fortunes. Nineteenth-century Bombay sheriff and city chronicler, James Douglas documents her in one of his books. While on a train journey to Sion Station in 1884, he writes:

> The ground as one can see from the carriage window, rises in a ridge, on which is visible the Catholic Church, and on outlying knob a watch-tower, in a corner of which has lived for many years a witch who, in this age of enlightenment, professes to spy fortunes or otherwise diagnose the future. If she had predicted the fate of the Sion Fort, which is now, in this month of March 1884, being consummated before our eyes, she would have been a remarkably clever woman, and have saved us trouble of comment. Here is a picturesque old fort. You cannot see it from the station, but it is discernible far and near, by land and by sea,

---

85. S.N. Sharma, *History of the GIP Railway (1853-1869)*, Part 1, Volume 1 (Bombay: Chief Public Relations Officer, Central Railway, 1990), pp. 36-38.

crowning with its battlements this projecting woody ridge of
Bombay Island, a fort interwoven with our earliest history and
almost coeval with the arrival of the English race in this quarter,
now being levelled with the dust. The fiat has gone forth, and
already the work of demolition has commenced, for the
iconoclasts are at their work tearing down in fury what their
genius will never be able to put together again.[86]

There are disagreements among archaeology experts regarding whether
the watchtower is the old Rewa Fort, or the fortification near the
Dharavi Bus Depot further ahead is the *actual* Rewa Fort. Maharashtra
archaeology department expert, Dr B.V. Kulkarni, claims that it is the
latter, but others would disagree.

At Sion, therefore, the railway line passes between two old historic
forts—one at Dharavi and the other, the watchtower overlooking the
line. It's as though the watchtower is still guarding the entrance of
Bombay city, as the train leaves Sion, the last station in city limits, to
enter what once was Salsette—a cluster of sixty-six villages, and now
the suburbs.

The Remains of the Day

There are echoes of the past at Sion Station—a few pillars across the
first three platforms have the inscription, 'Tata Iron and Steel
Company' (albeit without the year); platform four has eleven wrought
iron pillars with decorative work on the brackets of the roof; beneath
the new footbridge spanning all the four platforms are old stone
bricks, absolute originals. There is also a century-old overbridge (now
extended) with arches, a semi-spiral stone staircase landing into the
station premises and an inscription in one corner that advertises
Frodingham Iron and Steel.

The station master's office on platform one comes with original
wooden brackets, GIPR logos and a pitched roof. Back in the day, this
must have been the only significant structure at the station. If we

---

86. James Douglas, *Bombay and Western India: A Series of Stray Papers*, Volume 2
(London: Sampson Low, Maeston and Company, 1893).

observe the façade, we spot something akin to a window for the dispensation of tickets. Years of land-filling though have raised the platform height so enormously that the old window sill is almost touching the floor!

Decorative Work Near Sion Station's Roof

Parallel to the rail line, close to N.S. Mankikar Road, lies an undocumented 200-year-old milestone, dating back to 1817. Discovered by a group of college students during one of their projects, the milestone bears the inscription 'IX miles from St Thomas'. A bit ahead on the same road lies an octagonal solid structure that many say belongs to the era of the Second World War. It is a garrison, probably used to store ammunition, now maintained as a family dwelling. Treasures indeed!

KURLA STATION: SALT AND SHALLOW CREEKS

The line moves out of Sion Station. When the lines had been built, the topography of the area had been entirely different. There was no Eastern Express Highway, but smaller roads leading to the village of Chembur and the Central Salsette Tramway. There was no Kurla East, only a vast expanse of salt pans.

The oldest relic that used to exist (until recently), just after Sion Station, was an enormous 129-foot-long iron mast, holding overhead wires and spanning across all eight tracks. Reporting on the inauguration of the first electric railway in India between Victoria Terminus and Kurla, the *GIP Railway Magazine* of 1925 had said that this particular mast had the largest traction span in the world at that time. The massive gantry stood out amidst the single poles like a crown over the eight lines. But it was unceremoniously pulled down one night in the recent past, cut into pieces and carted away to be sold as scrap, paving way for new technology.

As the line moves ahead, an abandoned stone cabin without a roof is found hidden behind overgrown bushes. These are remains of an old level-crossing that was once located here, near the old Swadeshi Mill premises. Further ahead, at what is called the Sarveshwar Mahadev Temple junction, a footbridge with stone ramps passes over the line. This is, according to railway records, one of the oldest existing footbridges, built around 1904, with wrought iron lamps and balustrades. It faces the tracks, and possibly exists for those who love the simple pleasure of train spotting.

The Sarveshwar Mahadev Temple was built in 1883, thirty years after the first rail run, on land donated to workers of Swadeshi Mill and Kurla Spinning Mill by the Wadia Trust, so they could have a place of worship. Interestingly, the temple's archives mention that the old Kurla Station was originally located opposite this very temple.

As trains approach today's Kurla Station, they pass small hillocks blanketed with makeshift dwellings. In fact, when the first line was being laid, archives suggest that the land between Kurla Station and Ghatkopar had a small chain of mountains and salt pans. These mountains had to be cut to make way for a double line. To date, the old Kurla Village road, parallel to the railway line, is at a gradient, harking back to the erstwhile ridge.

An abandoned and solitary platform, just before Kurla Station, is a legacy of the old salt trade that once flourished here. It witnessed the conveyance of salt from the pans to the city. With the emerging network of railways, some of the salt pans had to be acquired by the government, and one of the largest proprietors to be affected was Hormusjee Bomanjee. In 1848, much of Bomanjee's land had developed as salt pans. The government's desire to acquire his land for the railways, he claimed, would lay waste more than 145 salt pans with nearly 1,600 mounds. The compensation offered for Bomanjee's lands led to further differences between him and the collector of Thana, J.S. Law.[87] Bomanjee asked for compensation of Rs 2,537 per annum, but had to settle for a far lower amount after arbitration. Bomanjee's other demand—to sell toddy from his land at Kurla—also came to be rejected.

~

Salt pans, shallow creek water and fish—these words shaped the names of Salsette's surburbs. Indeed, 'coorli' and 'chimbori'—two words that could very well have been the etymological roots of Kurla or Coorla and Chembur—were local names for the crabs found in large numbers in the shallow creeks in the vicinity.

When the first line was built, the area between Kurla and Thana was described as the 'flats', and after the Sion viaduct, the only significant work of railway engineering was the viaduct of Thana. The flats were wide open spaces with marshes and mangroves, flirting with the sea and the salt pans on the east. How much has changed since! Today, the site between Kurla and Vidyavihar, the next north-bound station, is a huge rail jungle. To the west is the sprawling Kurla

---

87. Mariam Dossal, *Mumbai: Theatre of Conflict, City of Hope: 1660 to Present Times* (India: Oxford University Press, 2012), pp. 116-17.

car-shed, and to the east is a large rail yard with some of the earliest electric gantries, all hidden behind thick bushes and overgrowth.

Kurla Station, which came up in 1856 (and was probably shifted to its present site in the 1890s), was the first station within Salsette. Kurla was also the destination of the country's first electric railway run in 1925.

Moreover Kurla had a key position within the city's water transport network. As the city expanded in the 1880s, and the rail lines and mills multiplied, the needs of the people increased; the supply of water from the Tulsi and Vihar Lakes fell short. Consequently, the first Tansa water supply pipeline project was proposed and work began in 1889. It was opened by Lord Lansdowne in 1892 and was estimated to supply the city of Bombay with 46,00,000 gallons of water per day, through pipes that were eighty-eight kilometres in length. This pipeline passed (and still passes) over the rail lines across an iron bridge. The year 1889 was carved on the iron pipes that were shipped to Bombay. A small narrow-gauge rail line was laid on the iron bridge, next to these pipes, for maintenance; there was a time when this would carry water maintenance trains.

Kurla was also notorious as the city's dump. According to an 1867 report on the Bombay Presidency's sanitary conditions, solid refuse was collected and carried by carts and rail to Kurla, sixteen kilometres from Bombay, to a tract of swampy ground belonging to the municipality. Today, the dump is located at Deonar, close to Govandi Station, along the Kurla-Mankhurd line.

The Remains of the Day

The ten-platform Kurla Station is a mine of relics. Let's begin with the old stone buildings at Kurla Station—isolated Gothic structures made of Malad stone, with semi-circular arches. For the most part, they're dwarfed by the ugly constructions in the locality. However, let it rain, and the stone in the old buildings sparkles, and assumes prominence. One of these structures is now used as the electric department's office. In the middle is a beautiful iron spiral staircase, and at the back is a wrought iron fence with floral designs. Two other stone buildings, which are now used as rail trade union offices, have quoins on them, indicating that they were built with some architectural thought. Both, now dilapidated, could be pulled down anytime.

Then there is platform 1-A. Residents remember that this platform was originally used by the Central Salsette Tramway run by the GIPR, connecting Mahul (near Chembur) to Andheri, somewhat parallel to today's metro. Kurla had been the interchange point. The thirteen-kilometre standard-gauge Central Salsette Tramway, with nine stations, was the brainchild of Lord Sandhurst's Bombay Improvement Trust. It was believed that the line would encourage more people to take to the planned suburbs. However, the strategy came to naught, as six years later, in 1934, the lines had to be shut down to make way for the Santacruz Airport.

Platforms nine and ten, now abandoned, were used till the mid-1990s to run shuttle trains from Kurla to Mankhurd. In fact, it was on platform nine that one found the foundation stone of the Mumbai (Bombay) Railway Vikas Corporation, and it was from platform ten that former railway minister Mamata Banerjee flagged off a local train service to New Bombay. The foundation stone was demolished around 2004, and the platforms subsequently forsaken.

In 2011, when the railways were building a new footbridge at Kurla Station and were excavating the area, remains of an old stone platform were found below the existing platform surface! There was even a solid stone wall, with design elements typical of the early days of railway construction. The rough stones were 'dressed' in order to fit the platform wall, cut precisely into regular shapes resembling triangles.

Kurla, as the destination of the country's first electric railway run, holds a number of vestiges of this technological leap. For instance, it has a power substation built in 1925, located just opposite platform eight. This artefact can also be spotted in the GIPR's publicity and promotion photographs released after the opening ceremony and inaugural run between Kurla and Victoria Terminus. Another substation, adjacent to it, came up in 1953, a year after the Kurla-Mankhurd line was electrified.

A little beyond Kurla Station, one spots abandoned lines and an old electric car shed that came up after 1925 to maintain the electric trains that had started arriving in ships from England. There is also a small, rusted iron signal box that offers important leads to the electrification of the first railway. Back in 2002—before its cover, chock full of inscriptions, was stolen—it carried the word 'Westinghouse', followed by an illegible smudge, and then, 'Signal Co Ltd, 1930'. Correspondence with Westinghouse Company revealed it was one of the major businesses of the 1930s responsible for the early electrification of the lines.

Further ahead, there used to be, until very recently, a structure resembling an old carriage. A still closer look disclosed that this was actually the remains of an old four-wheeled wooden wagon, with GIPR written across—possibly the oldest of such wagons. Today, one can find a similar forgotten flat cargo wagon at the diesel loco shed near the station.

During the days of the GIPR, it was fashionable to name running locomotives after important stations along the line. In the 1870s, one of a series of twenty-six six-coupled engines with six-wheeled tenders, supplied by Kitson and Hewitson of Leeds, was named Kurla and used for yard duties at Parel. Another set of engines of a similar class was named Bombay.[88]

VIDYAVIHAR STATION: THE MARSH THAT BECAME A SCHOOL

Vidyavihar is not a GIPR station, but a Central Railway one that opened on 16 August 1961. (As you may recall, the GIPR was renamed Central Railway in 1951). It was never a suburb in itself, just marshy land. However, it became the local hub of education, after the Somaiyas of Bombay developed educational institutions in the precincts around 1959. This explains the name, which, when loosely translated, means 'a suburb of knowledge'. It also explains the need for a station to be set up here, for there was a whole student population to cater to.

In the 1960s and 1970s, the railways had lost land on both sides of Vidyavihar Station due to encroachments. The railways had to devise a plan, and fast, to protect their territory. Theirs was a stroke of genius. The railways divided the plot—they built a hostel for their technical apprentices and railway quarters for their staff on one side;

---

88. *The Locomotive*, 15 September 1926, p. 290.

on the other, they set up a plant nursery, one that was nourished by a small rivulet that ran right through it. From this nursery, small pots would be sent regularly to the administrative offices of various railway stations.

However, neither the hostel nor the nursery would last. With the railways hoping to increase the capacity of the existing corridor between Kurla and Thana, work on a new set of lines began in full swing. The hostel for technical apprentices was demolished and so was the nursery.

In 2011, the commissioning of a fifth and sixth line has been the latest addition between Vidyavihar and Thana Stations to Clark's original blueprint of the GIPR. The construction of these two new lines was a challenge, as apartments and people had to be relocated and public utilities shifted. When the land was clear, there was another error—track crossovers weren't laid! Finally, after several hiccups, the lines opened.

The east side of today's Vidyavihar Station is the beginning of the old Ghatkopar suburb. Back in the day, the land here was dense with trees. In the 1940s, this vegetation was cleared to make way for residential houses for government servants displaced during Partition. This colony is today called Chittaranjan Nagar. A large section of the land also purportedly belonged to Raja Gaekwad of Baroda, who had given it as 'jagir' (a feudal land grant) to a prominent local family. The family seems to have lost some clout, and the land was acquired by the Bombay Municipal Corporation in 1950. On a part of this stands Rajawadi Municipal Hospital, functional since 1958.

The Remains of the Day

Today, the single-island Vidyavihar platform has a footbridge and two booking offices. The bridge has inscriptions of Lanarkshire Steel Company and the platforms hold circular seals with inscriptions of the Central Railway Engineering Workshop, Manmad.

GHATKOPAR STATION: A LINE FOR TRADE

Originally, Ghatkopar was part of Thana district, with salt pans in the east and Kirol Village to the west. Railway archives state that to lay the original line near Ghatkopar, mountainous rocks had to be cut.[89] Not surprisingly, as the line rushes past Vidyavihar, towards Ghatkopar, passing through a cleft in the mountains, one can spot hard rock projections. One also notices that the land on both sides of the rails is at a much higher elevation. The mountains end at Ghatkopar, which literally means the 'edge of the ridge'. The remains of these old mountains can still be seen as one travels by the city's metro just after it moves out of the Ghatkopar Metro Station.

Built in 1877 following requests from the resident community, Ghatkopar Station—with four platforms today—is busy on the best of days. Once upon a time, the small cluster of homes along the Rajawadi area and Agra Road were the only settlements here. As the area mushroomed, a number of businessmen from the Bhatia community built mansions and residential complexes along the stretch. A popular local alley, Hingwala Lane, is named after one such merchant, Ranchoddas Hingwala who purchased land in Ghatkopar. Indeed, the Hingwala family once owned a seven-storey mansion here, Billi Bungalow, that was destroyed in a fire in 1941.

The Bhatias had their trading houses and businesses in South Bombay, around Masjid Bunder. It was merchants from this community who petitioned the GIPR for a train from Ghatkopar Station. Once the line was activated, it came to be popularly known as the 'Bhatia local'.

In 1882, following a request from the salt merchants in the area, the GIPR had contemplated having rail sidings from Ghatkopar Station to the salt works in the east for examining and weighing salt before it was transported. However, this plan never materialized as the salt commissioner was against dispatching salt from Ghatkopar; he believed that the loading and unloading of salt was being satisfactorily handled at Kurla Station, probably from a solitary platform in the southeast that stands abandoned today. C.B. Pritchard, the commissioner of customs, opium and 'abkari', in a letter dated 30 April 1882, told the consulting engineer for railways in Bombay:

89. K.R. Vaidyanathan, *150 Glorious Years of Indian Railways* (India, English Edition, 2003).

[Besides the fact that] there is no real need for the incurrence of additional expenditure that the maintenance of this additional establishment [a rail siding and a salt station at Ghatkopar], the arrangement is also objectionable on the score of danger to the salt revenue and the salt department will not be willing to issue the permits for salt to be loaded up at Ghatkopar station or any sidings that may run from it[...] The arrangement would not also, I submit, be a profitable one for the railway company, as the position of salt works that would be affected by it is such that the salt to be loaded up at Ghatkopar would simply displace an equal quantity of salt that is now loaded up at Kurla station.[90]

Today, Ghatkopar Station is flanked by high footbridges running parallel to the line on both sides, now called skywalks, a twenty-first century term for pedestrian bridges. But these are seldom used. We also see the presence of the Versova-Andheri-Ghatkopar metro line, which terminates here.

The Remains of the Day

As reminders of the past, we see twenty wrought iron roof brackets on platform one; rails with 'GIPR-1890' running across them; nine old iron pillars with ornamental brackets; and a stone signal cabin.

VIKHROLI STATION: INTO THE FOREST

The trains move out of Ghatkopar and towards Vikhroli. Till the late 1930s, there was nothing along this stretch, with the exception of the tiny Vikhroli Village and Agra Road (or LBS Road). Today, all along the route, on both sides, one can spot the sprawling Godrej Industrial Complex with residential towers, factory units and public amenities.

The Godrej archives state that in 1942, Pirojsha Godrej, in the name of his son Naoroji, purchased all of Vikhroli Village[91] to set up

---

90. GIPR railway correspondence, documented circa 1882 from the Maharashtra Archives Bulletin of the Department of Archives.

91. Interestingly, Vikhroli Village was one of the original revenue villages to find mention in the fourteenth-century *Mahikavati's Bakhar*, where it is referred to as 'Vikharoli'.

an industrial township. However, the process of buying land wasn't easy. Newspapers state:

> He [Pirojsha] bought a tract of land in Vikhroli village at a public auction. There were several pockets of settlers in the neighbouring areas whom he bought off one after the other, paying more in the process than he had done for the original piece of land. Considering today's prices, what he paid was a pittance, yet he had to sell his shares and almost everything he had to defray the cost, besides taking loans.[92]

The Godrej plant was set up adjacent to rail sidings at Vikhroli, so that manufactured goods could be easily shipped. Indeed, the ballot boxes for India's first general elections were dispatched from precisely these sidings. It's said, in 1951, Pirojsha Godrej received a contract to manufacture ballot boxes valued at Rs 44 lakh for elections within the different state assemblies and parliament, with a delivery estimate of three months. A letter from Pirojsha Godrej on the movement of ballot boxes, dated 8 February 1952, celebrates the success of this national project:

> In connection with elections being held for different state assemblies and the House of People, 12,83,371 boxes had to be moved from Godrej Manufacturing Company siding at Vikhroli to different parts of country, excluding 15,000 ballot boxes which were transported by road for Bombay state and nearby. For moving of 12,58,371 boxes, 532 wagons were loaded at siding, of these 157 before November 1951, and 200 in November, and 175 in December. After the middle of December, different state governments placed indent at short notice and to keep up the schedule, the material had to be rushed to the factory and loaded wagons with ballot boxes had to be specially moved by passenger trains. All despatches were completed within sixty-eight working days.[93]

---

92. Nauzer K. Bharucha, '35 Acres for Homes, Offices in Vikhroli by Year-End', *The Times of India*, 14 April 2010.

93. 'Godrej Company Archives', *Western Railway Newsletter*, January 1952.

Vikhroli's humble sidings played a role in establishing democracy in India.

~

The four-platform Vikhroli Station was once a structure in the wild. Back then, the only prominent settlement in the vicinity was Hariyali Village. Gradually, things changed, largely on account of a rapidly growing rail network. Archives state that as early as 1907, the process to quadruple the lines between Currey Road and Kalyan had been approved. A mammoth sum of Rs 38 lakh had been agreed upon for this purpose, but the budget was later cut, delaying all plans. Finally, in 1910, land was acquired in the east, between Kurla and Thana, to widen the network.

Back then, the area between Kurla and Thana had a canopy of trees. Old records of the area state, 'The station masters used to lock themselves in at the station office as it was regularly visited by wild animals'.[94] Their fear wasn't unfounded. Skim through archives and you might come across an article from 9 October 1850: 'A tiger at Bandoop leaped upon the mail cart and upset it, and the gharry-wallah was little injured'.[95] Now, there are no tigers, but leopards sometimes do make it to the headlines!

The Remains of the Day

Today, the carpet of green had receded, replaced almost entirely by human dwellings. The station too has changed, and much has disappeared—an old well by a platform, for instance, or a signal cabin with a GIPR bell.

If we hunt for relics from the past, we find that platform four has the remains of a sloping roof with nine antique pillars and inscriptions advertising Glengarnock Steel (akin to those at Byculla and Parel). Among the oldest existing structures is the middle footbridge which, as per the railway records, had been built in 1923 to cover the two original platforms. This was subsequently extended to cover two

---

94. Vimal Mishra, *Mumbai Local* (India: Western Railway, 2008), p. 81.

95. James Douglas, *Glimpses of Old Bombay and Western India with Other Papers* (London: Sampson Low, Marston and Company, 1900), p. 108.

more platforms, and then in 2010, to shelter *two more* lines in the station's backyard.

KANJUR MARG STATION: REALIGNING A CITY

Historically, Kanjur or Cawnjoor was the original name of one of the ancient revenue-earning villages; this has been mentioned in the fourteenth-century *Mahikavati's Bakhar*. The road (marg) that led to the village came to be known as Kanjur Marg.

The railway station of Kanjur Marg was opened on 26 January 1968. In the late 1990s and the first decade of the twenty-first century, Kanjur Marg struggled with one of the biggest resettlement schemes for displaced families under an ambitious World Bank-funded initiative—the Bombay Urban Transport Project. Also called 'The Kanjur Marg Experiment', the objective of the rehabilitation project was to resettle 900 families in a low-cost, participatory manner with the willing consent of the community and the cooperation of the relevant governmental agencies; this was to facilitate the laying of new tracks between Thana and Kurla. Kanjur Marg stood out 'for the speed of resettlement (less than a year) and for the absence of police or municipal force to "manage" the physical resettlement. People moved voluntarily and demolished their own houses along the tracks.'[96] Today, a row of buildings along the east and the west highlights the success of the Kanjur Marg experiment.[97]

The Remains of the Day

Close to Kanjur Marg Station, we see the remains of an old level-crossing and a deserted cabin. As the train moves on, and just before it enters the next station, Bhandup, we also spot rail sidings that once entered the sprawling premises of Guest Keen Williams (GKW) Limited through a huge iron gate. Last, we see a large number of old, lightweight rails used by the GIPR in its earliest days.

---

96. Sundar Burra and Sheela Patel, *Norms and Standards in Urban Development: The Experience of an Urban Alliance in India*, May 2001.

97. Sundar Burra, *Resettlement and Rehabilitation of the Urban Poor: The Story of Kanjur Marg* (India: Society for the Promotion of Area Resource Centres, 1999).

BHANDUP STATION: THE ORIGIN

If Sion is the birthplace of the Indian railways, Bhandup is the genesis. As we know, a rail alignment between Bombay and Thana had been worked out in the 1840s by one of country's founding engineers, Colonel George Thomas Clark, on a visit to Seth Framji Cawasji Banaji's estate at Bhandup.[98] (The Bhandup of the 1850s is today's Powai; Kanjur Marg was yet to develop as a full-fledged suburb.)

Powai was important as it had two key lakes and a tenth-century temple dedicated to Goddess Padmavati. Indeed, this presiding deity granted Powai its name—she was colloquially referred to as Poumvi, rounded off to Powai. Powai has been witness to some rather interesting excavations. In 1925, along the dry bed of Powai Lake, stones were found resembling Shiva lingas, with six-line inscriptions in Sanskrit. Experts deciphered these inscriptions and concluded that these lingas were about 700 years old.[99] Later, in 1965, another stone inscription found in the bed of Powai Lake recorded that those who failed to maintain the local temple would be cursed. The north of Powai—that is today's Bhandup—grew into one of the key salt extraction and dispatch centres. Consequently, Bhandup Station grew in strategic importance—a fact that becomes all too apparent when we study an old footbridge in the station built in 1925. It is one of the longest engineering creations of that time, spanning six tracks—a construction feat that acknowledges the economic significance of Bhandup. To date, the suburb has numerous salt pans, and houses offices and bungalows of the Central Salt Department.

The Remains of the Day

The railway station at Bhandup is small. But it does have few relics of the old GIPR, including the remains of a pitched roof; GIPR brackets; and antique pillars. Some GIPR brackets were removed in 2004 and dumped in the station's backyard to be sold as scrap. These were later

---

98. Teresa Albuquerque, *Urbs Prima in Indis: An Epoch in the History of Bombay* (India: Promilla and Co Publishers, 1985), p. 4.

99. *The Times of India*, 13 December 1964.

found with a scrap dealer in Ulhasnagar, who had put them to good use by converting them into table stands. A drawing room in Bombay might well have these treasures!

Several relics breathe *under* the station. In July 2010, a structure with twenty-two stone-and-brick arches, resembling an old bridge, was unearthed under a platform in Bhandup Station during the construction of new railway lines. Similarly, there is an old stone well buried deep within the earth. In the late 1970s, this well had fallen to disuse and had been filled up; a peepal sapling had been planted at the site, which grew into a gigantic tree. This tree has survived the onslaught of modern construction projects—even the skywalk curves around it, out of deference. Many such wells dot Bhandup—some lost, some still in use, with water being drawn out with whirring diesel pumps.

NAHUR STATION: INTO THE TWENTY-FIRST CENTURY

One of the youngest stations on the old line, the halt-point at Nahur opened on 21 April 2006. Though the station is new, Nahur Village, documented as Nawoor, was one of the ancient revenue villages.

The Remains of the Day

Today, the only GIPR relic close to Nahur Station is a cluster of stray abandoned lines. Until 2003, there had also been an intact stone signal cabin; from here, the then railway minister had surveyed the land on which Nahur Station was to be built. Today, another cabin probably belonging to the salt department, with teakwood pillars and a roof of Manglorean tiles, lies in ruins next to the lines. Ironically, it is on the Bombay Municipal Corporation's heritage list.

MULUND STATION: WATER FOR THE THIRSTY

Mulund Station opened in 1931 and catered to one of the earliest planned suburbs of Bombay. For, Mulund follows a gridiron plan (that is, it has a grid-like layout), designed by architects Crown & Carter in 1922.

Before the station was even born, Mulund was in the news. In the mid-1920s, Bombay was at the brink of a serious water crisis. The

First World War had ended, huge numbers of people were teeming into the city, and they were all, without exception, starving and thirsty. The monsoons in 1918 had, for all practical purposes, failed, and some serious damage to the old Tansa aqueduct in 1919 had only made the situation worse. The alarmed Bombay Municipal Corporation had to act quickly. It took up a project—Tansa Completion Works—to get more water. Between 1923 and 1927, steel plates were supplied by the celebrated British firm, Dorman, Long & Co. On arrival in Bombay's docks, these plates were transported by the GIPR to Mulund, from where they were taken across a special rail siding into Messrs Braithwaite and Co's factory for fabrication. This factory, consisting of five workshops and a power station, was 'equipped with the most modern tools and machinery for rolling the plates into cylinders, riveting them with hydraulic riveters into lengths and assembling the lengths into pipes about 56 feet in length.'[100] Tansa Completion Works accomplished its mission by 1927; it provided water to the thirsty city.

These rail links were retained till recently.[101] Faint remains of the old sidings can still be found, just as the train leaves Mulund Station for Thana, as protruding pieces of iron rails along the sides of the road. These are firm reminders of the city's growth.

The Remains of the Day

At Mulund Station, as markers of our past, we can find ancient iron pillars with octagonal bases, nine on each platform, with inscriptions advertising Glengarnock Steel—similar to those found at Byculla, Parel and Vikhroli. Furthermore, the 'backyard' of the station master's office has a few abandoned and derelict stone buildings.

THANA STATION: FOR THE LOVE OF A DAUGHTER

As the train passes under an overbridge and zooms towards Thana, it crosses an abandoned water tank. Just ahead, there is a forgotten subway.

---

100. 'Condensing and Utilization of Exhaust Stem in Locomotives', *The Engineer*, 23 March 1923.

101. *Land Revenue Administration Report (of the Bombay Presidency, Including Sind)* (Bombay: Government Central Press, 1935), p. 40.

The story goes that a British gentleman, W.H. Ruxley[102] was to go to the Santacruz Airport to bid farewell to his daughter, who had already reached the terminus; she had been on a visit to India and was now on her way back to England. A distraught Ruxley missed seeing his girl off, as the railway crossing had remained closed for an unusually long time that day. The next day, along with a few local residents, he met the railway manager, told him about the erratic level-crossing timings, and took it upon himself to get a small subway built at the site. Till late 2000, the subway was used by two- and three-wheelers, but later, an overbridge came up and the subway was rendered useless. Subsequently, two new rail lines were laid, blocking its entrance completely. Today, Ruxley's subway is little more than a drain with plastic and filth; no one remembers its touching history—that it emerged because a man loved his daughter.

The train moves ahead on a high three-arch stone bridge, with a detailed carved inscription: 'RL, BF, TF'—technical specifications about rail levels and the depth of foundation that had to mandatorily be mentioned as per the *Indian Railways Bridge Manual* of 1998. This bridge is the administrative border between Mulund and Thana city.

~

The T-81 reaches Thana at 4:20 p.m., exactly fifty-seven minutes after it begins its journey at Victoria Terminus— the first ever journey, too, had taken fifty-seven minutes. Back in the day, in 1853, a row of durbar tents had been erected at Thana to welcome the first train; the tables had literally groaned under the weight of every delicacy of the season. Major Swanson, the senior director of GIPR who officiated as the chairman on the occasion of the first train run, toasted to the health of the queen. It was one of the most memorable days in India's transport history.

Today, by contrast, there are crowds of office-goers at Thana Station; there's traffic, a maze of pedestrian and vehicular bridges, and of course, the station escalator (a first for Bombay's railways).

---

102. Film Reference: *Mulund*, directed by Sashi Sreedhar.

The only open spaces are the parking lots (when not in use) and the only tents are those put up by the railway maintenance staff, dangerously perched between the tracks.

Thana remained the country's only railway terminus for nearly a year. The first railway tracks were laid such as they entered Thana's koliwada, the fishing village, to split it into two—east and west. The area near the station today is still called koliwada, but the sea is much further away, and fishing is hardly the main occupation here.

Once the railway started regular runs, there was need to upgrade the station. Additional land of about four acres was acquired. Of this, about three acres was owned by thirty residents; the GIPR acquired it at a cost of Rs 1,000 per acre of agricultural land and Rs 500 per acre of barren plots. The acquisition was complete by 1891.

In December 1926, the GIPR began electric locals for Thana.[103] In the light of such developments, an old stone warehouse—a work of beauty—that once stood near today's platform nine, came to be demolished.

The Remains of the Day

Thana, today, is a ten-platform station, but the ghost of the GIPR still lingers here, with relics dotting the premises, more so along the western periphery from platforms one to four, which are comparatively older. The first platform, in fact, is probably an old cargo station or a siding; it holds double-headed rails, belonging to the earliest days of the GIPR, that have been creatively shaped to form the station's pillars and roof. Some rail pillars carry telling inscriptions—'BV & Co Ltd', for instance, or 'Moss Bay Co'. BV & Co Ltd, or Bolckow, Vaughan and Company Limited, was a huge iron and steel firm based around Middleborough, registered in 1864, based on a partnership between Henry Bolckow and John Vaughan since the 1840s; the two lived side by side in two town houses. They were possibly competitors to Moss Bay Hematite Iron and Steel Company.

---

103. Dr A.K. Arora, *History of Bombay Suburban Railways: 1853-1985* (Bombay: The Indian Railway Electrical Engineers Association, 1985), p. 44.

Another significant inscription found in the station on a few
pillars is 'Barrow Steel'. Barrow Hematite Steel Company, set up in
Barrow-in-Furness in the UK, was a 1850s 'greenfield project'— that
is, a facility in an area where no previous conveniences existed. It
developed fast to become a site with sixteen blast furnaces and the
largest steelworks factory in the world in the 1870s. It also became
one of the key suppliers of rail infrastructure to India.

BEYOND THANA STATION: KALWA, MUMBRA, DIVA, KOPAR, DOMBIVLI, THAKURLI AND KALYAN

From Kurla to Thana, the line passes along the eastern shore and salt
pans with little difficulty. After Thana, the train has to enter what was
described as Concan in the 1800s. Entering Concan (or Konkan) was
tricky. Two huge viaducts had to be built, over which the rail lines
would run; tunnels had to be made through Parsik Hill to reach the

Courtesy: Central Railway Archives

The 'Deccan Queen' Outside Parsik Tunnel

bottom of the massive Sahyadri ranges. British railway contractor, George Wythes had to build the line from Thana to Parsik.[104]

Building the creek bridge and the tunnels was a huge task; dealing with the labour force that had gathered in large numbers and lived together at the construction site was a further challenge for British engineers. Work was often affected due to strikes; one such uprising can be traced back to 1855.

> Everything was going on as smoothly as usual at the Tannah Viaduct. The masons were dressing and scrabbling; the bricklayers turning their arches; the coolies toiling up the stages with their heavy loads; the women grinding chunam and carrying the lighter materials to the groups of workmen, when suddenly a loud chattering arose and the female labourers one and all threw down their baskets and refused to work. The cause of the rebellion was a worker who had been guilty of an act of indiscretion towards one of his numbers which the fair community immediately resented by an unanimous outburst of virtuous indignation and it was only upon the delinquent making amends for his misbehaviour that they consented to resume work.[105]

After the Thana creek bridge, the line splits into three corridors. While one corridor continues straight to Kalwa Station, the other two corridors bifurcate—one becomes the line used for outstation trains and fast locals, and the other becomes the Trans-Harbour Line (opened in November 2004), linking Thana to the satellite city of New Bombay. Both these meet a bit ahead of the Parsik Hill near Mumbra Station to reach Kalyan together.

George Wythes' team, while boring tunnels, seems to have demolished a seventeenth-century Portuguese fort that was once on

---

104. The lines had extended to Kalyan (Callian) about a year after the first run. From here, the railway line branched in two directions: the northeast line leading towards Kasara-Igatpuri-Bhusawal, and the southeast line to Karjat-Pune-Solapur. Another single line moves from Karjat and goes to Khopoli at the base of the Sahyadri ranges.

105. *Bombay Quarterly Review*, July-October 1855.

Parsik Hill, in a bid to get stones for the tunnel's construction. The fort, when documented in 1818, had walls that were three feet thick![106] Today, the battles of the Portuguese and the Marathas led by Sambhaji, Shivaji's son, at this precise site, have been forgotten. The fort probably lives in some other form under the rail-track foundations and in the tunnel walls, looking over millions of passengers who pass by in electric trains.[107]

~

Where does the old line go from Thana Station? To a small two-platform Kalwa and then to the historic Mumbra—a key station for early British rail engineers, who wove grand plans of establishing rail connectivity from here to Panvel and 'Concan'. In the 1880s, this was where the original blueprint of the Concan Railway was spun.

Next there's Diva, followed by Kopar, a new entrant in 2007, to ease the burden on the 1887-opened Dombivli Station that comes next. And there's Thakurli, with an old railway colony, Bawan Chawl. Finally, there's Kalyan, which came up in 1854, a year after the first run. Here, the line bifurcates, rushing towards either Karjat or Kasara.

Platforms may be getting longer and trains may be growing swifter, but Berkley's original blueprint of the GIPR continues to ferry more than three million passengers each day. This blueprint, in due course, grew into a network of railway lines all over the country. Today, the Indian railways feature as the largest rail network in Asia, covering 65,000 kilometres[108] and 7,500 stations—the fourth largest in the world after the United States of America, Russia and China.[109]

---

106. B.V. Kulkarni, *Mumbai Parisaratil Arthath Ek Kal Chya Firanganatil Kille* (India: Government of Maharashtra, 2008), pp. 447-52.

107. Today, a new set of tracks and a creek bridge are coming up next to the old railway lines.

108. S.K.S. Yadav, Kum Kum Chaudhary and Somnath Kisan Khatal, 'Issues and Reforms in Indian Railways', *International Journal of Trade and Commerce*, January-June 2012, Volume 1, pp. 106-125.

109. *The World Factbook: 2013-14,* in <https://www.cia.gov/library/publications/the-world-factbook/rankorder/2121rank.html? countryName=China&countryCode=ch&regionCode=eas&rank= 3#ch>, accessed on 20 July 2014.

THE ROMANCE OF THE HARBOUR LINE

Bombay is home not only to the Main Line, but also to the Harbour Line. In 2010, the city's Harbour Line turned 100. 12 December 1910 saw the first section of the line officially open between Kurla and Reay Road Stations—the latter being the original terminus. From Reay Road Station, one had to take a tram to continue the journey into Bombay.

Since the Harbour Line's passenger network ended rather abruptly at Reay Road, there was urgent need to extend it to Victoria Terminus. But procuring land in the southern part of the city was almost impossible. With no land available, an elevated railway was the only option. But this posed a practical problem, with the gradients too steep for steam engines to climb. Therefore, electrification became all the more necessary. This explains why the Harbour Line is elevated, and by 1925, it became the first passenger railway in India to be powered by electricity.

~

In the early years of the new millennium, the first electrically operated tram car appeared on the streets of Bombay. It was 1907; the railways were yet to follow suit. Though railway electrification had been on every official's agenda since the early twentieth century, a number of impediments thwarted swift decision-making.

In 1904, W.H. White, chief engineer of the Bombay Presidency, proposed the electrification of the two Bombay-based companies, GIPR and BB&CI Railway, and a joint terminus for both. The companies were in favour of electrification, but expectedly, there were differences regarding the request for a joint terminus. It took another year to obtain permissions from the British government to upgrade Bombay's railway infrastructure. The government of India appointed Charles Hesterman Merz—a British electrical engineer who pioneered the use of high-voltage three-phase AC power distribution in the United Kingdom—as a consultant. However, Merz resigned before tabling his ideas. (All he recommended was the replacement of the first Bassein or Vasai Bridge.)

To complicate matters, before any plan could be executed, the First World War broke out and early dreams of railway electrification were temporarily shattered. All costs towards railway production were diverted to meet the needs of British forces outside India. By the end of the war, the Indian railways were in a state of disrepair. But by 1917, the railways attempted a quick recovery; work picked pace and the quadrapulation (four-tracking) of the lines was completed till Kalyan. This had been one of the prerequisites for electrification. Two years later, in 1919, the Bombay Municipal Corporation passed a resolution making it mandatory for the GIPR to electrify its lines till Kalyan.

The railways turned back to Merz, who by 1920 had formed a consultancy firm of his own with a partner, William McLellan. The government secured the help of this firm, and drew up plans for electric infrastructure for the Bombay-Poona/Igatpuri/Vasai and the Madras-Tambaram routes. The secretary of state in India sanctioned these schemes in October 1920.

What were the technical specifications? Well, a 1,500-V DC power mode was adopted and easy speed control was embraced. Power was to be supplied by the Tatas, while the GIPR built its own in-house power-generating plant at Thakurli. All inputs for electrification, except power supply, were imported from various companies in England.

The electric coaches that had arrived a month before the electric lines' inauguration were then the widest in India (twelve feet in width, and sixty-eight feet in length). Each unit had four coaches, including a motor coach with automatic couplers. The third-class coach had as many as ninety-six seats each. They were provided by Cammell Laird in the UK and the 1898-founded German train builder, Waggonfabrik Uerdingen AG, now a part of Siemens. Best of all, the trains were capable of running smoke-free. The era of clean transport had arrived in Bombay, as had the age of electric multiple units that still run packed with commuters. India became the twenty-fourth nation in the world to have an electric railway, and the third one in Asia.

Much like the first ever railway train run from Bombay (to Thana) on 16 April 1853, the first ever electric train in India also ran from Bombay. The debut journey, however, was a shorter one, with the train covering the sixteen-kilometre distance between Victoria Terminus and Kurla, at the remarkable speed of eighty kilometres per hour. The date is etched in railway history: 3 February 1925; and the first motorman was Jahangir Framji Daruwala. The journey was inaugurated by then Bombay governor, Leslie Orme Wilson.[1] In memory of this governor, one of the first electric freight locomotives to reach Indian soil in 1928, built by Swiss Locomotive and Machine Works, with electrical equipment by Metropolitan-Vickers, England, came to be named Sir Leslie Wilson. This proud locomotive that once used to navigate Maharashtra's winding ghats, now rests at the National Rail Museum, New Delhi.

The Kurla-Chembur section ran on steam, even as the line was extended further[2] to Mankhurd on 1 July 1927. It was only post-Independence, in 1952, that the Kurla-Mankhurd section was electrified.

In 1956, the government decided to adopt the 25-kV AC single-phase traction as the norm for the Indian railways to meet the challenge of increasing traffic. An organization named the Main Line Electrification Project, which later became the Railway Electrification Project, and still later, the Central Organization for Railway Electrification, was established. The first 25-kV AC traction section in India was Burdwan-Mughalsarai via Grand Chord. The conversion to 25-kV is still an ongoing process in Bombay.

The Harbour Line segment that was the first to get electrified in

---

1. Dr A.K. Arora, *History of Bombay Suburban Railways: 1853-1985* (Bombay: The Indian Railway Electrical Engineers Association, 1985).

2. *Ibid.*, p. 44.

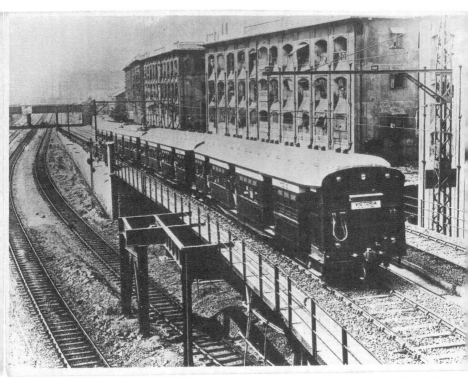

Courtesy: Central Railway Archives

The First Electric Train between Victoria Terminus and Kurla

India would, ironically, be amongst the last to get upgraded in the country with new power technology.

~

Today, the Harbour Line connects the satellite cities of New Bombay and Thana. It ferries more than 10 lakh passengers between thirty-eight stations. Let's travel with these commuters down the sea-spanning line, shall we?

SANDHURST ROAD (UPPER-LEVEL) STATION: NERVES OF STEEL

The Harbour Line starts from Victoria Terminus, runs parallel to the Main Line for a couple of kilometres, then rises via a steel viaduct to reach the Sandhurst Road (upper-level) Station. This rail alignment was formed as early as the 1920s.

Sandhurst Road, as we know, is India's first two-tier station. The upper-level station is a maze of steel frames and pillars. Indeed, the viaduct has a whopping 2,788 tonnes of steel and is 1,728 feet long; back then, it cost Rs 20 lakh to build. Sandhurst Road, as you might recall, also holds the distinction of hosting the first electric railway in India; its overhead electric masts were a novelty for passenger railways and these hold national heritage value.

The Remains of the Day

The past comes alive in Sandhurst Road (upper-level) Station. Here, we find original steel pillars, with plaques bearing the name 'MacLellan', dated 1921. We also find a few of the oldest overhead wire masts, with ancient signage.

DOCKYARD ROAD STATION: OF HATRED, WAR AND ETERNAL LOVE

The viaduct takes the train straight towards the Dockyard Road Station over the railway yard at Wadi Bunder. Opened in 1931, the station has two small, ancient, wooden cottages—one used as a station master's cabin and another utilized as a booking office. The platform and the track are on a huge stone rampart, along the base of an ageless hillock. This hill, which once held Mazgaon Fort, has witnessed glorious stories of hatred, war and romance.

~

In the seventeenth century, the British (through the East India Company) and the Mughals were perennially at war with each other. To make matters worse for the British, the fierce Siddis, who were of African descent, had allied themselves with the Mughals. Faced with the Siddis' unrelenting attacks in 1672, the British constructed several fortifications in Bombay, among them Sewri Fort and Mazgaon Fort.

In 1689, the Siddi general, Yakut Khan, with an army of 20,000 men, invaded Bombay, captured Sewri Fort, then Mazgaon Fort, and moved south to bombard the rest of Bombay. The British, on their part, tried raising a local army of kolis with the help of Parsi leader Rustomji Dorabji Patel; but this did not yield the results they hoped for. Almost all was lost for the British. At this point, the British governor John Child made a plea for mercy, begged Mughal Emperor Aurangzeb to reign in his forces, and offered him Rs 1.5 lakh. Aurangzeb accepted the offer on the condition that Child be sacked. Child's untimely death in 1690, however, resulted in his escaping the disgrace of being fired.

Why did Emperor Aurangzeb relent? Perhaps, he was distracted by his battle against the Marathas; maybe he needed British protection for trading with Arab countries; possibly, he viewed the British as useful allies who could get the Mughals revenue through trade. Whatever the reason, Aurangzeb's decision changed the course of history. Yakut Khan, in the meantime, furious about the barter, withdrew his forces on 8 June 1690, after razing Mazgaon Fort.

With the fort gone, the forlorn sea-facing hill of Mazgaon was soon taken over by bungalows—one of which was painted white to act as a 'lighthouse' for ships.[3] It was also overrun with plantations— Mazgaon mangoes were sent to the queen. Between 1880 and 1884 the hill was converted into a water reservoir, over which was laid a garden named after civic chief John Hay Grant. The reservoirs were upgraded in 1925 by the popular S-bridge contractor, Teju Kaya; this was also the year that witnessed the electrification of the Harbour Line. After Independence, the garden was renamed after Barrister John Baptista, born at Matharpacady in Mazgaon; he was the mayor of Bombay between 1925 and 1926 and was closely associated with the Home Rule Movement.

~

About 100 years after Yakut Khan's fierce attack, the hill—where the fort had been—was taken over by bungalows. A fascinating eighteenth-century love story unfolded on this hill, one that continues to be

---

3. J.M. Campbell, *Materials towards a Statistical Account of the Town and Island of Bombay*, Volume 2 (Bombay: Government Central Press, 1893), p. 530.

retold in England and Bombay even today, in the twenty-first century. The tale goes that on the night of 14 January 1773, Eliza Draper, wife of Daniel Draper, the East India Company's senior official in Bombay, descended from the bedroom of her sea-facing bungalow on Mazgaon Hill, down a rope ladder, into a boat waiting below—to elope with a naval officer, Commodore John Clarke, whose flagship *H.M.S. Prudent* was then at harbour. She left a brutally honest note for a husband in her room: 'Draper, my heart bleeds for what I suppose may possibly be the sufferings of yours, though too surely had you loved, all this could never have been.'[4]

When on a visit to England earlier in 1766-67, Eliza Draper had met Laurence Sterne, vicar of Coxwold and celebrity author of *The Life and Opinions of Tristram Shandy*. They 'took fire at each other at the same time' and spent much of the next three months together in a relationship which for Sterne soon became all-consuming.[5] Sterne wrote to Eliza every day. His letters were developed into *The Journal to Eliza*, a fictionalized chronicle of their relationship. Both Sterne and Eliza were already married—Sterne to a woman who had gone to live in France with their daughter, and Eliza to a man thirty years her senior. Eliza was twenty-three; Sterne was fifty-four and a clergyman.

After Eliza left for India, Sterne longed for his beloved and made a 'sweet little apartment'[6] for her at Shandy Hall, which is known as 'Eliza's room' to this day. The Drapers, on their part, took up residence in a whitewashed bungalow called Manor House (also, Belvedere House) on Mazgaon Hill. Here, Eliza became more and more estranged from her husband, who had grown choleric and displayed nothing but indifference towards his wife's ennui. It was this that prompted Eliza to flee Manor House, seek the protection of Commodore John Clarke, and elope with him.

---

4. N.P. Chekutty, 'The Life and Letters of Elizabeth Draper', *Himal*, 13 January 2013, in <http://himalmag.com/life-letters-elizabeth-draper/#sthash.xdos86T2.dpuf>, accessed on 4 September 2014.

5. 'Sterne Letters from Yorick to Eliza', *WorthPoint*, in <http://www.worthpoint.com/worthopedia/sterne-letters-yorick-eliza-1773-400007471>, accessed on 4 September 2014.

6. Wilbur L. Cross, *The Life and Times of Laurence Sterne* (London: Forgotten Books, 2013), pp. 422-23.

Today, where her house stands, there is a solitary stone plaque recalling her story: 'Near this spot stood Manor House, the residence of Eliza Draper, immortalized by Sterne, 1773'. The edge of the cliff by which the whitewashed Manor House stood has been lost, having been quarried to build rail lines, docks and roads.

~

By the mid-1840s, Mazgaon—already a ship-building site since the eighteenth century—began to change in shape. In 1843, a rich mogul, Aga Mohammad Rahim, on the orders of the government, spent approximately Rs 9 lakh to build docks here. The process took almost six years to complete due to the depth of the waters. Soon, the British Peninsular and Orient (P&O) Company set up office by renting a portion of the docks.[7] Thus was born the Mazagaon Docks Ltd— built by the P&O Company to maintain their ships in Indian waters. The P&O Company's docks birthed the name 'Dockyard', and this dictated the GIPR's choice of name for its station.

While the name endures, the topography has changed. There was a time when the sea was closer to Dockyard Road and the waves lashed against Mazgaon; however, city planners pushed the mighty ocean back in the mid-nineteenth century to reclaim land, build roads and construct rail lines. Today, on both sides of Dockyard Road Station, one can still find old houses of the Portuguese and British eras, tree-lined narrow streets and colonies stuck in a time warp. Here, we also have the heritage zone of Matharpacady, an area populated by Marathi-speaking East Indians, also (as mentioned earlier) the birthplace of Barrister Joseph Baptista.

Inside the maze of old settlements is a playground with an antique iron garden roller, one of the oldest of its kind in the city, dated 1894. The playground was originally named after Tipu Sultan's relative, Nawab Ayaz Ali, who had migrated to Mazgaon after the British

---

7. Govind Narayan Madgaonkar, *Mumbaiche Varnan*, edited by Narhar Raghunath Fatak (India: Marathi Granth Sangrahalaya, 1863), pp. 75-76. Translated by the author.

defeated the ruler in 1799.[8] Locals say that Ayaz Ali's descendents and family moved out of India in the early twentieth century.

In another of Dockyard Road's narrow alleys, along Nesbit Lane, was located the firm, Messrs Marshland Price & Co, that manufactured India's first monorail that ran through Patiala in Punjab between 1910 and 1927.[9] Popularly known as the Patiala State Monorail System (PSMT), the train and tracks now rest at the National Rail Museum, New Delhi.

The Remains of the Day

Close to Dockyard Road Station are three steel bridges. The first two bridges do not have significant markings on them, but the third one holds six P&W MacLellan plaques, and the stamp of that famous nineteenth-century English firm Dorman, Long & Co.

REAY ROAD STATION: THE ORIGINAL TERMINUS

The train negotiates a curve with roads, apartments and warehouses on either side, and glides down a bridge to land into Reay Road Station, the original terminus of the Harbour Line. The station opened as a terminus on 12 December 1910 and was named after Donald Mackay, the eleventh Lord Reay, who was the governor of Bombay between 1885 and 1890.

When it first opened, Reay Road Station, flanked by warehouse platforms, was a hub of activity, with workers and contractors, cargo trains and trucks. Today, the platforms here are relatively empty, and we find local kids using the abandoned warehouses either as open-air libraries during exam time, or as a cricket pitch during holidays.

The Remains of the Day

On paper, Reay Road's station structures are listed as grade one heritage constructions. However, little is done to conserve these

---

8. Samuel T. Sheppard, *Bombay, Place Names and Street Names: Excursion into the Byways of the History of Bombay City* (Bombay: The Times Press, 1917), p. 106.

9. Today, the site is a storehouse of metal roads.

relics, and shanties and illegal settlements have crowded around them. The elevated building that is Reay Road Station is a basalt stone structure and has faded letters reading 'Reay Road, GIPR'. While the building itself does not carry a date, the steel girders of the bridge in the vicinity state: 'Bombay Port Trust, 1915', with the port trust emblem.

Close to Reay Road Station, an old and lonely water fountain stands just next to the lines, surrounded by once-formidable warehouses. The water fountain was built by a merchant in memory of his daughter, for warehouse workers and animals that ferried cargo-laden carts. A plaque reads: 'The public gift of Mr Lowji Megji, J.P., in loving memory of his late daughter Kusumbala, AD 1924'.

COTTON GREEN STATION: WHAT'S IN A NAME?

Now, the train rushes over a stone-and-iron bridge to reach the elevated Cotton Green Station. This halt point had been created as the locality had been the hub of cotton trade in the early twentieth century.

But why Cotton *Green*? To answer this we need to go back to records from the mid-eighteenth century. John Henry Grose, that intrepid traveller and a civil servant of the East India Company, offers the clearest, simplest and most acceptable explanation, as a part of his two-volume book, *A Voyage to the East Indies*. He says:

> The only English church at Bombay, and which is full sufficient for any possible congregation at it, is a building extremely neat, commodious and airy; being situated on what is called the Green; a spacious area that continues from the fort thereto, and is pleasantly laid out in walks planted with trees, round which are mostly the houses of the English inhabitants.[10]

---

10. John Henry Grose, *A Voyage to the East Indies: Containing Authentic Accounts of the Mogul Government in General, the Viceroyalties of the Decan and Bengal, with Their Several Subordinate Dependances, with General Reflections on the Trade of India*, Volume 1 (London: S. Hooper, 1772).

This might provide a clue. The area around the 'only English church' (today's St Thomas Church at Fort) was called 'Bombay Green'. Due to the area's proximity to the docks and the bales of cotton being piled up there for trade, it came to be referred to as 'Cotton Green'.

There were plans to convert the area around the Green into a garden surrounded by buildings; Lord Elphinstone, then Bombay's governor, was in favour of the proposal. Consequently, when a garden emerged in 1869—with trees, manicured lawns and perfectly laid out pathways—it came to be referred to as Elphinstone Circle. Post-Independence, the circle was renamed in honour of Benjamin Horniman, the British editor of *Bombay Chronicle* who supported the Indian freedom struggle; it is known as Horniman Circle to this day.

By 1844, cotton trade from the old Cotton Green had shifted further south to Colaba. The new locality, rather predictably, came to be called 'New Cotton Green'. Following further remodelling and reclamation, New Cotton Green shifted to the Sewri-Mazgaon reclamation area, where a spacious Cotton Exchange Building was built.[11] The rail station that came up opposite this Cotton Exchange Building was, for now obvious reasons, named Cotton Green. The cotton exchange hub would move once more—this time to Kalbadevi—but there would be no more shifts in names.

The Remains of the Day

Cotton Green Station is a steel giant; the only remains of value here are twenty-one original pillars, some old wrought iron fencing and a few double-headed rails that have been used as street furniture and road dividers.

Just below the station is the office of Sewri's fire brigade; attached to this is a small, abandoned one-storey structure—once the office of the Fire Salvage Association. A heavy iron plaque in a corner remembers the ship, SS *Fort Stikine*, and the brave fire fighters who laid down their lives to rescue those on board. The tragedy dates back to 1944, when the freighter, SS *Fort Stikine*—carrying cotton bales, raisin,

---

11. 'A Map of Bombay, Specially Drawn for the East India Cotton Association Ltd, 1947', *Bombay Explorer*, Number 42, June 2004, p. 32.

gold ingots and ammunition, including around 1,400 tonnes of Category A explosives (the most sensitive kind)—caught fire and was destroyed in two giant blasts.

> [...] tonnes of explosive went off in the evening, blasting the ship into the sky, ripping through the docks, lifting the adjoining ship, the *Jalapadma* (6,450 dead weight tonnage) clear out of the water and landing it on a dock nearby. The explosion set off a reaction in the city: partitions fell, and the evening sky was lit up as bales of burning cotton and oil drums set ablaze flew through the air.[12]

Courtesy: Mumbai Port Trust Archives

A Bridge Near Cotton Green Station (Now Partially Demolished)

12. Jerry Pinto, 'The Day it Rained Gold Bricks and a Horse Ran Headless', *Bombay, Meri Jaan: Writings on Mumbai*, edited by Naresh Fernandes and Jerry Pinto (India: Penguin Books, 2003), p. 140.

So powerful were the two explosions that they came to be recorded by seismographs at the Colaba Observatory, and the earth trembled at Shimla, over 1,700 kilometres away.

Just before the train leaves Cotton Green Station, two roads pass below that connect the city with the docks. Both these bridges were built in the early 1920s, with faint, cracked plaques spelling out, 'Rowji Sojpal & Co Contractors, 1923-24'. Rowji Sojpal was a Jain philanthropist who had come down to Bombay from Kutch to work as a contractor. Today, several old housing tenements still bear his name, the biggest of them at Sewri.

SEWRI STATION: THE LAND OF THE FLAMINGOES

The train passes the Cotton Exchange Building, an abandoned office of the Japan Cotton Trading Company, the barricaded premises of the equipment depot of the Indian Air Force, and finally, the rail lines of the Bombay Port Trust (stuck in a time warp with semaphore signals).

Now we spot Sewri, derived from Sivadi or Sivavadi (the place or garden of Shiva).[13] The two-platform Sewri Station is plain and unexceptional, except for an ancient iron footbridge.

Sewri was originally a small hamlet along the eastern shore on Parel, one of the original seven islands of Bombay. The sleepy village developed into a bustling town during the Mazgaon-Sewri reclamations. It grew further when tenements emerged, constructed by the Bombay Development Department set up by Governor George Lloyd in 1918. Outside Sewri Station, one can still see tenements belonging to the Raj, with 'BDD, 1925' carved on their façade.

~

Less than a kilometre from the station is the abandoned but state-protected seventeenth-century Sewri Fort. The fort that was once of key strategic significance for Bombay's defence is today a playground for local kids. The fort overlooks the sea and the ecologically vital

---

13. Samuel T. Sheppard, *Bombay, Place Names and Street Names: Excursion into the By-ways of the History of Bombay City* (Bombay: The Times Press, 1917), p. 129.

mangrove mudflats; occasionally, one has the privilege of witnessing flamingoes. Numerous small, but formidable black basalt hills can still be spotted around the fort, giving us a vague sense of how Bombay was centuries ago. Today, the east holds oil refineries and the Bombay Port Trust, and the west has a Christian cemetery.

Prior to 1865, there had been no cemetery, only the Agro-Horticultural Society Gardens. The garden was obtained by Arthur Crawford, Bombay's municipal commissioner, from Bomanji Framji Cama, to build a European cemetery. There was urgent need for such a cemetery. Until 1760, the English had buried their dead at Mendham's Point at Colaba (named after the first man interred there, and near today's Regal junction). Due to strategic considerations, the British later shifted the cemetery to Sonapur (Marine Lines) next to a Muslim cemetery and the Hindu burning ghats. But as the city burgeoned, residents began to complain.

> It can well be imagined therefore that by 1855 the juxtaposition and constant use of these cemeteries had given rise to serious complaints both from the public and the municipal authorities, who declared that the high mortality of the Girgaum section at seasons when cholera was epidemic was primarily due to the miasmata wafted from the cemeteries and mortuaries on the Back Bay foreshore.[14]

A Burial Commission appointed in 1863 declared that all the city's cemeteries ought to be clustered near Matunga. The project, including the construction expense of the Tower of Silence and the provision of railway communication, was estimated to cost Rs 47 lakh. The price was prohibitive. In a bid to find a solution to the impasse, Arthur Crawford, the then municipal commissioner, obtained the old Agro-Horticultural Society's gardens. The site was consecrated in March 1867 and has since served as a final resting place for innumerable Europeans and, later, Indians. Pertinently, this is where the architect of Victoria Terminus, F.W. Stevens is buried.

---

14. S.M. Edwardes, *The Gazetteer of Bombay City and Island*, Volume 3 (India: Cosmo Publications, 2002).

The Remains of the Day

The original shell of the small Sewri Station can be easily identified through thirteen steel pillars, a few of them bearing inscriptions of 'Tata Iron and Steel Company'.

Sewri Bridge also has a rare engraving: 'GIPR. Joseph Westwood & Co Ltd, London, 1897'. This date is intriguing, since railway records state that the station was born in 1922, and the Harbour Line itself took shape in the early twentieth century. What could 1897 refer to? British industrial records state that ship-builder Joseph Westwood's independent firm was founded in 1883, and became a private company in 1897—the year inscribed on Sewri Bridge. The pillars of Sewri Bridge—that have completed more than 110 years if we go by the inscription date—were probably built in London, shipped to India and assembled in Bombay: a rich global legacy for the humble station of Sewri.

Close to Sewri Station and the Bombay Port Trust line, we find a rare set of century-old four-wheeled wagons, now abandoned, belonging to a time when the docks we see today had not yet completely developed. Just a few yards away lie other neglected pieces of the past in the form of war cannons—two of them on a footpath along the Bombay Port Trust Colony road. These could well have been a part of that historical old fort of Sewri.

WADALA STATION: ALL THINGS RECENT

Old maps tell us that Wadala Station was once called Gowari, ahead of which was Raoli, where the GIPR was linked to the BB&CI Railway. Today Gowari is considered an archaic name, though Raoli remains, as does the link with the BB&CI Railway.

The sprawling Wadala Station is comparatively new. However, its yard does come with an abandoned steam engine water pipe; this suggests that the Bombay Port Trust's steam locomotive shed was once in this station.

The Remains of the Day

Near Wadala Station is the old scrap yard of the Bombay Port Trust railway, where old fire wagons, iron sleepers and steam pipes lie in a heap waiting to be scrapped. The lines here are littered with garbage and tenements; even the old GIPR stone signal cabin is lost in the sea of tin sheds and informal settlements.

KING'S CIRCLE AND GURU TEGH BAHADUR NAGAR STATIONS: WHERE EMPERORS WALKED

King's Circle is a name that evokes curiosity. Why was the station named thus? The author, Samuel T. Sheppard tells us that at a meeting of the Bombay Improvement Trust held on 20 April 1911, the chairman described the development of the Dadar-Matunga scheme and the gardens to be laid out east of Matunga Station. In honour of the king, it was decided that a circular garden would be named 'King's Circle'. The avenue from Crawford Market to Sion Causeway would be known as 'King's Way'.[15]

If we go back in time to recover Guru Tegh Bahadur Nagar Station's original name, we learn that it was called Colwada or Koliwada, after a small hamlet of the fishing community of the kolis, the original inhabitants of Bombay. It was only in July 1979 that its name changed to commemorate the ninth of the ten gurus of Sikhism.

The Remains of the Day

At the base of the Victoria Terminus-bound platform of King's Circle Station, there is an old abandoned booking office dating back to the 1940s—now a site for gossip and social gatherings.

The route from here to the next station, Guru Tegh Bahadur Nagar, is replete with interesting structures, including the Shanmukhananda Auditorium, built in the 1960s on land originally allotted for a girls' school. Apart from hosting some of India's best-known artistes, the hall has also been home to political conventions that come with fascinating anecdotes. It's said, in 1963, the All India Congress Committee, with over 4,000 delegates, decided to hold its session in the auditorium. Air conditioners had not been

---

15. Samuel T. Sheppard, *Bombay, Place Names and Street Names: Excursion into the By-ways of the History of Bombay City* (Bombay: The Times Press, 1917), pp. 88-89.

commissioned, and the sweltering heat of Bombay was unbearable. Therefore, the auditorium managers came up with a novel solution—truckloads of ice blocks were dumped into the water tank every hour to cool the water, which then chilled the air in the packed auditorium. 'Never in the history of air conditioning has a building been cooled by ice!'[16]

Besides this hall, there is the ancient shrine of Sheikh Misri, close to the rail road. Legend has it that Sheikh Misri was a saint who migrated from Egypt (then Misr) over 500 years ago. Today, his dargah is visited by those with thwarted wishes, for the belief is that he fulfills the prayers of his devotees.

As the train stops at the island platform of Guru Tegh Bahadur Station, flanked by Sion in the west and Antop Hill in the east, one comes across some heritage surprises, including fourteen pillars of the original station shed.

CHUNABHATTI STATION: INTO THE LIME KILNS

The train zooms into the next station, Chunabhatti. An extension of an old Kurla village, the railway station at Chunabhatti was inaugurated on 15 June 1960, almost nine years after the GIPR ceased to exist.

What does Chunabhatti mean? It is actually a matter-of-the-fact translation of 'lime kilns'. Why was the station named so? Because, the area known as Chunabhatti today, held one of the key lime kilns of old Bombay. After quarrying the hills, the lime extracted was used for the majestic buildings coming up in the south of the city.

The line between Guru Tegh Bahadur Nagar and Chunabhatti Stations was once surrounded by so many informal settlements that the railway safety commissioner had to threaten to stop services to get them removed. The clearance of those tenements menacingly close to the lines was followed through in the 1990s. Despite this, new dwellings emerged, and the area next to Chunabhatti's rail line remains a bustling community hub, with markets and houses running in close proximity to the lines.

---

16. *The Shanmukhananda Hall*, in <http://www.shanmukhananda.com/Profile.html>, accessed on 12 August 2012.

The Remains of the Day

The pillars for Chunabhatti Station have been built using discarded rails and iron imported from England, and bear a strong resemblance to those at Thana and Kalwa Stations. These are the only significant 'heritage items' to be found here, with most other structures being fairly new. The pillars carry engravings such as 'Cammell Sheffield Toughened Steel, GIPR, 1886'.

Cammel rails have been a rarity along this side of the railways. The popular ship-building and iron-works firm from Sheffield was founded by Charles Cammell, and was in competition with John Brown, who on 1 May 1861, rolled the world's first commercially made Bessemer rails, to supply quality rails across the world. In 1866, Brown and Cammell divided 22,000 tonnes of rails for the GIPR in India.

> At that time, Cammell's had 28,000 tonnes of orders on its books. By autumn 1868 it was remarked that though the previous three years had been generally regarded as depression years in the UK iron and steel trades, in those same years, John Brown paid an average annual dividend of 6 per cent and Charles Cammell 10 per cent. In the late 1860s Sheffield made almost half the steel rails rolled in the UK.[17]

Traces of the fiercely competitive deal between Cammell and Brown can be found in Chunabhatti Station today.

BEYOND KURLA STATION: CHEMBUR, MANKHURD, VASHI, BELAPUR AND PANVEL

After Chunabhatti Station, and then Kurla, the harbour branch continues along what was the old garbage line of the Bombay municipality in the first decade of the twentieth century.

In the late nineteenth and early twentieth centuries, garbage used to be dumped outside the city's limits. It used to be collected from a central point at Mahalaxmi in small, stinking wagons referred to as the 'Deccan King', and discarded, initially at a Sion dump, and later,

---

17. Kenneth Warren, *Steel, Ships and Men: Cammell Laird, 1824-1993* (UK: Liverpool University Press, 1998), pp. 58-59.

beyond Chembur's salt marshes. Shortly before the Harbour Line from Kurla to Reay Road was opened, in 1909, a single garbage line from Kurla to Chembur had already been constructed. It took (and still can be seen taking) a sharp curve from Kurla to reach Chembur.

The practice of running garbage trains is prevalent to this day, with coaches of old electric trains collecting refuse along the tracks. It was in 1921 that the process of strengthening the Kurla-Chembur garbage track was taken up. The plan was to extend the line for approximately ten kilometres till Trombay and develop the latter as a residential and business suburb. On 4 December 1924, the Kurla-Chembur track was finally upgraded for passenger service and merged with the Harbour Line. An old resident of the locality recollects that in the 1930s the guard would issue tickets on the train every Saturday; Chembur was so serene that one could hear the whistle of the train when it started from Mankhurd.

On 1 July 1927, this line was extended further to Mankhurd for steam locals, and in 1952 it was electrified. Forty years later, in the 1990s, the line was extended beyond the creek, into the mainland of India—from Mankhurd to Vashi—to reach New Bombay. In 1993, the line was further extended to Nerul and Belapur, and two years later to Khandeshwar. By 1998, the line spanned Panvel in the Raigad district of Maharashtra, where the British had once planned to lay rail lines to bring in cotton.

THE PORT AND ITS RAILWAY

Bombay's eastern shore, facing the mainland, has been the site of headlines, legends and stories, a place of battles, love and commerce. It has witnessed shipwrecks, emerging trade routes and vessel-building. Indeed, the shipwrecks[18] of the pre-steam period, before 1850, are heavily concentrated south of Mazgaon and Colaba.

The island of Bombay is the story of reclamation. Indeed, it wouldn't be an exaggeration to say that the reclamation of the inland

---

18. B. Arunachalam, *Mumbai by the Sea* (India: Maritime History Society, 2004), p. 209.

seas by filling breaches and blocking tidal water gave shape to the city as we know it today.

Two hundred years after Bombay's then governor, Gerald Aungier, submitted a plan for the city to the court of directors, one saw the birth of the Bombay Port Trust in 1873 with schemes to comprehensively develop the docks and related connectivity. The rail lines that emerged here are the legacy of port expansion. Today, a ten-kilometre-long only-freight Port Trust Line runs between Indira Dock (formerly Alexandra Dock) and Wadala, parallel to the passenger line that connects South Bombay to the mainland at Vashi (and beyond).

Courtesy: Mumbai Port Trust Archives

The Construction of Rail Lines by the Docks

Since the sea was a major mode of transportation till the mid-nineteenth century, rail links and sidings connected it to the main lines. These sidings were constantly being upgraded, and in 1899, a rail link was planned between Sion and Ballard Pier. Lord Sandhurst's Bombay Improvement Trust, which aimed to build planned suburbs beyond the old fortified city, also emphasized developing existing communication links.

By the beginning of the twentieth century, the docks were growing and improved connectivity was the need of the hour to ferry cargo to and from the ports. The Bombay Port Trust already had elaborate sidings and goods yards connected to the GIPR's Main Line. Rail connectivity to Prince's and Victoria Docks had been achieved by three sidings crossing Frere Road (now P. D'Mello Road). But with time, it was found that the sidings could accommodate only a fraction of the import and export traffic. Most of the items of trade were conveyed from ship to rail and vice versa in bullock-carts that were not only cumbersome but also expensive—their use doubled handling charges.

Plans for connecting the goods yards of the main railways with dock sidings also proved to be problematic. The goods yard of the GIPR at Wadi Bunder was aligned at right angles with the sidings serving the dock berths, while the BB&CI Railway goods terminus could be linked to the western lines only by crossing over the GIPR. By the late nineteenth century, with cotton trade moving to Sewri, a 1914 report of the Bombay Development Committee (penned by the superintending engineer of construction, R. Whately, on 6 November 1913) elaborated on the need for a rail link to this side of Bombay:

> There is under consideration a short link connecting the BB&CI Railway main line at Mahim with the Port Trust siding at Wadala; this link is necessary owing to the removal of the cotton trade to Sewree and to the Port Trust Scheme for sorting sidings at Wadala. An independent line is necessary in order to avoid delays which would occur at a junction with the harbour branch. The proposed line will run parallel to the GIP Railway link and through the area being laid out by the City Improvement

Trust north of the junction between the harbour branch and the GIP link to Mahim.[19]

Eventually, a new rail link connecting the BB&CI Railway along the western shore and the harbour railway along the eastern shore in the vicinity of the docks was planned. The line cut across the GIPR just after Matunga Station to reach the BB&CI Railway lines at Mahim. The Wadala-Mahim section that we see today was formally opened on 11 August 1914. A separate Port Trust Line interlinking the Harbour Line and the Main Line of the GIPR, and the BB&CI Railway, was opened a year later, based on an early plan made in 1894.

Initially, these moves were opposed by the GIPR, but a persistent government handed over the plans to a Commission of Inquiry in 1900, which was headed by Arthur Trevor. Studying the existing rail arrangements to the port and the growing traffic, Trevor's commission recommended the need for a separate port railway to the government. The new line was to be in two sections:

(1) The GIP Harbour Line extending from Kurla to a proposed new goods depot of the Port Trust at Mazgaon, with a chord connection to the BB&CI Railway;

(2) The Port Trust railway extending from the Prince's and Victoria Docks to a goods depot to be constructed at Mazgaon [a length of five kilometres, involving the purchase of private properties for a length of about a kilometre].[20]

The Bombay Gazetteer correctly predicted:

When finished, the line will offer suitable accommodation for the increasing trade of the port by affording greater facilities for the convenient shipment of produce. It will also develop a most important suburb and make considerable areas of land available for residential and other purposes which now lie unoccupied for

19. 'Note on the Development of BB&CI Railway on the Local Section since 1909,' *Report of the Bombay Development Committee*, 1914.

20. S.M. Edwardes, *The Gazetteer of Bombay City and Island*, Volume I (India: Cosmo Publications, 2002).

want of easy means of communication with the business parts of the city, and will thus assist in relieving the congestion of population in the city of Bombay.[21]

Subsequently, it was decided to extend the second section (from Prince's and Victoria Docks to the goods depot at Mazgaon) to Wadala, where a capacious marshalling yard was provided. Work began fast. The Port Trust Line was commissioned with effect from 1 January 1915,[22] and ten stations emerged.

Courtesy: Mumbai Port Trust Archives

A Train at a Quay Station

~

21. *Ibid.*, p. 358.

22. Shantaram Chittar, *The Port of Bombay: A Brief History (For the Trustees of the Port of Bombay to Mark the First Centenary of the Bombay Port Trust, 1873-1973)* (India: S.Y. Ranade, 1973), pp. 35-36.

British rail historian, Paul Atterbury states in his book, *Along Lost Lines*, that the idea of running special trains to carry passengers to and from ships and ferries dates back to the 1840s. Initially, they served ports along the Thames and the west coast of Scotland. By the 1880s, 'boat trains' were running to ports and harbours all over Britain, serving ferries and ocean liners.

The first railways in India were a version of this, but proper and 'branded' boat trains were replicated in Bombay in the early 1920s, loosely based on the model followed by Pullmans. (Pullmans were luxury carriages developed by George Pullman that were independently staffed and offered a comfortable night's sleep on the run. This American idea was taken to Britain in the 1870s.) An elaborate port railway network was put in place, connected to the main lines of the GIPR and the BB&CI Railway.

Mole Station at Ballard Pier was a wharf that not only used to ferry cargo, but also troops and passengers from steamships to destinations in the north, including Karachi (now in Pakistan). The Punjab Limited train was inaugurated on 1 June 1912 from Ballard Pier Mole Station, as a 'limited' service on certain days. It journeyed to Peshawar and took several days to get there. Today, it is known as the Punjab Mail and takes thirty-six hours to cover the 1,929 kilometres between Bombay and Ferozepur.[23]

Another popular boat train was the Bombay to Peshawar Frontier Mail. She made her maiden run from Colaba Station on 1 September 1928; however, during the winter months, between September and December, she used to depart from Ballard Pier Mole Station. The Frontier Mail was introduced for a significant reason: the BB&CI Railway wanted to give its arch rival, the GIPR, a run for its money, and the BB&CI Railway's agent, Ernest Jackson, believed that the introduction of the Frontier Mail would offer stiff competition to the Punjab Limited train. After all, the GIPR's Punjab Limited took several days to get to the north, while the Frontier Mail was substantially faster, reducing transit time to a mere seventy-two hours.

---

23. *Indian Railways Fan Club Association*, in <http://www.irfca.org/~shankie/famoustrains/famtrainpunjmail.htm>, accessed on 18 July 2012.

It is interesting to note, though, that when the Frontier Mail left Ballard Pier Mole Station, it traversed over the tracks of the Bombay Port Trust railway lines, then the GIPR lines, and only after that did it cross over to the BB&CI Railway lines.

On the Frontier Mail's return from Peshawar, Churchgate Station's building would be lit to announce the safe arrival of passengers, thus setting into motion a new tradition of lighting public railway buildings. Today, the Frontier Mail runs out of Bombay Central and terminates at Amritsar; it carries the name, Golden Temple Mail.

Ballard Pier Mole Station was an ideal hop-on point for the British passengers arriving from England by steamer. It was also a pick-up point for mail brought in from Europe by the P&O mail steamer.[24] By 1920, Ballard Bunder Gatehouse had been built to commemorate Ballard Pier's development into the Ballard Estate; it was designed by George Wittet, the chief architect of the Bombay Port Trust. After Independence, the Gatehouse became part of the naval dockyard and fell into disuse. In 2005, the Indian navy restored it, opening it to the public as a maritime museum.

Today, much has changed. Trains that once ferried passengers from Ballard Pier have been discontinued, and so have steamships. The twenty-first-century Port Trust Line, stripped of its old glory, runs a ten-kilometre straight route. It is still connected to the main lines of Central and Western Railways, but owns a fleet of only five diesel locomotives.

The Mumbai Port Trust today caters to only 10 per cent of the country's sea-borne trade (in terms of volume). But in forgotten corners and abandoned sidings, history still lives. Century-old wagons used during the First World War, steam water pipes and old semaphore signals dot the line, reminding us of the glorious past.

---

24. *Ibid.*, in <http://www.irfca.org/~shankie/famoustrains/famtrainfrontier.htm>, accessed on 18 July 2012.

THE WONDERS OF THE BB&CI
RAILWAY LINE

28 November 2013: the Western Railway completed 150 years since the first train chugged down its lines in 1864.

Two years after the first train ran successfully on Indian soil—specifically on 21 November 1855—the East India Company signed an agreement with the BB&CI Railway to 'lay and construct a railway line between Surat to Baroda [now Vadodara] and Ahmedabad.'[1] Therefore, one witnessed the construction of a forty-six-kilometre broad-gauge track from Ankleshwar to Utran in Gujarat. Four years later, Bombay entered the scheme of plans, when the BB&CI Railway signed a contact with the East India Company to build a railway line from Utran to Grant Road in Bombay. This line was vital, since it would help the British transport cotton that grew in Gujarat to the port city, from where it would be taken to England in ships and steamers. By 1864, the plan became reality, with a line that extended all the way to Bombay—first to Grant Road (which was initially a terminus); then to Backbay, a station between today's Marine Lines and Churchgate; and eventually to Colaba, the southernmost tip of the island (where Cotton Green was then located). The 1864 timetable has only one train on this line, between Grant Road and Ahmedabad, that took approximately forty-six hours to complete a journey; the train would start at Grant Road at 7 a.m. and reach Ahmedabad at 5 a.m. on the third day. Similarly, on its way back, the train would begin its journey from Ahmedabad at 7 a.m. and arrive at Grant Road on the third day at 5:30 a.m.

---

1. S.M. Edwardes, *The Gazetteer of Bombay City and Island*, Volume 1 (India: Cosmo Publications, 2002).

Like the GIPR that morphed into the Central Railway, the BB&CI became the Western Railway. The first suburban service in Bombay, with steam traction, was introduced in April 1867, with one train plying each way between Virar and Backbay Stations. Three years later, the line extended to Churchgate. By 1900, forty-four trains each way carried over one million passengers annually.

The first (three-coach) electric multiple unit service was introduced between Andheri and Colaba in 1928. Today, the suburban section extends from Churchgate (the city's business centre) to Virar, covering a distance of sixty kilometres and twenty-eight stations. Recently, the lines have been extended to Dahanu Road, adding ten more stations and sixty more kilometres.

The GIPR and BB&CI Railway companies were in fierce competition with each other and there were severe restrictions on the extent to which trains could run on rival lines. While goods trains of the BB&CI Railway were allowed to use the GIPR line only between Dadar and Carnac Bridge, passenger trains of the BB&CI Railway were allowed to use the GIPR line strictly between Mahim and Gowari (now Wadala). As for GIPR trains, only goods trains were allowed to run on the BB&CI Railway lines, and that too from Dadar to Colaba.

CHURCHGATE STATION: THE BEGINNING

Named after the old gate of a now vanished fort, the seven-storey building of Churchgate Station came up in the 1950s. It has several firsts to its credit—it is the country's first network to run on AC-DC current modes; it had the very first pedestrian subway; and the world's first 'ladies special' train operates from here.

The Remains of the Day

The solid iron hydraulic buffer beams at the end of Churchgate Station's platforms have been manufactured by 'Ransomes & Rapier, Ipswich', the iconic firm that supplied locomotives for the first railway line in China. This firm was founded by four engineers in 1869— James Ransome, his son, Robert Ransome, Richard Rapier and Arthur

Courtesy: Western Railway Archives

Courtesy: Western Railway Archives

Churchgate Station Under Construction

Churchgate Station, late 1920s

Bennett. They manufactured railway equipment, as also shells, guns and tank turrets during the First World War. The firm shut shop in 1987.

Courtesy: Mumbai Municipal Corporation Archives

A Footbridge Outside Churchgate, Now Replaced by a Subway

MARINE LINE STATION: THE BACKBAY BUNGLE

Marine Lines Station is close to Marine Drive, the site of the enchanting 'Queen's necklace', with a line-up of lights by the horizon. Marine Drive comes with a rather interesting story. In 1917, a proposal was put forward by a syndicate of prominent citizens for the reclamation of 1,500 acres of land between Colaba and Backbay. The execution of the idea was beleaguered with losses and delays. In 1926, it was estimated that the work, given the rate at which it was proceeding, would be completed in 1945 at a cost of Rs 11 crore, four times the estimated cost! The Backbay Enquiry Committee was set up, spearheaded by K.F. Nariman and Manu Subedar. It uncovered financial irregularities; besides, the construction of the sea wall was inadequate and 9 lakh cubic yards of mud had escaped through it. The project came to be known as the Backbay Bungle, or Lloyd's Folly (after George Lloyd, then the governor of Bombay). Eventually, four blocks were completed in 1929, a total of 439.6 acres. Of this, 234.8 acres were sold to the military at a cost of Rs 2.06 crore, and 16.6 acres were incorporated into Marine Drive and its sea wall.[2]

> By 1940 the construction of Marine Drive was complete. It was, the *Indian Concrete Journal* proclaimed, the 'Finest promenade in the East, built in concrete.' Lining the Drive were Art Deco apartment blocks, looking out to the Arabian Sea. Behind them, on Queens Road, were also modern buildings of steel and concrete, staring across the Oval Maidan at the medievalism of the Gothic Revival buildings. The new built form represented an architectural shift from Victorianism to modernity.[3]

The Remains of the Day

Marine Lines Station still holds a few relics of the BB&CI Railway, including wooden benches and furniture, an old lantern by the station master's cabin and original wrought iron railings that act as a fence

---

2. 'Mumbai: From Simple Beginnings to Bustling Metropolis', *Issuu*, in <issuu.com/dragonov/docs/mumbai/1>, accessed on 3 September 2014.

3. Gyan Prakash, *Mumbai Fables* (USA: Princeton University Press, 2011).

between the platform and the road. The fast-line tracks are, in fact, original BB&CI Railway tracks.

CHARNI ROAD: ANIMAL FARM

The story behind Charni Road goes back to 1830s. Cattle belonging to the local inhabitants of the congested Fort area used to graze freely at Camp Maidan (now Azad Maidan). In 1838, the British introduced a 'grazing fee' that several cattle owners could not afford. A few records state that Jamsetjee Jeejeebhoy spent Rs 20,000 to buy a verdant patch of land near the seafront at Thakurdwar to ensure that no one had to pay to graze starving cattle. Later, the area came to be known as 'charni' (grazing), and when a railway station came up forty years later, it was recognized as Charni Road.

The Remains of the Day

Rare findings at Charni Road Station include huge iron balustrades, now painted yellow; old benches; and a signal lamp in the station master's cabin.

GRANT ROAD STATION: THE FIRST TERMINUS

Grant Road, named after Robert Grant, the governor of Bombay between 1835 and 1839, used to be the terminus of the erstwhile BB&CI Railway. The terminus, established in 1859, would connect Bombay to Surat. Over the years, this terminus moved to Bombay Central, and Grant Road Station oversaw cargo operations.

The Remains of the Day

The first terminus, Grant Road, occupies an old stone building, more or less intact. Indeed, a horse-carriage pathway of cobblestone, until recently, was still in place. The station master's cabin and the booking offices have majestic teakwood furniture and floral bell hooks; there is also an ancient gangman's shed, and a police station built of stone and Manglorean tiles (unfortunately, now covered with tar to avoid leakages).

The office of Jackson Cooperative Bank—a bank for rail employees—can be spotted in this station; it has been named after Ernest Jackson. Jackson took over the responsibility of chief auditor of BB&CI Railway in 1911. Deeply concerned about the well-being of the lower- and middle-classes, Jackson founded the first credit cooperative at the Calcutta Port Trust within a few years of the enactment of Cooperative Act of 1904. He rose to the position of an 'agent' of the BB&CI Railway, and oversaw the emergence of the Bombay Central Station, the rebuilding of the Bassien Bridge and the advent of the boat trains of the BB&CI Railway. To many, Jackson remains the father and sponsor of the credit cooperative society of India.[4]

BOMBAY CENTRAL: THE PLACE OF FORGOTTEN COINS

Bombay Central (now Mumbai Central) came up in the 1930s, even as Colaba Station closed. Under the supervision of the renowned

Courtesy: Western Railway Archives

Bombay Central Under Construction

Courtesy: Western Railway Archives

Bombay Central Station, 1931

---

4. *The Jackson Credit and Cooperative Society of the Employees of the Western Railway Ltd,* in <http://www.jacksonsociety.com/HTML/History.htm>, accessed on 4 September 2014.

firm, Gregson, Batley and King, the station was ready in twenty-one months, and was inaugurated on 18 December 1930.

Interestingly, a brass cylinder with the names of the officers connected with the construction of the station, as also coins carrying denominations of one rupee, and eight, four, two, one, half and quarter annas, were placed in a grove beneath the foundation stone of Bombay Central Station.

The Remains of the Day

Apart from those ancient coins, stray relics at the Bombay Central Station include an old seal of BB&CI Railway; an iron bell outside the station master's cabin; and teakwood benches with 'only for ladies' inscribed in Gujarati. The railings of the fence outside the station are actually the remains of old tracks.

MAHALAXMI TO ELPHINSTONE ROAD STATION: TIME STANDS STILL

It was from Mahalaxmi that the first electric train of the BB&CI Railway had run. Onward, one reaches Lower Parel and Elphinstone Road. The latter originally consisted of two stations separated by half a kilometre, with an independent issuing and collecting staff. Today, of course, this has changed, as we see one cohesive station.

The Remains of the Day

Mahalaxmi Station has an old signal cabin, complete with antique levers; wooden benches; and ancient queue separators.

Lower Parel Station holds several remains from the past, from forgotten sleepers (pot, clip and even simple iron sleepers), to heirloom furniture in the station master's cabin, to bricks that carry the letters 'BB&CI'.

As for Elphinstone Road Station, it holds a few scattered relics— such as ancient tracks, now used to fence out slum settlements; a 1911 plaque on a pillar outside the station master's office; and balustrades dating back to 1878 at the base of a footbridge.

DADAR AND MAHIM STATIONS: WHERE THE CROWDS MILL

Dadar and Mahim are enormously busy stations. While Dadar Station, as we know, is a maze of platforms and bridges, Mahim Station is distinctive because of its building made of massive stone blocks. Mahim's thatched roof was once the pride of the station, but today, it is dwarfed by its mushrooming premises.

Govind Narayan Madgaonkar, in his book documenting Bombay in 1863, states that the original Mahim Station (belonging to the GIPR) was located near the Custom House or 'mandvi', close to where today's Mahim Causeway starts.[5] However, this original station seems to have been swallowed by time, for there are no traces of it.

Old records of the Bombay Municipal Corporation's water department also document the existence of a Persian wheel at the station, connected to water tanks in the area. Water trains used to get filled here and supply water to the island city of Bombay during times of near-drought.

The Remains of the Day

Few know that a little before the approach of Dadar Station, one can find one of the oldest plaques in Bombay, with the engraving, 'Darlington Engineering Company and BB&CIR, 1900'. One can also find an ancient abandoned British cabin with letters carved in wood: 'Dadar Jn North Cabin'. Further, there is a huge circular well, now buried, that in its days of glory used to fill water steam engines.

Mahim Station holds old-fashioned queue separators and pillars reading 'Dalzell Steel'—which, by the First World War, was the largest individual steel works factory in Scotland; it is now a part of British Steel.

Parallel to Mahim Station, along Lady Jamshedjee Road, is one of the last remaining relics carrying evidence of Bombay's topographical history—evidence of the weaving together of islands. Here, a six-foot stone plaque, dated 1846, commemorates the linking of Mahim and Bandra.

---

5. Govind Narayan Madgaonkar, *Mumbaiche Varnan*, edited by Narhar Raghunath Fatak (India: Marathi Granth Sangrahalaya, 1863). Translated by the author.

BANDRA AND KHAR ROAD STATIONS: LEGACIES OF THE PAST

Bandra Station is in the Bombay municipal list as a grade one heritage structure and has been recently restored by the railways. This station has a beautiful arched roof and lofty towers. Indeed, rail records state that the entire roof was assembled in London, transported to Bombay by steamer and placed over the standing pillars.

Back in the day, from the slaughter house at Bandra, the BB&CI Railway used to run 'meat trains' across dedicated rail sidings to deliver fresh meat to Bombay city. Today, the old slaughter house no longer exists, and has been taken over by the city's municipal bus (BEST) depot and a host of slums. The sidings are buried deep under electric cables, water pipes, sewage and tar.

The next station, Khar Road was opened in July 1924 for 1,700 expected passengers of the new town-planning scheme.

The Remains of the Day

What are the remains of the day at Bandra Station, apart from the magnificent heritage building? To answer this question, one has only to look at the pillars holding the roof, which are, in fact, six double-headed rails bound together, with 'BB&CI 1888' engraved across; the heavy iron fences at the various entrances of the station; and the pillars of the middle footbridge reading 'Dalzell Steel'. Outside the station lies a century-old plaque to mark the opening of Turner Road. And at the Bandra yard we have one of the oldest relics of the past—a locomotive turntable (till recently in use and operated manually).

The tiny station of Khar holds a few stone structures, etched name boards and decorative iron pillars. Platform one—that is used by the Harbour Line—seems to be an original construction of the BB&CI Railway.

FROM SANTACRUZ TO VIRAR

The train moves swiftly through a range of stations within the island city—Santacruz, Vile Parle, Andheri, Jogeshwari, Goregaon, Malad, Kandivali, Borivali, Dahisar, Mira Road, Bhayandar, Naigaon, Vasai

Road, Nallasopara and Virar. It's a long journey for the average city-dweller.

The Remains of the Day

Let's document what remains of the past, station by station.

The most prominent feature at Santacruz Station is the row of bungalows, belonging to the British era, in the railway colony.

Vile Parle Station carries an old signboard of a third-class ticket booking window, almost forty years after the third-class was abolished.

The station building at Andheri, once built of stone and now completely demolished, had a rare plaque commemorating the year of construction—1902. The old station was pulled down as additional tracks are being laid to extend the Harbour Line to Goregaon. As tokens of the past, we can find discarded iron sleepers along the station premises.

The unassuming Jogeshwari Station, interestingly, has the oldest BB&CI relic found so far during this study—an iron bell dated 1868 with the engraving, 'BB&CIR Contract No.10. 1868'. This hangs outside the station master's office.

While Goregaon Station can still be found within an ageing stone building, at Malad Station, the pillars are made of double-headed rails, while Kandivali and Borivali Stations have antique iron bells.

Moving on to Dahisar Station, a beautiful, arched iron footbridge has been lost to station expansion. At Mira Road, however, the original line and remains of an old bridge can still be spotted, while at Bhayandar Station, fire buckets are in use! As we travel from Bhayander to Naigaon to Vasai, we spot the Vasai yard, which holds a treasure trove of relics, including an abandoned power station and a number of stone buildings.

The railway station of Nallasopara, a vibrant port in the fourteenth century, still carries decorative pillars and a fire bucket, while Virar Station is a capsule of the past—it has Manglorean tiles, a long-standing water tank, wooden benches and an iron bell.

EXTENDING THE SUBURBAN LINE

In 1999, the ministry of railways proposed an extension of the suburban corridor all the way to Dahanu, sixty kilometres beyond Virar. A plan was chalked out; it was determined that the railways required a widening of all track centres—after all, mail and express trains are ten feet in width, as against the original British design of electric multiple-unit local trains that are twelve feet in width. The first direct suburban local train between Churchgate and Dahanu Road was inaugurated on 16 April 2013.

A TWELFTH-CENTURY MYSTERY AT THE
WESTERN RAILWAY YARD

In November 2010, the Western Railway found a rather intriguing relic under a tree in the Mahalaxmi railway scrap yard, which was being cleared to build a new power substation. Old railway employees claimed that the relic had been at the Mahalaxmi scrap yard for nearly forty years, and that it had been brought in a rail wagon from Nallasopara Station (about fifty-six kilometres away from Churchgate) after an excavation. In the recent past, the relic had been worshipped with garlands.

The relic captivated a number of archeologists. Some turned to the renowned historian, Dr D.M. Mirashi, and his book *Silhara Rajvanshacha Itihas Ani Koriv Lekh* or *The History and Inscriptions of the Silhara Dynasty* for answers. Dr Mirashi described a lost artefact that belonged to the era of the Silhara dynasty (810 and 1240 AD)—specifically to King Haripal Dev.[6] Made of stone, he claimed this artefact was rather impressive—about two feet wide and five feet high; towards the top, it carried engravings of a mangal kalash (sacred pitcher), a sun and a moon, while the lower edges held the picture of 'gardabhshap' (a donkey). Towards the middle, there was an inscription, no longer readable.

---

6. The Silhara dynasty ruled the region around present-day Bombay. Split into three branches, one ruled North Konkan, the second South Konkan, while the third ruled what is now known as Satara.

However, when Mirashi's sketch was matched against the relic at the Mahalaxmi scrap yard, archeologists found that the supposed inscription and the sacred pitcher were missing; further the relic didn't fit Mirashi's listed dimensions.

In which case, could a stone artefact closer to Mirashi's description also be lying in the Mahalaxmi yard? Who can tell?

As for the relic that was found, it came to be divided into two segments, with the top end separated from the rest. There are plans to move it to the Western Railway heritage room at Churchgate.

NOSTALGIA ALONG THE LINES

'I SAW BOMBAY'S FIRST TRAIN'

Dinshaw Wacha (1844-1936), a social reformer, politician and a businessman—whose tall statue today stands looking over the traffic outside Churchgate Station—was a young boy when the first train ran in Bombay. He was one among the thousands standing at Byculla, gazing at the city's latest invention!

His memoir, published in 1920, documents how he perceived this 'wonder of the world'.

> Locally the commencement of the decade (1850-60) must have been full of the highest significance to the ruling elders and the elderly Indian population. There was to be noticed that novel system of locomotion—a steam engine in front puffing and emitting a suffocating smoke, and a few carriages being dragged along in its train on iron rails. It was the wonder of the world of Bombay. I can recall to my mind even today the scene which was vividly impressed on my memory as I stood midst an admiring crowd, a few yards from the old level-crossing at Byculla (just near the southern spur of the Nesbit Road over bridge) as the first train was opened for passenger traffic to a short distance. The railway was a new impression and a new dispensation, the unlimited potentiality of which for universal beneficence was, of course, unthinkable to my boyish imagination. Only there was a very pleasant feeling akin to a sensation that on that eventful opening day something titanic was seen passing over a crowded part of Bombay.[1]

---

1. Sir Dinshaw Edulji Wacha, *Shells from Sands of Bombay; Being My Recollections and Reminiscences: 1860-1875* (Bombay: The Bombay Chronicle Press, 1920).

Wacha was one of the many who witnessed the crucial years of the birth and growth of the railways in India, from the first train run to the lines' electrification. He also rose to become a member of the Bombay Improvement Trust that later planned new suburbs.

'MY DAD IS THE FASTEST'

Norma Probert, who passed away in 2014, was the daughter of 'Speed King Percy', Percival Middlecoat, the senior pilot driver of the 1928 Bombay-Peshawar Frontier Mail. Middlecoat held the record of driving the train fastest; he drove the Frontier Mail well beyond Rawalpindi, towards the Khyber Pass. He passed away early in 1936 after having contracted pneumonia, incurable at that time.

Norma Probert grew up in pre-Partition India. After studying in St Denys' School in Murree (now in Pakistan), she settled in the UK. From England, she recalled, 'The Frontier Mail made its debut in 1928 and was praised in 1930 by *The Times* as the fastest train in the British Empire. I would like to think this accolade was partly due to my father, who was a senior driver of this very train between 1930 and 1936. As far as I know, his speed record was never beaten in his lifetime. My father loved living life on the fast lane—he owned the swiftest motor bike of the time and the fastest racing car. He was a speedfreak, but he was also a scholar.

'The Frontier Mail was a luxury passenger train, pulled by the enormous steam engines of the day. In 1934, it was also the first train in the Indian Peninsula to have an air-conditioned compartment. During the Raj years, the train was partly used for the convenience and speed of troops boarding ships to and from the UK and, of course, for the swift transfer of mail. The soldiers travelled by third- and second-class tickets; the officers and civilian railway personnel travelled first-class.

'The Frontier Mail ran like clockwork, arriving at each station on time. Of course, there were the usual hold-ups, such as signal failure, or cattle crossing the tracks at villages. But the main objective—to arrive at all the main stations on time—was usually met.

'I remember travelling by the Frontier Mail train as a child. We moved from place to place, and so we had our own bogey—part of it for our goods and furniture, and a six-berth compartment for the family. Dad did not always drive during these journeys as he had to help my mother look after us.

'Every driver travelled with his "batman" or assistant. Well, in any case, that was the name my father used for his helper, because my father's family came from a military background. The assistant did odd chores—he ran across platforms when the train was stationary, getting anything that was needed, and in general, looked into the welfare of the driver's family.

'We travelled in style. Our compartments had leather (or its facsimile) berths, with backrests that could be folded down—these could therefore be used as beds or kept upright during the day as couches. Each compartment had its own WC and washbasin with running water.

'The train was not a walk-through one. The bogeys were all separate carriages. Before the advent of ACs, we had electric fans. I think there were six in each six-berth carriage. The windows had two kinds of shutters—of mesh to keep the insects at bay, but let the air in; and of polished wood. Besides, there were pull-down blinds. The shutters were maneuverable, and the slats could be opened or shut to invite the sun or ward off the heat. There were locks on the doors and the windows for additional safety.

'Sleeping on trains was a joy to me. I loved the rhythm of the wheels on the track, the chugging of the steam locomotives, and the rocking motion of the train. It was like a sedative and we kids all slept well.

'We were served food by liveried bearers on silver trays, with silver cutlery; even the crockery was of bone china! The meals were strategically ordered—the waiters would board at one of the stations; we would place our orders after going through à la carte menus; the waiters would then relay the order to the next station, and we would be served the choicest food at the following stop—steaks, grills, casseroles, stews, delicious fish and some Indian dishes too! The used trays and crockery would be cleared at yet another station. The timings of the stops would coincide with meal times, as the journeys were long, sometimes running into forty-eight hours depending on one's destination.

'Since I travelled by the train up to the age of eleven, I have clear recollections of those exciting and memorable journeys. We children loved the noise, the hustle and bustle of the various platforms we stopped at—the naming of wares, the shouts of "garam garam chai", and the sudden appearance of sellers of sweets and delicacies which we were not allowed to eat, much to our disappointment!

'All told, my childhood and the North Western Railway are tied up. My early years were privileged, and for this I must thank my father for those wonderful railway journeys.'[2]

'THE MAN AT THE MATUNGA CROSSING'

Dr Ardeshir B. Damania, once a Matunga resident, now associated with the University of California (Davis), has vivid memories of the suburb's level-crossing. As a young boy, he used to wait there with his father, Behramji M. Damania, who was an engineer, aviator, entrepreneur, adventurer and businessman.

Dr Damania recollects, 'My father and I used to wait for the level-crossing to open, sometimes for half-an-hour. The level-crossing used to be operated manually with two large "keys", as big as your palm. There was a very small "kholi" or cabin where both keys had to be inserted for the signal to change to green on either side of the level-crossing. Once the keys would be released from the "lock", the signals would change to red on both sides. With each key in hand, the gateman would run to open the level-crossing gates on either side. This foolproof mechanism prevented accidents from happening at level-crossings.

'Between 1930 and 1959, the man who operated the gates was physically challenged—he possessed only one leg, having lost the other during a shunting accident. Any railway yard employee who'd lose a leg would be given a job at a level-crossing. The man at this particular crossing would run with a wooden leg across four tracks, from one gate to another, to open them. He'd give a stiff salute to my father as we'd drive across in our big black car. Then a bell would start ringing and the gateman would start closing each gate, one at a time.

---

2. Personal correspondence.

'On those occasions when we'd wait interminably at the crossing, we'd see a small diesel locomotive pulling a string of about twenty wagons, filled to the brim with refuse meant for dumping at the Sion-Dharavi refuse grounds. My father and I would have to hold our breaths as the train would crawl at snail's pace, at about 10 mph. My father would tell me, "Hold your nose, the Deccan King is passing by!" And I would.'

In the early twentieth century, the siding tracks would enter the Tata Power Co receiving station through a metal gate. Dr Damania, whose father was the superintendent of the receiving station, recalls, 'Whenever a wagon containing machinery or cables for the power station would emerge, a small shunting engine would place the wagon on the siding outside the gates. The engine would depart quickly because it would be holding up the lines between Matunga and Sion Stations.

'After that, my father would ask for the wagon to be hand-pushed into the power station. For this, thirty to forty labourers would be hired. They would sing in unison as they'd push the heavy twenty-two-tonne railway wagon. I can still remember their cries and the strain on their poor, thin bodies, glistening with sweat; the recalcitrant wagon would budge inch by inch. As a young boy I felt very sorry for the labourers. Once the wagon got unloaded inside the power station, the men would have to push it back outside the gates promptly, in a day or two, to avoid paying penalties to the railways. They'd then have to wait for the shunting engine to come and take it away. The GIPR workshop was just next door, so finding an engine was never a problem. But once the wagon left the power station's premises and the gates were shut, it was the railway's responsibility to take the wagon away.'

Dr Damania looks into the distance and asks, 'I wonder if the siding still exists?'

The old siding still exists, I tell him, but it is now walled over. Its remains can be found under overgrown bushes.[3]

---

3. Conversations and personal correspondence.

Courtesy: Western Railway Archives

Workers Unloading a Narrow-Gauge Locomotive

'MY GREAT-GRANDMA WAS NOT AN ENGINEER'

Lawrence Lemmens, the great-grandson of Alice Tredwell, who built the difficult rail inclines of Bhor Ghat, clears the air about his great-grandmother's life.

'I have always been troubled by overenthusiastic young engineers who have, for utterly unfounded reasons, hailed my great-grandma as a "great lady engineer". This is not quite the truth, nor did my great-grandma ever make such claims. A document of the era puts things in context, when it states, "Mrs Tredwell [Alice Pickering Tredwell], with a high spirits [...] conducted the business of the contract." Which of course she did—there was a lot of money involved!'[4]

The story goes that once the lines trundled fifty-three kilometres from Bombay to Kalyan, they diverged—one line went towards the northeast for forty-two kilometres to Thal Ghat, and another went southeast for sixty-one kilometres to the foot of Bhor Ghat.

---

4. Personal correspondence.

Contract number eight of the GIPR—the construction of lines across Bhor Ghat—is popular in the history of the Indian railways, not only because the project was labour intensive, but also because the lines were to be built by a woman.

Let's uncover the full story. The contract for the first twenty-four kilometres along Bhor Ghat had initially been taken on by William Frederick Faviell, the same contractor who had built the first thirty-four kilometres between Bombay and Thana. But Faviell, for a variety of reasons, abandoned the contract midway. It was then, on the recommendation of Robert Stephenson, given to another well-known English contractor, Solomon Tredwell, who reached Bombay on

Courtesy: Central Railway Archives

A Train Negotiating the Ghats

29 October 1859; he died two months after his arrival due to an illness, probably cholera, acquired in the ghats. It was his widow, Alice, who then took over the contract. With the help of former GIPR engineers, Swainson Adamson and George Louis Clowser, she eventually met the demands of the contract successfully.

Whether Alice Tredwell is an engineer is irrelevant. Today, she is remembered for her courage. After all, it's not every day that someone takes on a challenging project in a strange country.

'WE ARE THE DESCENDANTS OF VICTORIA TERMINUS' ASSISTANT ENGINEER'

The descendants of the assistant engineer of the glorious Victoria Terminus, Raosaheb Sitaram Khanderao Vaidya, remember him as being tall and well-built, and a meticulous planner, carefully implementing each of chief engineer, F.W. Stevens' designs. They also remember Vaidya mentioning that portions of the Victoria Terminus remained incomplete for a long time. Vaidya later drew up the original plans for the construction of the Taj Mahal Hotel, where we see a similar 'floating staircase'. Besides, he was associated with the Bombay Municipal Corporation's headquarters and the Council Hall, which is the present headquarters of the Maharashtra State Police.

Vaidya was supposed to have been a man of deep integrity. The Bombay Municipal Corporation building, of which he was the resident engineer, was ready after four years, at a cost of Rs 59,000—less than the estimated budget. Vaidya was offered gifts and tokens of gratitude, but as a rule, he returned everything. If he feared causing offence to the donator, he'd keep a symbolic fruit and hand back the remaining contributions.

Vaidya's descendants (recalling memories handed down by their grandmother) say that the family had a bungalow in Sion. The entire household used to stay there, until the 1930s or 1940s (when they grew in number, and had to shift to smaller houses). The plot of land, which belonged to the Bombay Improvement Trust, was surrendered to the organization. It's said, there used to be huge portraits of Vaidya and his wife at the Sion bungalow. But sadly,

these were given away, nobody knows to whom. According to one of
Vaidya's descendants, his only belonging in the family's possession is
a 'thali' or a silver plate in which he used to eat his lunch—mainly
fruits.[5]

---

5. Based on an email conversation with a direct descendent of Raosaheb Sitaram
Khanderao Vaidya, Vidyadhar Vaidya in 2013.

FORGOTTEN LINES AND LOST JOURNEYS

COLABA STATION: IN ENDS, BEGINNINGS

Colaba Station was the southernmost terminus of the old BB&CI Railway. The station opened in 1873, but shut down in 1930 as a part of the second phase of the Backbay reclamation project.

Ironically, it was the first phase of the same project that led to the opening of the station. In the 1860s, the fortifications of Bombay were being pulled down; the city was expanding, and new roads and buildings were coming up. In light of this, after prolonged discussions and correspondence, the Bombay government authorized an extension of the BB&CI Railway line from Grant Road to Chowpatty, and from here, following the Backbay shore, to Colaba. The extension split Chowpatty, and important streets in the area had to be crossed by two overbridges.

Cotton Green, the business hub of cotton trade—that until then was to be found in front of the Town Hall (where Horniman Circle stands today)—was shifted to a few kilometres of reclaimed land on either side of the new Colaba Causeway. The new cotton hub called for more facilities, and the causeway was further widened and rebuilt by 1863. To give it an additional boost, the Bombay government designated the area as a separate ward in 1872, and a year later, in 1873, a horse-drawn tramway was opened, with offices at Colaba. The same year, Colaba Station emerged. The horse-drawn tramway and the railway line brought a certain romance to travel within the area. As the crowds increased, the railways decided to convert the small Colaba Station into a major terminus.

It took three decades but a majestic building and a large station, equipped with a yard, was opened on 7 April 1896; this was the year when the city was badly hit by the plague. The station with a stone façade, adjacent to Wodehouse Road near Sassoon's Dock, had a carriage porch, a high tower and a tiled roof. The building had waiting rooms, ticket counters and offices with three broad platforms, 500 feet in length. By the turn of the century, in 1900, of the forty-four trains that plied to Virar, almost forty were from Colaba Terminus.

In the 1920s, the Backbay project of the 1860s, which had reclaimed land for the line, was revived by the development directorate of the Bombay development department. This department pushed for further reclamation of the Backbay foreshore. This was when the terminus at Colaba became a hurdle.

James Mackison, special engineer of the municipality, submitted a proposal for an underground railway between Churchgate and Grant Road. While this was initially approved—on grounds that the enhanced value of properties above the line would meet the cost of the line—the government shelved the entire project due to a shortage of funds.

In the meantime, the Backbay project was pursued wholeheartedly and the railways were asked to close their line between Churchgate and Colaba. A notice was served to the BB&CI Railway in 1920. On the New Year's morning of 1931, the BB&CI track finally terminated at Churchgate. Colaba Station had closed the previous night, on 31 December 1930.

Churchgate was remodelled; the level-crossing and footbridge closed. The entire strip of land ceded by the railways to the development directorate was taken over by a range of art deco buildings by 1938. Today, the Fateh Chand Badhwar Railway Colony, built over the old Colaba Station and the yard, is home to numerous high-profile railway officials and their families. Few would know that Fateh Chand Badhwar, a 1955 Padma Bhushan recipient, who died at the age of ninety-five in 1995, was the first chairman of India's railway board and had played a key role in standardizing the look of railway coaches in free India.

Today, at Colaba's old station premises, all we find are the original wrought iron fences that used to border the station building and a few ancient rails.

BOMBAY BACKBAY STATION: CLAIMING THE OCEAN

The word 'back bay' has several connotations in Bombay. Today, it's a reclaimed area in the southern part of Colaba, which itself is the southernmost tip of the island city. Historically, as we now know, it was a reclamation project that happened in phases, starting in the 1860s.

During the planned extension of the BB&CI Railway within Bombay, the railway's pioneering engineer, Colonel P.T. French, sought a rail line from Grant Road that would pass through the crowded districts of Girgaum, Sonapur and Esplanade—instead of one that went straight to Colaba. But Charles Forjett, who was then the commissioner of police, prepared a report and found that the suggested route was impractical and expensive, since land between Grant Road and Esplanade would have to be purchased.

The only practical option was to recover land from the Backbay region and lay a line to Colaba. Even as this was in progress, it was suggested that a temporary terminus could emerge at Chowpatty. But then Bartle Frere's Ramparts Removal Committee opposed the proposal, citing that the station and the crowds it would attract would hurt the city's aesthetics.

Finally, in 1866, the line was extended south of Grant Road to a station called Bombay Backbay, with three suburban trains plying in each direction. A year later, on 12 April 1867, regular suburban trains between Virar and Bombay Backbay commenced.

The opening of Bombay Backbay Station was a part of the company's ambitious plan to reclaim the large, natural bay along the western seafront. The station was primarily used to run ballast trains carrying material for reclamation. The location of the station was just outside the western side of the old Fort, alongside the bay, somewhere between present-day Marine Lines and Churchgate. The station was subsequently shifted southwards, closer to Town, and called Churchgate.

The Backbay Reclamation Company was one of the many firms established during the commercial boom in the city that began in 1861 with the commencement of the American Civil War. When the civil war ended in 1865 and the international supply of cotton exceeded demand, the market in Bombay collapsed and the Backbay Reclamation Company, like many others, got liquidated. The government took over the company's projects. The only scheme it completed was the reclamation of a narrow strip of land, wide enough to lay the tracks for the BB&CI Railway line's extension from Churchgate to Colaba. This triggered the development of the city's western shore.

BALLARD PIER MOLE STATION: COMINGS AND GOINGS

The Port Trust Line was once used not only to ferry cargo, but also troops and passengers from steamships at Ballard Pier, via long-distance trains to destinations like Karachi. It remained one of the city's lifelines till the 1940s, when it was closed.

Courtesy: Mumbai Port Trust Archives

A Rare View of Ballard Pier Mole Station, Early 1900s

'Mole' is of Latin origin, and means a massive structure, usually of stone—such as a pier or a causeway—between places separated by water. Two major trains that plied from Ballard Pier Mole Station, as we know, are the Punjab Limited and the Frontier Mail.

Old sepia-toned photographs of Ballard Pier Mole Station show a two-platform station sheltered by a roof. One can imagine ships standing on one side and a deserted road on the other side. Today, the erstwhile station premises can be found behind the tall walls of the Bombay Port Trust, away from public view.

Close to the site where the station once stood, is the Ballard Bunder Gatehouse, built from Kurla sandstone; it is today a listed heritage structure. It served as the public access point to Ballard Pier, and a popular arrival point for passenger steamers. After India's Independence, the gatehouse became part of the naval dockyard. It was obscured from view and public memory for over fifty years, until 2005, when the Indian Navy, as we now know, restored the building and opened it to the public as a maritime museum.

MAZGAON STATION: A MIXED DEMOGRAPHIC

The Bombay Gazetteer of 1909 lists Mazgaon as second of the important nine stations in the city limits, besides Victoria Terminus.[1] The original Mazgaon Station catered to the teeming local population on one side of the line, and the old Portuguese and British suburb on the other.

Mazgaon Station was located to the north of today's Sandhurst Road, approximately at the base of Hancock Bridge. Indeed, old US military survey maps of Bombay, dated 1914-18, and made with precision during the First World War, distinctly show this location for Mazgaon Station. Around 1915 or 1920, the Mazgaon Station of that era made way for the new two-tier Sandhurst Road Station, to match the alignment of the newly planned Harbour Line. Today all you can find of Mazgaon Station are stone arches, which are probably remains of the old retaining wall.

---

1. S.M. Edwardes, *The Gazetteer of Bombay City and Island*, Volume 1 (India: Cosmo Publications, 2002), p. 348.

BORI BUNDER STATION: GROUND ZERO

A photograph that looks remarkably like a pencil sketch captures a rather quaint scene—a fence made of dense, wooden sticks; a row of low sheds; a wide road with cannons buried muzzle down; a telegraph line passing overhead; and a small cart. This is the earliest available photograph of what was Bori Bunder Station. Taken probably in 1854, when photography had recently arrived in Bombay and Daguerreotype images were only just evolving, this long-shot picture was taken by W.H. Stanley Crawford. The photograph was published in India by local scholar Krishnashastri Bhatwadekar in 1854,[2] a year after the first official train run. Bori Bunder was clearly at the brink of massive development, with temporary structures and open spaces.

Note: In the Public Domain

W.H. Stanley's Bori Bunder Station, circa 1854

---

2. *A Short Account of Railways, Selected from Lardner's Railway Economy*, translated by Krishnashastri Bhatwadekar (Bombay: Ganpat Krishnaji Press, 1854), p. 19.

What was Bori Bunder like, before the station emerged? *The Handbook of Bombay Presidency* describes the wharf in the early 1800s as, 'the place from which Panwell [Panvel] steamers formerly departed several times daily—the direct distance across being only 22 miles [35 kilometres].'[3] Back then, Panvel was viewed as the 'mainland'. The steamers carried goods and supplies for Fort's township, and also transported people. With solid rocks on one side and a small hillock on the other, the Bori Bunder jetty had limited landing facilities and people used to alight from small boats and jump over numerous rocks to reach the shore. Around 1852, the hillock was flattened, the rocks removed and a massive wharf built, to facilitate the movement of larger cargo-laden boats.[4] Bori Bunder was eventually the harbour where the material required for building the first rail lines was unloaded as it came from England in steamers.[5]

By the vicinity of the jetty at Bori Bunder, there was a wide 'esplanade', a large clear ground. Let's go back in time and observe this site, which had different uses for different people. In the early nineteenth century, when Bombay was a walled city, the esplanade was popularly known as 'pawan chakki' or literally 'the grindstone of wind' among the locals. After all, there was a huge windmill positioned by the shore.[6] While the English put up tents in the vast open area to beat the heat and get fresh sea breeze, the military saw the space as a clear firing range from the fort, for purposes of defence. Much land was also cleared and kept free for safety; this was after disastrous fires had swept through the dwellings in Fort in the late eighteenth and nineteenth centuries. During the mutiny, specifically on 15 October

---

3. George Bradshaw, *Handbook to the Bombay Presidency and North West Provinces of India* (London: W.J. Adams, 1864), p. 34.

4. Balkrishna Bapu Acharya and Moro Vinayak Shingne, *Mumbaicha Vrutant* (India: Maharashtra Rajya Sahitya Sanskriti Mandal, 1889), p. 281.

5. Captain Edward Davidson, *The Railways of India: With an Account of their Rise, Progress and Construction, Written with the Aid of the Records of India Office* (London: 1968), p. 245.

6. James Douglas, *Bombay and Western India: A Series of Stray Papers*, Volume 2 (London: Sampson Low, Marston & Company, 1893), p. 218.

1857, at exactly 5.10 p.m., it was here that Bombay's police commissioner, Charles Forjett, gunned down Drill Havaldar Sayyad Hussein of the Marine Battalion and Private Mangal Gadia of the Tenth Regiment Native Infantry, for taking part in a conspiracy against the British government. The punishment hoped to 'teach a lesson' to the natives for challenging the British Empire.

Today, the open spaces of the esplanade still exist, dotted with wells; these have been divided into four grounds—Cross, Oval, Cooperage and Azad Maidans. They are intersected by busy roads and junctions, and it's hard to picture them as a single large unit. Near Azad Maidan, where Indian soldiers were killed in 1857, stands the Amar Jawan Memorial in their honour.

~

Ground zero of the railways sliced through Dhobi Ghat ('washermen's lines', which later moved north, near today's Metro Big Cinema, and is still referred to as Dhobi Talao or 'washermen's tank') and the parade ground of the native infantry regiment. Not surprisingly, making space for Bori Bunder Station itself was a massive effort. Streets leading to Fort had to be shut, and existing roads realigned. A newsletter released on 29 October 1852 during the construction of the original Bori Bunder Station declares:

> The road from Mazgaon to Fort George will be closed for vehicles and also for passengers until a footbridge is put across; all the traffic must in future go round by the road in course of construction between the regiment lines and the dhobi lines.[7]

On 16 April, 1853, the GIPR operated the first passenger train in India from Bori Bunder to Thana with fourteen bogies and 400 passengers. However, it seems, the temporary structures that we see in W.H. Stanley Crawford's photograph remained in place for quite some time. As late as 1860, the GIPR's chief engineer, James John

---

7. *Allen's Indian Mail, and Register of Intelligence for British and Foreign India, China, and All parts of the East*, Volume 10, January-December 1852.

Berkley was found describing the original Bori Bunder Station's edifices as temporary.[8]

But development and upgrades were soon to follow, with the American Civil War fuelling change. When the American Civil War broke out in 1861, and the southern ports of America were blocked, the supply of cotton to England also stopped. As the war continued, the English turned to India to avert a 'cotton famine' in their local textile industry. Cotton bales arrived in huge quantities from India's interiors and got dumped at Bori Bunder Station and all along the ports; from here they had to be shipped to England. Consequently, the station was literally choking for want of space, and for lack of storage options! Huge sheds and godowns had to be erected to protect the cotton from wind and rain, and later a goods terminus specially came up at Wadi Bunder near Mazgaon, originally marshland, to store firewood. These sheds and goods termini were the first major upgrades to the Bombay terminus.

With such improvements, by 1864, the small Bori Bunder Station became remarkably spacious. 'Bori Bunder station is a commodious edifice, with well-furnished reception rooms and well calculated to carry out the arrangements necessary for vast and extensive office,' certified English cartographer, George Bradshaw.[9]

~

Like Dhobi Ghat that made way for Bori Bunder Station, old slaughter houses near Bori Bunder—whose reek often offended passengers— were eased out to clean the area, and create a spacious station. Arthur Crawford, who took over as Bombay's first municipal commissioner around a decade after the station came up, moved the 'irritating and stinking' slaughter houses out of the city to Bandra, around 1866, where they remained for a while.

---

8. 'The GIP Railway: Description of the Line and Works by J.J. Berkley', *Professional Papers on Indian Engineering*, Volume 3, edited by Major J.G. Medley (India: Thomason College Press, 1866).

9. George Bradshaw, *Handbook to the Bombay Presidency and North West Provinces of India* (UK: W.J. Adams, 1864).

Three structures emerged there, one for storing beef and the other two for mutton. These were designed by Bombay's then-renowned municipal engineer, Russel Aitken— the genius behind the port city's wet docks—and constructed by Messrs. Wells and Glover with rail sidings that branched into two lines.[10] It was from the slaughter house at Bandra that the rival BB&CI Railway was to start 'meat trains' and dedicated rail sidings to deliver fresh meat to Bombay city.

Today, as we know, the old slaughter house has ceased to exist.

~

Right until the 1870s, Bori Bunder Station kept being renovated, changed and modernized. Soon, the site of the original station underwent a literal 'sea change'; vast tracts of land were reclaimed (during the Mody Bay Reclamations), pushing the sea further back from Fort to Mazgaon, and changing the face of the eastern shore entirely. It was now time for the humble Bori Bunder Station to get a complete makeover! A new majestic station emerged, called Victoria Terminus, laboriously built to the south of the old terminus.

Today, at the site where the old Bori Bunder Station once was— somewhere near the electric locomotive shed, close to signals S-54 and S-48—Victoria Terminus-bound trains, fast and slow, halt before entering the mega terminus. Operationally, this is to get a 'line clear' and a platform signal; metaphorically, this acts as a mark of respect for the original Bori Bunder Station.

~

What remains of history? Today, a handful of old cargo sheds can be found next to platform eighteen—the legacy of the cotton boom. Built of stone, they have high, pitched roofs and antique fittings. They display the construction techniques of the latter part of the nineteenth century—teakwood fixtures; large metal straps to bind the six-framed,

10. Rahul Mehrotra and Sharada Dwivedi, *A City Icon: Victoria Terminus, 1887 (Now Chhatrapati Shivaji Terminus Mumbai, 1996)* (India: Eminence Designs, 2006), pp. 31-32.

massive doors, windows and vents; and cobblestone flooring. When the BB&CI Railway later came up, these sheds became a part of its railway yard.

At the site of the old Bori Bunder Station, there are two cobble-stoned platforms, now completely abandoned. A rotten wooden board in one corner of says 'Ludhiana fast or ordinary service'— a legacy of organized cargo transport by rail.

As Bori Bunder Station and the railways grew, it was not just public roads that were diverted and closed. Quite a few occupants and settlers, and their enterprises, were disturbed—a slaughter house, a meat and fish market, a washermen's settlement. Even before the arrival of the railways, in 1766, the temple of Goddess Mumbadevi— where Bori Bunder Station would later emerge—had shifted to the 'native township' further north, to strengthen the fortifications of Bombay's fort.[11]

However, two Muslim shrines have withstood the ravages of time. An 1827 revenue survey map of the fortresses of Bombay documented two dargahs next to Fort George as 'Musulman Tombs.' This was more than twenty-five years prior to the arrival of the railways. While one dargah was located very close to the fort wall, the other seemed to be positioned at the northern end of the fort. Try retracing their locations on today's maps, and you will still find the two shrines—one inside today's Victoria Terminus, called the Baba Bismillah Dargah; another outside Victoria Terminus' premises, referred to as Pedru Shah Baba Dargah. The dargahs—having been there much before the railways had been conceived of—were taken into consideration while planning the new terminus, and survived the changes around them.

The Baba Bismillah Dargah is a curious place. Not many know its significance—it is older than some UNESCO-listed structures and the railway line. Devotees crowd inside, most of them regular visitors. Outside, at any given point, you find scores of people casually lounging, sitting on railings, smoking and chatting on mobile phones; around them, there are parcels, drums and mugs of water. The air is generally thick with the smell of hot brewing tea.

---

11. K.K. Chaudhari, *Greater Bombay District Gazetteer*, Volume 1, 1986.

The story goes that when the government acquired land to expand Bori Bunder Station in 1877 under the Land Acquisition Act, it decided not to remove the dargah following petitions from local Muslim citizens. It then decided to enclose it within the station premises as a small, covered building.[12] The dargah remains to this day, silently witnessing change and growth.

Today, the dargah is flanked by the remains of British engineering relics. An antique iron footbridge, now a part of the dargah, suggests that the site of worship was once surrounded by rail lines and one required a footbridge to access it. 'There were railway lines that went straight to the GPO from where trains picked parcels. Now they are buried seven to eight feet below the road,' says Imam Abdul Karim, who stays inside the dargah.

The other holy site, Pedru Shah Baba Dargah, has been around since the 1790s. This dargah is 'a cottage-like shrine of Pedro-Shah, a Christian convert to Islam, who obtained the honour of sanctity,' says S.M. Edwardes.[13] This site, too, has remained undisturbed for centuries.

SALSETTE TROMBAY RAILWAY: CONNECTING THE DOTS

The Salsette Trombay Railway, also known as the Central Salsette Tramway, ran from Wadhavli near Trombay to Kurla, and then through the Sahar area between the GIPR and BB&CI Railway, to Andheri. The line was opened in January 1928, and was run by the GIPR. It operated eight steam engines, built in 1921 in England by W.G. Bagnall. The Salsette Trombay Railway was a part of a larger plan of the Bombay Improvement Trust that wanted to link up the west and the east—Andheri and Trombay Stations.

Inhabitants of the city recall that the thirteen-kilometre line was frequented by picnickers, who used to travel to Trombay to buy toddy or palm liquor. However, in 1934, the line was shut to make way for

---

12. Rahul Mehrotra and Sharada Dwivedi, *A City Icon: Victoria Terminus, 1887 (Now Chhatrapati Shivaji Terminus Mumbai, 1996)* (India: Eminence Designs, 2006), p. 103.

13. S.M. Edwardes, *The Rise of Bombay: A Retrospect* (Bombay: The Times of India Press, 1902), p. 62.

the Santacruz Airport. Most of the locomotives used were returned to England.

INDUSTRIAL LINES: THE MAKING OF A BUSINESS CAPITAL

Back in the day, there were several industrial rail lines with different gauges, with their own locomotives criss-crossing almost the entire length and breadth of Bombay. To begin with, the Bombay Backbay Reclamation Scheme had its own rail line to facilitate reclamation and construction. Then the Bombay Improvement Trust, the Bombay Reclamation Company (with four locomotives), the Elphinstone Land Company (with two locomotives), Esso Company near Mahul, the Fertilizer Corporation of India Ltd in Trombay, and the Anik Quarry followed suit.[14]

WATER TRAINS: QUENCHING A CITY'S THIRST

The GIPR was in charge of ferrying water when Bombay was in the throes of a water crisis. To deal with the scarcity of water and protect existing water resources, a separate water supply committee—with various city authorities, including the GIPR superintending engineer—was constituted. In 1855, this committee proposed to act in a joint venture with the GIPR. The GIPR would assist in the conveyance of water by trains—more convenient, expeditious and economical than any other mode of transportation. It would also help construct a large wooden reservoir on the platform of Mahim Station. Since Mahim had several tanks, water would be drawn from these tanks with the help of a Persian wheel and animal carts, and poured into the reservoir at Mahim Station. The reservoir would hold water for one train, and this would prevent any possible delay in loading water once the train reached the station.

The water trains that plied from Mahim were in service between 2 and 9 June 1854. In this short period, about twenty-three trains were

---

14. *Indian Railways Fan Club Association*, in <http://www.irfca.org/docs/locolists/industrial/display.php?file=Maharashtra.txt&title=Maharashtra>, accessed on 25 January 2013.

run. Of these, twenty-one ran from Bombay to Mahim (and back), one from Bombay to Ghatkopar (and back), and a last from Bombay to Bhandup (and back). The quantity of water conveyed by each train averaged 10,000 gallons and a double or return journey would cost Rs 80 to Rs 100. The total charge for twenty-three trains was Rs 1,880; this amounted to about an anna for eight gallons of water. In 1854, it was officially recorded that the total amount received by the railways for the carriage of water was Rs 10,700—equal to about an anna for eighteen gallons.[15]

BHOR GHAT'S REVERSING STATION: THE ASCENT

The century-old Bhor Ghat 'Reversing Station' of the GIPR was situated near Khandala, between Bombay and Pune (then Poona). It was demolished in 2002 for the construction of the Bombay-Pune Expressway, despite protests.

To navigate heavy inclines across the mountain ranges, the station had a 'reversing facility', with a turntable at the top for steam engines. The principle was simple. Each train had two locos, one that led, and one at the rear (called the 'banker loco'). The reversing station was shaped like an inverted 'V', a triangle without a base. The locos used to go up and wait. Then they'd get uncoupled, move to the turntable, get turned, and assume their normal positions as lead loco and banker.

Following electrification, the reversing station was discontinued and a new alignment of tracks was built below it. To date, the arches of the reversing station can be seen, having been preserved as heritage structures.

---

15. Varsha S. Shirgaonkar, *Exploring the Water Heritage of Mumbai* (New Delhi: Aryan Books, 2011), pp. 44-47.

THE TRAMWAYS OF BOMBAY

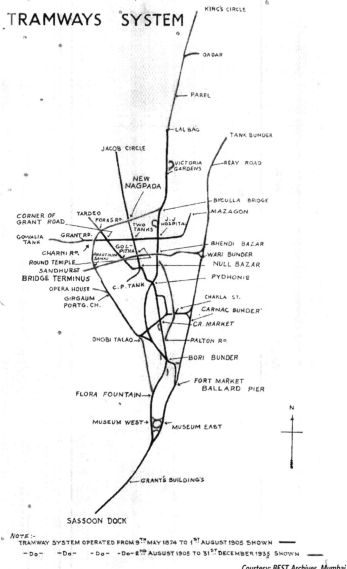

TRAMWAYS SYSTEM

KING'S CIRCLE

DADAR

PAREL

LAL BAG

TANK BUNDER

JACOB CIRCLE

VICTORIA
GARDENS

REAY ROAD

NEW
NAGPADA

BYCULLA BRIDGE

CORNER OF
GRANT ROAD

TARDEO

FORAS RD.

MAZAGON

GOWALIA
TANK

GRANT RD.

TWO
TANKS

J. J.
HOSPITAL

CHARNI RD.

GOL-
PITHA

BHENDI BAZAR

ROUND TEMPLE

PRARTHNA
SAMAJ

WARI BUNDER

SANDHURST

NULL BAZAR

BRIDGE TERMINUS

OPERA HOUSE

C. P. TANK

PYDHONIE

GIRGAUM
PORTG. CH.

CHARLA ST.

CARNAC BUNDER'

C. R. MARKET

DHOBI TALAO

PALTON RD.

BORI BUNDER

FORT MARKET
BALLARD PIER

FLORA FOUNTAIN

MUSEUM WEST

MUSEUM EAST

N

GRANT'S BUILDING'S

SASSOON DOCK

NOTE :-
TRAMWAY SYSTEM OPERATED FROM 9TH MAY 1874 TO 1ST AUGUST 1905 SHOWN ——
- Do -   - Do -   - Do -   - Do - 2ND AUGUST 1905 TO 31ST DECEMBER 1935 SHOWN ——

Courtesy: BEST Archives, Mumbai

From Pestonji D. Mahaluxmivala's *History of the Bombay Electric Supply & Tramways Company Limited*
(Bombay: 1936).

The railways were in place by 1853, but road public conveyance remained poor. Apart from the two-wheeled bullock 'reklas', there were horse-drawn four-wheeled carriages that accommodated five passengers (four inside and one outside); double-decker horse-drawn omnibuses plying between Mumbadevi and Elphinstone Circle, Girgaum and the Cathedral; and buggies and palanquins for hire.

In January 1865, twelve years after the first rail run, Messrs Stearns, Hobart, & Co, an American trading firm, applied to the government for concessions to lay and operate a tramway system in Bombay; they called their new enterprise the Bombay Horse Railway Company Limited. They obtained a deed of agreement rather soon, on 28 February 1865. However, fate had other plans. The American Civil War had ended and Bombay's financial markets crashed. The scheme did not fructify.

Five years later, in 1870, Messrs Stearns, Hobart, & Co wrote to the municipal commissioner reiterating their intention to put the agreement into force. By this time, another firm, Messrs Lawrence & Co had applied for similar permissions. Therefore, the matter was referred to the select committee of Justices of the Peace in 1871, to decide whether street tramways were desirable in Bombay. The select committee, in turn, submitted a detailed presentation of terms and conditions, and Messrs Stearns, Hobart, & Co expressed their willingness to accept these.

By this time, however, word had spread and a whole host of companies had started applying for the permit. They had to be objectively assessed, and after a detailed appraisal, a whole new front-runner emerged, along with Messrs Stearns, Hobart, & Co—Mr George Alvah Kittredge.

Finally, a deed of agreement was signed on 1 March 1873, granting both William French Stearns and George Alvah Kittredge the right to construct, maintain and operate tramways on the streets of Bombay. They were to pay an annual rent of Rs 3,000 per mile for a double track and Rs 2,000 per mile for a single track, payable on a half-yearly basis. Stearns and Kittredge floated a company in New York called the Bombay Tramway Company Limited and registered it in Bombay in March 1873.[1]

The construction of the lines was entrusted to Messrs Glover & Co. Built with teakwood, the lines were seven feet long and six inches wide, and were placed about four feet apart. On the top of these teakwood sleepers, Belgian steel rails were placed.

The section between Colaba and Pydhonie was opened to the public on 9 May 1874. At the end of the first day, 451 passengers had travelled by tram and the Bombay Tramway Company had collected Rs 80; by the end of the first week, 3,135 passengers had travelled on a total of 294 trips. The trams charged three annas to cover the distance between Colaba to Pydhonie, and half an anna to take commuters from Victoria Terminus to Pydhonie. From 1899, the fare was reduced to one anna, no matter the distance.[2]

The tram's cars belonged to one of three categories—closed double-horse cars, open double-horse cars and open single-horse cars. The first batch of twenty-three double-horse and open single-horse cars was imported from America. The closed double-horse cars could seat twenty-four passengers and there was standing room for a dozen more. Subsequently, all cars were built in Bombay; only castings and wheels were imported from America.

The Bombay Tramway Company started operation with 200 horses—Gulf Arabs for double-horse cars (bought at Rs 400), and Walers for single-horse cars (bought at Rs 600). The number of horses increased exponentially to 1,360, by the end of the tramline's life.[3]

Close attention was paid to the purchase and care of horses. For single-horse cars especially, every aspect was looked into—from the horse's weight (it could not be under 900 pounds), to its girth (it could not be under sixty-eight inches), to its age (between five and

---

1. *BEST Undertaking*, in <http://www.bestundertaking.com/history.asp>, accessed on 2 September 2014.

2. 'History of Modern Maharashtra', *Mumbai University*, in <http://www.mu.ac.in/myweb_test/FYBA%20-%20History%20of%20%20Modern%20Maharastra.pdf>, accessed on 9 September 2014.

3. Official archives from BEST Museum, Mumbai.

seven years), to its colour (it could not, under any circumstance, be black). For double-horse cars, since two horses were being employed as against one, the weight or size of each animal was not accorded the same degree of importance.

The Bombay Tramway Company maintained a whole stable department to look after its horses, and had a veterinary and stall superintendent at its stables at Tardeo and Parel. One 'ghorawalla' was employed for four horses and he was responsible for their safe custody, their grooming at least thrice a day, and the cleanliness of the stalls. He was required to see that the collars and blinkers of each of his horses were in perfectly good order, and was obliged to feed them as per company specifications—grains such as gram, barley and corn (across four feeds), hay (across six feeds), 1.5 ounces of salt, and two to three pounds of carrots (specifically during summer).

On 19 July 1899, the company applied for sanction to convert the tramways in the city from horse- to electric-traction. But before this proposal could become a reality, the company collapsed, and was taken over by the Bombay Electric Supply & Tramways Company Limited (BEST Company Limited).

The order for the first electric tramcar for Bombay was placed with the Brush Electrical Company, London. The vehicle arrived in the city in January 1906. City-dwellers gave a warm welcome to the electric tramcar. On 7 May 1907, at 5:30 p.m., the tramcar, specially decorated for the occasion, started its journey outside the municipal office, went as far as Crawford Market, and returned to the point it had started from. After this inaugural run, four tramcars were kept plying along various routes daily till 11 p.m.

The trams were a novelty, and added excitement to everyday life. People crowded around stops, jostled one another to board them, and enjoyed the trams' speed, comfort and low fares.

The enthusiastic welcome of this new mode of transport is especially incredible if we consider the fact that on the very first day of its operation, a passenger, who we only know as Malvankar, fell off a running tram and lost his leg. His story was not unlike that of the British statesman, William Huskisson, who died during the inaugural run of the world's first twin-track inter-urban passenger railway, the

Liverpool-Manchester Railway. Malvankar's accident was written about and discussed threadbare. The BEST Company Limited was flooded with suggestions on how best to prevent such accidents in the future. A few of these were implemented—for instance, some trams were gifted doors.

Even as the crowds increased, the BEST Company Limited introduced a double-decker tramcar on Bombay's roads in September 1920. There had been simultaneous talks in favour of motor buses; these plans saw the light of day in 1926. The buses were to run, as an experiment, on three routes—between Afghan Church and Crawford Market, Dadar Tram Terminus and King's Circle, and Opera House and Lalbaug. From 15 July 1926, with a modest fleet of twenty-four vehicles, motor buses became a part of Bombay's transport network.

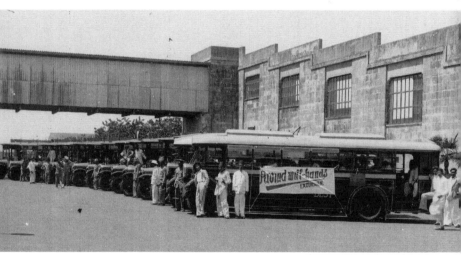

Courtesy: Western Railway Archives

BEST Buses Outside Bombay Central Station Taking Mill Workers for a Picnic

In 1952, a survey of tram traffic was conducted. On the basis of these findings, the BEST Undertaking[4] decided to release fewer trams on routes with insufficient traffic. This did not cut losses. The harsh truth was that tramways had become outdated modes of transport. So, in 1953, non-viable routes were closed, the first being the one between Null Bazaar and Jacob Circle (route number twelve); a bus began plying this circuit instead. With time, the number of tram routes closing increased dramatically. Finally only one remained— between Bori Bunder and Dadar. On 31 March 1964, at 10 p.m., the last tram, packed to capacity, left Bori Bunder.

It was the end of an era.

---

4. On 7 August 1947, the Bombay Municipal Corporation took over the BEST Company Limited, to form the Bombay Electric Supply and Transport Undertaking, which was again renamed Brihanmumbai Electric Supply and Transport Undertaking (BEST Undertaking) in 1995. BEST celebrates 7 August annually as 'BEST Day'.

INTO THE FUTURE

October 2007—it was an unusually hot day. But excitement was building up for the night, as I had procured permission to witness and be part of the trial runs of a new, technologically superior train that had arrived in Bombay. Not since 1925, when the lines got electrified, had the city's railway network seen such a huge upgrade.

By the time I reached the Kandivali railway workshop along the former BB&CI Railway lines, it was almost 1 a.m. The new train was strikingly different from the ones I had seen thus far. Violet-silver in colour, Bombay's next generation train no longer carried those regular dust-brown and dull yellow hues. This was brave, since the old colour had cleverly camouflaged betel-nut stains, so commonly found across the city's public infrastructure. What's more, the new train had large windows, elegant interiors and was much brighter and roomier than its predecessors.

The motor coach was strewn with wires, beeping devices and a laptop with flickering graphs. When the engineers got to work, the train started slowly. But soon, it sped through several isolated stations in the night. It zipped past Mira Road Station at 100 kmph, braked and picked up momentum again.

The new train had electrical equipment from Siemens and worked with the help of software and simulation. The remarkable 'iron horse' had been bought for Rs 20 crore with World Bank aid, as a part of a massive project—the Bombay Urban Transport Project—to upgrade the city's transport infrastructure.

As we know, Bombay had been the birthplace of railway electrification in India, with 1,500-V DC technology being preferred in 1925. As we also know, around the 1950s, the railways shifted to the modern and newer 25-kV AC technology that saved power. Bombay, however, could not upgrade its systems—any reconstruction would inconvenience the travelling public. Electric trains coming from other parts of India had to change their locomotives at Bombay's threshold—an area referred to as the 'neutral zone'—and switch to significantly older technology. This was certainly a hassle. So finally, in the new millennium, the Bombay railways began to convert their obsolete DC devices to AC ones—but in phases.

To keep train operations running during this period of transition, the Bombay railways developed local trains and locomotives that could run on both DC and AC. These local trains, known as MRVC (Mumbai [Bombay] Railways Vikas Corporation) trains, could not only reach a maximum speed of 100 to 110 kmph (as compared to the 80 kmph of their predecessors), but could also save more than 35 per cent of power through 'regenerative braking'—each time the trains braked, they'd generate power that could be sent back to the systems.

The GIPR completed conversion of the first suburban section between Kasara and Titwala from 1,500-V DC traction to 25-kV AC traction in November 2006. The process is by no means complete, and the last section to get upgraded will be the Harbour Line.

THE METRO AND THE MONORAIL

More than 150 years after Clark and Berkley's pioneering GIPR lines, and the subsequent emergence of BB&CI Railway lines, Bombay has begun building new rail networks. This has been long overdue, given the explosion of the city's population and the immense strain on Bombay's railway infrastructure.

In this context, Bombay's metro is worth a mention. An urban metro rail service, with multiple corridors across the island and suburbs, has been planned, offering east-west connectivity (as against the present north-south connectivity). The system, designed to reduce traffic congestion, will be built in three phases over a fifteen-year period, with completion expected around 2021.

When complete, the system will comprise three high-capacity metro railway lines, spanning a total of sixty-three kilometres. The first line, the Versova-Andheri-Ghatkopar Corridor Mass Rapid Transit System (MRTS) project—the original project to be awarded within a private-public partnership framework—is a (roughly) twelve-kilometre elevated metro with twelve stations. Work on this corridor began in February 2008, and six years later, in June 2014, the line opened. Twenty-seven-year-old Rupali Chavan operated the inaugural train.

Thanks to the metro, railway turntables, a nineteenth-century invention to move trains, are back in the city. The railway department has procured turntables, so trains can change tracks; one of them is already in place at the Versova car shed. Old battery-operated shunters also seem to be in fashion! In the absence of diesel and electric power, these shunting engines are handy for pushing and pulling empty wagons. Nearly a century ago, the BB&CI Railway has two such battery-operated shunters, imported from England in 1927. These were used while the railways were moving from the era of steam to electricity. Both 'revived relics' will now be of value—highlighting the fact that old technology is still relevant.

~

The city's monorail—a train that straddles a single concrete or steel guideway—is the second huge development that needs acknowledgement. The monorail has been planned across those stretches of the city that the metro cannot reach, such as Chembur, Wadala and Mahalaxmi, and is a first of its kind in present-day India. When the monorail opened to the public on 2 February 2014, a day after its inauguration, the response was overwhelming and crowds thronged the station in huge numbers. Twenty-three-year-old Juilee Sameer Bhandare was the pilot of the city's first monorail.

There is a sense of déjà vu when one sees the monorail trundle past Chembur and Wadala. A century ago, in the north, Patiala had an eighty-kilometre-long state monorail system that had operated for nearly seventeen years between 1910 and 1927. It had been the only operational railway built on the Ewing System—a principle of balancing monorails developed by British inventor W.J. Ewing in the late nineteenth century. Most of the monorail, if you recall, had been put together in Bombay; indeed, the rail tracks had been built in Mazgaon. It was only fitting that the first monorail in contemporary India emerged in its mother city.

~

There is a third development we need to make note of. In a bid to strengthen the old suburban railway network in Bombay, the ministry of railways decided to go vertical in a land-starved city. It proposed an elevated corridor over the existing lines—the first over the Western Railway, from Virar to Churchgate, and then to Oval Maidan—close to the spot where a rail line used to run to Colaba about ninety years ago.

However, the plan faced its first hiccup. Due to restrictions on road bridges, most of this Rs 21,000 crore project would have to become an underground rail corridor, rather than an elevated one.

This, too, comes with a sense of déjà vu. A proposal for an underground railway network for Bombay has emerged at least once every 100 years—a proposition per century. In the 1890s, the British, obsessed with the popularity of the London Underground that had opened in the nineteenth century, suggested a similar network in Bombay. Then, in the late 1920s, the British proposed connecting Churchgate and the other business districts with an underground railway network. Independent India of the 1950s and 1960s heard similar murmurs, and there emerged detailed proposals, work studies, and demos on how an underground railway could be built without disturbing other underground utilities. (A miniature model of this demo can be found to this day at the BEST Museum in Sion.) The former railway minister, Lalu Prasad Yadav, revived the idea in the twenty-first century. Strangely, none of these plans has seen the light of day. Now, in the second decade of the twenty-first century, concerted efforts are being made to *actually* build the underground rail corridor.

History has the uncanny knack of repeating itself. One can only hope that this time around, these strategic plans meet with success.

EPILOGUE

Bombay's rail network was the first to emerge in the country, the first to witness some of the most path-breaking upgrades. Age has not withered the lines' spirit. Today, Bombay's trains are known not only for their pioneering position in railway history, but also for their robustness.

On 26 July 2005, around 2 p.m., Bombay was struck with heavy rainfall, a virtual storm.[1] By 27 July, the Indian Meteorological Department in Santacruz had logged a record 944 mm of rain. The city looked like it once had—a cluster of sinking islands. Sion turned into the swamp it had been. Trains came to a halt and power cables got dismantled. More than fifty electric trains went into a state of disrepair. Within a week, however, services bounced back. Perhaps, it is for this reason that Bombay's train network is viewed as an extension of the city—it never sleeps.

Let's fast forward to 11 July 2006 and then, 26 November 2008. On 11 July 2006, the suburban railway network of Bombay witnessed a series of seven bomb blasts over a period of eleven minutes, claiming the lives of several commuters.[2] It was a catastrophe—one that the nation followed with shock. Yet, Western Railway services were restored within a few hours of the serial attack. 864-A, the first-class coach damaged due to the bomb blast at Matunga Road Station, was the only train (of those devastated) to survive. After being restored at

---

1. 'Heavy Rains Paralyze Mumbai', *Rediff.com*, 26 July 2005, in <http://in.rediff.com/news/2005/jul/26mumbai.htm>, accessed on 9 September 2014.

2. 'At Least 174 Killed in Mumbai Train Blast', *CNN*, 12 July 2006, in <http://edition.cnn.com/2006/WORLD/asiapcf/07/11/mumbai.blasts/>, accessed on 9 September 2014.

a cost of Rs 1.2 crore, and converted to AC traction, it now runs on the Central Railway lines.

On 26 November 2008, two of the ten terrorists who attacked Bombay blindly sprayed bullets in the concourse of Victoria Terminus. As we know, the attacks, that began around 9:30 p.m. and ended more than an hour later, killed fifty-eight people and injured 104 others.[3] Once more, the railways offered a fitting reply to terrorism, by restoring services within a few hours. The bullet marks on the walls of Victoria Terminus were patched up in 2010.

The Bombay rail network may have been weakened by time and fate. But it is strong in will.

~

The oldest train line in India has witnessed the steady progression of time. It has beheld love stories, misfortune and adventure. When one walks along the first line, one hears whispers from the past, murmurs of forgotten tales. One perceives the lines:

> The railroad track is miles away,
> And the day is loud with voices speaking,
> Yet there isn't a train goes by all day
> But I hear its whistle shrieking. [...]

> My heart is warm with friends I make,
> And better friends I'll not be knowing;
> Yet there isn't a train I wouldn't take,
> No matter where it's going.[4]

The trains of yore live on—in reality, in our collective unconscious.

---

3. 'We Have Got Justice: 26/11 Victim's Wife', *Sahara Samay*, 21 November 2012, in <http://www.saharasamay.com/regional-news/others-news/676518074/we-have-got-justice-26-11-victim-s-wife.html>, accessed on 4 September 2014.

4. Edna St Vincent Millay, 'Travel', *Poets.org*, in < http://www.poets.org/poetsorg/poem/travel>, accessed on 2 September 2014.

ACKNOWLEDGEMENTS

This work would not have been possible without the railways and its men. As a kid, travelling all the way to school and back on Bombay's trains had been a joyful experience; the mysterious sidings and the tracks always had something to say. Later, when I discovered that the very rails I had traversed every day were the oldest in Asia, my mission became clear. I decided to record the fascinating story of the emergence of the railways in India, and the tales of love, labour and war that defined them.

A chance discovery of ancient bullhead rails near Bhandup served as an incentive to write this book. I received encouragement from colleagues at the Indian Railway Fans Club Association (IRFCA), such as Satish Pai, I.S. Anand, Apurva Bahadur, Ashish Kuvelkar, Ravindra Bhalerao and several others. Further, my senior architect friends Ulhas Rane, Pallavi Doke, Rajneesh Gore and Rahul Chemburkar hammered home the need to pursue this project.

The study would have remained just a compilation of scattered newspaper articles had the late Bombay historian, Sharada Dwivedi not encouraged me to collate my research into a book. Articles of late veteran railway historians G.D. Patwardhan and A.K. Arora provided inspiration.

This work would have remained incomplete without Rafique Baghdadi's inputs on Berkley's hotel at Byculla, and Mazgaon. My walks with city historian, Deepak Rao, and his constant feedback regarding the city's history and geography lent credibility to my findings. Meetings with railway historian, Ian J. Kerr during his Bombay visits granted me keen insight into my subject; he went over the initial draft of my manuscript and offered valuable guidelines.

I especially have to thank senior railway officers Pranai Prabhakar

and Sriniwas Mudgerikar, along with Sharat Chandrayan, Vidyadhar
Malegaonkar and Narendra A. Patil, who made this project a reality
by extending the full support of the railway family in Bombay and
kindly permitting me to use archival images and drawings. Others
from the railway public relations department, including V.
Chandrasekar, A.K. Singh, A.K. Jain, G.S.K. Iyer, Michael Manuelraj,
Nitin David, Gajanan Mahatpurkar, Hormazd Mohta, Sunil Singh,
Ajay Solanki, Smita Rosario, Anubhav Saxena and the late Bhagwat
Dahisarkar have been more than friends. I also thank the Western
Railway's former general manager, Anoop Krishna Jhingron, for all
his help. The chief public relations officer of the Bombay Port Trust,
V.R. Joglekar, has been most supportive.

It would have been impossible for me to finish this draft without
the support of my senior editors at *Mumbai Mirror, Mid-Day, DNA* and
Hindustan Times. Time Out Bombay's former editor Naresh Fernandes'
heartfelt support, by promoting my study and passing it to publishers,
took the project to a different level. I must thank my journalist
friends Kailash Korde and Shashank Rao, Prachi Bari and Pravin
Mulye, who endorsed my work, and critic Akshay Deshmane, who
read the early drafts and pointed out mistakes.

A special thanks to R.N. Bhaskar for putting in a word, without
which this manuscript would have remained unpublished.

I am grateful for the complete support extended by Sabyasachi
Mukherjee, director of the Prince of Wales Museum (now Chhatrapati
Shivaji Maharaj Vastu Sangrahalaya), and all my colleagues at the
museum studies department. Their guidance and training not only
helped me spot relics, but also empowered me so I could assist the
Central Railway with selecting artefacts for their heritage gallery at
Victoria Terminus. My museum colleague, Vivek Tetwilkar and his
father, historian Sadashiv Tetwilkar, also need special mention.

Thanks must be extended to Vrunda Pathare and Sanghamitra
Chatterjee of the Godrej Archives, whose exhibitions offered valuable
facts about Vikhroli.

A big thank you to the author of *City of Gold: The Biography of Bombay*,
Gillian Tindall, for going through excerpts of the draft and offering
priceless suggestions.

I'd also like to thank the commissioning editor of this book, Dharini Bhaskar.

I would not have been here without my late parents, Dr Bhalchandra P. Aklekar and Sanjivani B. Aklekar, who I miss every moment. I must confess that I have done an injustice to my wife, Priya, and sister, Pradnya, by constantly remaining preoccupied with the Bombay railway network!

Finally, I must thank my elder daughter, Tanvi, who typed the various drafts of this lengthy manuscript multiple times, and little Vaibhavi, who offered moments of relief during hectic writing sessions.

Printed in Great Britain
by Amazon

71473553R00139